Praise for Lorelei James's
Branded As Trouble

Gold Star Award! "...Branded as Trouble is a great story of two individuals who overcame drugs and alcohol proving that it is possible to find love while dealing with an addiction...This story deserves a Gold Star for Colt and Indy's journey from abuse, to friendship, to relationship, and finally to trust and commitment...a must read book for 2009!"
~ *Lt. Blue, Just Erotic Romance Reviews*

Rating: 5 Hearts, Top Pick! "...Even though you are reading about some serious issues, it's with done with some humor and heart felt emotions...you end up laughing at points and you are reaching for tissues at others...Overall though, this is a love story. India and Colt aren't perfect but they are wonderful characters..."
~ Terri, Night Owl Romance Reviews

Recommended Read! "...Ms. James tackles the issues of alcoholism...and the different aspects of this disease (personal, friends and impact on family) that I find this story not only super erotic but fantastic on another level..."
~ Tanya, Joyfully Reviewed

Rating: 5 Angels "...a splendid tale on trust, friendship, love, romance and finding the right soul mate...Ms. James pens emotions, warmth, and companionship...she was completely in tune with the characters' feelings in this believable story..."
~ *Linda L., Fallen Angel Reviews*

Rating: 5 Cups "...A spectacular novel, this breathless portrayal of love, life, and judgment in a small town will have you aching for a happy ending for these two characters that I can guarantee you will fall in love with..."
~ *Danielle, Coffee Time Romance*

Rating: Grade A "...the big draw to the Rough Riders series for Lorelei James fans is the erotic. Her heroes and heroines steam up the pages something fierce...but what I like just as much is the sense of family that has run throughout this series...just as powerful as all that lovin' that's goin' on."
~ *Sandy M., The Good, The Bad, and The Unread*

Rating: 4 Nymphs "Branded as Trouble...it's just as hot, sexy and fast-paced as its five predecessors. It's rare to have the hero and heroine of a contemporary romance have such addictive and flawed pasts, so I really appreciated the unique background these two characters brought to this new story."
~ *Mystical Nymph, Literary Nymphs*

Look for these titles by
Lorelei James

Now Available:

Rough Riders Series
Long Hard Ride
Cowgirl Up and Ride
Tied Up, Tied Down
Rode Hard, Put Up Wet
Rough, Raw, and Ready
Branded As Trouble
Shoulda Been a Cowboy
All Jacked Up

Wild West Boys Series
Mistress Christmas
Miss Firecracker

Beginnings Anthology: Babe in the Woods
Three's Company Anthology: Wicked Garden
Wild Ride Anthology: Strong, Silent Type

Dirty Deeds
Running With the Devil

Branded As Trouble

Lorelei James

A Samhain Publishing, Ltd. publication.

Samhain Publishing, Ltd.
577 Mulberry Street, Suite 1520
Macon, GA 31201
www.samhainpublishing.com

Editing by Angela James
Cover by Scott Carpenter

First Samhain Publishing, Ltd. electronic publication: March 2009
First Samhain Publishing, Ltd. print publication: January 2010

Dedication

To all the black sheep—everyone deserves a happy ending

Chapter One

In celebration of his first year of sobriety, Colt McKay climbed on the back of a bull and rode for a full eight seconds.

In celebration of his second year of sobriety, Colt McKay climbed in an airplane and parachuted out.

In celebration of his third year of sobriety, Colt McKay had hoped to climb on a woman and end his self-imposed sexual abstinence of the previous thirty-six months.

He imagined soft candlelight, soft kisses, a woman's soft skin and a soft bed beneath him.

At least that part of his fantasy had come true. Colt was in bed. He was even laying face down on a puffy tie-dyed quilt with a woman beside him. However, he was not basking in the afterglow of red-hot sex, rather, he was grimacing in pain from the sensation of a red-hot poker jabbing him in the butt for the millionth time.

"Fuck. That hurts."

"Almost done. Two more quick stitches and you'll be good to go," Doctor Monroe trilled in that annoyingly chipper voice of hers.

Go. Right. Where the hell was he supposed to go?

Snip snip. Murmured words. Everything was going fuzzy. With his previous substance abuse issues he'd refused the torturous Doc's painkillers, so he figured the adrenaline high was wearing off and he was about to crash. Hard.

Great. Just what he didn't need. To look even more pathetic, helpless and weak.

"See? That wasn't so bad, was it?"

Colt lifted his head and glared at the woman with the

whiskey-rough voice who'd dared to speak to him. Any other time the remorse swimming in those amazing sapphire eyes would sway him to be soft and sweet with her.

Not now. Maybe not ever again.

He kept his tone cool, even when he wanted to scream his fool head off at her. "Not so bad? For who? Jesus Christ, Indy, you shot me in the ass. It don't get a whole lot worse than that."

Chapter Two

"It was an accident."

Colt grunted.

"Why did you come barging in like that anyway?" India's pulse skipped when he cranked his head around and glared at her. Again.

"Are you serious? Three punks were hassling you. You were by yourself. At night."

"So? It's not the first time, nor will it be the last. Besides, I had it under control."

"Sure didn't look like it. Why didn't you shoot *them* with the nail gun?"

"I would have if I'd thought of it."

Dr. Monroe said, "Well, whatever her intentions were, you're very lucky she had a bad angle and the nail only went through the dermis and not into the bone."

"Lucky. Right."

"Done." The smell of antiseptic burned strong for a second. The sound of ripping paper was followed by the snapping removal of latex gloves. Dr. Monroe said, "You sure you don't want a painkiller, Colt? That local anesthetic will wear off in another two hours."

"I'll be fine."

"I thought you'd say that." She patted him on the shoulder. "I'll swing by tomorrow to check on you to make sure there's no infection."

"Wasn't that what the tetanus shot was for?"

"No. The only reason I'm not admitting you to the hospital is because of the...delicate nature of the wound's location. The gossipmongers in this town would have a field day with this incident, especially in light of your previous reputation, so I understand why your brother thought it'd be best if you were treated here." Her eyes narrowed. "That said, if you feel feverish and uncommonly sore at any time in the next twelve hours, you'd better get this butt to the ER. Pronto."

India said, "What does he do now?"

"Sleep. As much sleep as he can get. Motrin every six hours, if he'll take it." Doctor Monroe stood and fastened the metal clasp on her black medical bag. She said in a low voice, "I'm going to suggest you leave him be, India. Is there someone else who can keep an eye on him?"

"What? He's in my guest room!"

"I know, but you seem to...agitate him and he needs to rest."

Heat scorched her cheeks. Dammit. She wasn't completely inept when it came to caring for another person. She could do this Florence Nightingale shit.

Cam McKay ambled over. "After I drop the doc off, I can come back and watch him tonight if you'd like."

"Stop whispering. I'm right here in the room," Colt snapped.

India and Cam exchanged a look. When Colt attempted to lift up off the mattress, Cam put his hand in the middle of Colt's back and gently held him down. "Whoa. Take it easy."

"Yeah, I wouldn't want to *agitate* you any more than I already have," India retorted sweetly.

Colt locked his gaze to hers. She withheld a shiver at the command in the dark blue depths. "India stays. She's the one who went all psycho carpenter on my ass, she can damn well take care of me." He flashed her a smile reminiscent of a shark about to bite. "I sorta like the idea of you playin' fetch and carry for me, sugar."

"I'll just bet you do."

"Now that it's settled, we're off." Cam set Colt's cell phone within reach. "I'll check on you later." To India, he said, "You need anything, call my cell, not the station, okay?"

"Okay." She followed Cam and Doc Monroe down the staircase that opened into the back parking lot. She slid the deadbolt on the door and flipped the lock.

Man. What a wacky night. India sucked in a deep breath to

quell her sudden bout of nerves. It didn't make sense she was jumpy. She'd been alone with Colt McKay hundreds of times in the last three years.

But not after you shot him in the butt.

The whole thing bordered on surreal. Three guys had stumbled in demanding matching tattoos. She'd told them to leave, pointing to the sign she didn't ink anyone under the influence. After sweet-talking her didn't work, they'd become belligerent. India had dealt with enough drunks she took it in stride when they threatened her with macho bullshit. As if that Neanderthal behavior would somehow get her to change her mind? Please.

She'd just about convinced them to leave, when Colt and Cameron burst in. Colt's hostile posture was bad enough, but Cam had just gotten off duty with the Crook County Sheriff's Department and still wore his uniform. And his sidearm.

The guys panicked and ran out the back door, knocking over a makeshift sawhorse table loaded with tools.

Cam gave chase as well as a prosthetic-wearing cop could.

In the melee, Colt bent over to pick up the tools and India grabbed the big framing nail gun. As she was trying to avoid stepping on screws scattered like tacks, she tripped over the compressor hose and fell...right into Colt. More specifically, right into Colt's butt. Upon contact with a solid surface, the nail gun's triggering mechanism released a three-inch screw. Right through Colt's Wranglers, penetrating the bottom of his left butt cheek.

Colt hadn't screamed in agony. He'd just dropped to his hands and knees, asking her to put the nail gun on the counter.

By the time Cam returned, Colt's wound was seeping blood. Cam, being the levelheaded sort, tried to convince Colt to go to the hospital. Colt refused.

After a few minutes of fruitless arguing, Colt did the damndest thing. He pushed to his feet, snagged a pair of pliers from the jumbled tool pile and headed up the back staircase to India's apartment, almost at a dead run.

Cam and India raced after Colt and wrangled him to the closest horizontal surface—the bed in the spare bedroom—and Cam called his good buddy Doctor Monroe. India wondered just how good of "friends" Cam and the doctor were because the doc

13

showed up within ten minutes.

After Doctor Monroe pulled the nail out, she administered a local anesthetic and a tetanus shot, which appeared to cause Colt more discomfort than the injury.

India forced herself to watch him get stitched up even though it was only three stitches. Blood and needles were part of the tattoo business and had never bothered her. So why did the sight of Colt's blood cause her stomach to heave?

You weren't close to barfing. You sucked down too many Red Bulls, that's all.

If that was true, why was she cowering outside the room?

Guilt? Fear he'd light into her now that they were alone?

Screw that. Colt couldn't make her feel any worse than she already did.

She snuck back in and perched on the folding chair next to the bed Doc Monroe had vacated.

Colt's hair was damp and disheveled. The muscles in his jaw were bunched tight. His chest rose and fell quickly with every shallow breath. His entire body rivaled the bedside table for rigidity.

India wished she could soothe his pain. Would it relax him if she smoothed the frown lines from his feverish brow? If she ruffled her fingers through his glossy black hair would his eyes close in bliss? If she rubbed his broad shoulders would he groan with satisfaction? If she placed her lips on his would he welcome her kiss?

Kissing him? Where the hell had that idea come from? Colt was her buddy, her best pal, her sounding board, her client. Not to mention her A.A. sponsoree. She shot him a quick glance.

Sometimes that fact was a damn crying shame.

No doubt Colt McKay was a fine-looking man. Too good looking to be honest. He had the face of an angel—a fallen angel to be sure—a sinful smile rivaling the devil's for temptation, the muscled body of a disciplined athlete, and more charms than a damn jewelry store. He was, simply put, perfect.

Perfectly off limits, not that he'd ever given any indication he'd be interested in her beyond friendship.

There's the real reason to cry.

Colt's fiery blue eyes focused on her.

She had no earthly idea what raced through his brain when he looked at her like that, but she liked it. She set her hand on his shoulder, jerking it back when he flinched. "Sorry."

"Don't be. It just surprised me, that's all. You never touch me like that."

Do you want me to touch you like that? "I'm..." India blew out a frustrated breath. "Dammit, Colt. I'm sorry. So freakin' sorry. I'm such a klutz. I didn't mean to shoot you in the butt."

He merely stared at her.

"What?"

"You could kiss it and make it better."

"Funny. Does it hurt?"

"Like you wouldn't believe."

She winced. "I'm sorry."

"If you're not gonna pucker up, I'd be grateful for some Motrin."

India leapt to her feet. "No problem." She hustled to the nightstand for a glass of water and shook out two orange pills. "Here."

"Thanks." Colt popped the pills and took a big drink. The second gulp left him sputtering and water droplets clung to the bristle on his cheeks.

Without thinking, she wicked the moisture away with her fingers.

"God. Your hands are so cold."

"Sorry." India moved her hand but Colt caught her wrist.

"Don't stop. It feels good."

"It does?"

"Yeah. My face is on fire."

When she stroked his face, from his forehead to his chin, he expelled a long sigh. India couldn't tear her eyes away from how Colt's sharp facial features contrasted with his full lips. For the longest time she just touched him, studying him, sort of like she was seeing him for the first time.

Finally, he said, "You're quiet."

"You sound surprised."

"I am. You're never quiet."

"True."

"So talk to me."

"About?"

"Anything."

"Think you'll be better by meeting night?"

"Talk to me about anything *but* A.A." He shifted his position. "Tell me about the last tattoo you did."

"Nothing too exciting. Another college girl bringing in a Chinese symbol her friend had found online that 'means' something significant."

"In other words…"

"Complete and total bullshit. For all I know—and all she knows—I could've tattooed the Chinese symbol for outhouse above her butt."

Colt laughed softly.

Encouraged by his laughter, she kept talking. "A couple days ago a big, burly biker came in and wanted a bumblebee done on each thigh above his kneecaps."

"Why?"

"In an outburst of passion, some hot chick swore he was the 'bees knees' so he demanded the moment be forever immortalized on his hairy skin."

"You're kiddin' me."

"Of course I'm kidding. Damn, you're gullible, McKay."

He gave her a droll look. "Gullible ain't a word that's ever fit me, Indy."

"I don't imagine it has." She placed her palm on his cheek. During the three years Colt belonged to A.A., he'd told her some of the things he'd done while drunk or high or both. Granted, his past was tame compared to the shit she'd pulled, not that she'd shared the worst of it with anyone and she suspected he held secrets pretty close to his incredible chest too.

"I hate it when you look at me like that," he said.

"Umm. Like what?" *Like I wanna lick you up one side and down the other?*

"Like I'm a lab rat."

India let her thumb arc over his cheekbone. "Not a lab rat. A guinea pig."

"Great. That's so much better."

"I sketched a new tattoo design I'd like to try on you."

"Yeah? Maybe once my ass is healed you can turn the puncture wound into one of them cool, fake bullet holes you see on motorcycles and pickup tailgates."

"Please. I'm an *artiste*. I have something way better in mind. Something hip-fun-sexy-cool."

Suspicion clouded Colt's face. "I already told you. You ain't tattooing the area around my nipples. Ever."

"But this new pattern is so awesome. Turquoise and orange outlined in black and red, that looks like flames—"

"No way, no how."

"Just hear me out."

"Dammit, Indy, I said *no*. Why are you so dang fired up about doin' this?"

"Because you have great nipples."

Colt's ardent gaze dropped to her chest. "Bein's that I haven't seen your nipples, I'm afraid I can't return the compliment, sugar. But we could rectify that right now. Take off your shirt."

"Ha ha." To hide the fact he'd caught her off guard, and that single hot look caused her nipples to stand at attention, she snipped, "Fine. I'll just use my super cool new design on your cousin, Blake. I'm sure he'd be up for it. Especially since he's already here building some shelves."

"Maybe while he's debating ink colors, you could convince the slob to pick up his goddamn tools so innocent bystanders don't get nail shot in the ass."

Whenever India brought up Blake West's name, Colt became bad-tempered. Not a reaction she understood since Colt and Blake were related and hung out on occasion.

"While you're busy playin' with Blake's nipples, you could pierce them. With little tinkling golden bells. So he can't sneak up on his flock of sheep when he ain't pretendin' to be a carpenter."

Why had Colt gone beyond peevish to pissed off? "Look, I'm sorry. I was—"

"Forget it. I'm tired. My ass hurts like a mother and I'm supposed to be resting. So shut the light off when you leave."

"If you need anything—"

"I won't." Colt dismissed her by facing the wall.

Jerk. She had half a mind to retrieve the nail gun so she could nail his smart mouth shut.

You have no right to be indignant.

Still, Colt's erratic behavior stung. He was usually so even-keeled. So sweet and thoughtful with her. India retreated to her room.

She stared at the glow-in-the-dark stars glued to her walls and wondered if Colt would freak out when she told him about her date with Blake tomorrow night.

Way to act like a jealous asshole. If Indy hadn't guessed you are goofy in love with her before, she'll know for sure now.

Colt snorted. Right. He'd eat his hat if that happened. India hadn't a clue how he felt about her. She'd chalk up his reaction to stress. Or pain. Or frustration.

Which was fine with him. Better she pick any one of those excuses rather than know the truth: he'd fallen for her so hard he hadn't looked at another woman in the three years since she'd come into his life.

He knew it was stupid. Indy was his best friend. Their friendship was the most important thing in his life and he'd be a fool to jeopardize it.

The fact she maintained their friendship after hearing about his sordid past, made him extra cautious not to screw that up, like he'd screwed up every other relationship. Plus, since she was his A.A. sponsor, it'd put her in a sticky situation if they started knocking boots. India was too important to the local organization to chance taking a tumble with the infamous former bad boy loser Colt McKay.

If you're such a loser, why does India end up with you all the time anyway?

Good question. They were together at least three times a week—not all of them A.A. related. Colt knew her love life was as pathetic as his. Did her feisty, in-your-face personality scare men away? Or was it the tattoos, piercings, and hard-edged eyes that kept men wary? Hell, it was hard to pick which of those characteristics was his favorite when it came to Indy.

Yeah, they were a pair all right.

Sprawled in an unfamiliar bed, dissecting why his life was a mess even when he was clean and sober, Colt squinted at the caller ID when his phone vibrated. "Hey Cam. What's up?"

"Just checking in. How you feeling?"

"Shitty."

"I figured. Anyway, I called Dad and told him I'd run into

you at the diner and you were on your way out of town for the weekend. So you're clear until Monday."

"What did Dad say?"

"Nothin' worth repeating."

With some of the family issues he'd had recently, it was a relief Cam had his back, since his other brothers probably would say something smart about his weekend getaway. "Thanks."

"No problem. I'm working a twelve-hour shift from noon to midnight tomorrow. You need anything?"

"Yeah. Extra clothes. Bring me a pair of sweats since the ones that were in my gym bag stink."

"Will do. Anything else?"

"Where's my truck?"

"I moved it to the fenced lot behind the building. Why?"

"Just wanted to make sure it was outta sight."

"I *am* a cop. I did actually think about stuff like that."

"Sorry."

"Get some rest."

"It's about the only thing I can do." The second the words left his mouth Colt wanted to suck them back in. His piss-ant injury was nothing compared to what Cam had suffered. In combat. On the other side of the planet. Alone. Or what he suffered every day, dealing with his handicap, physically and emotionally. "Shit, man, I'm sorry."

"Nothin' to be sorry about, bro. See you tomorrow."

Chapter Three

Colt was bored out of his fucking mind.

He'd tried to sleep. But every time he'd dozed off, oh-so-helpful India popped in to check on him. And for some bizarre reason, checking on him meant touching him. She'd place her cool hands on his forehead. On his cheek. Then on the back of his neck. The last time she'd barged in, he barely stopped from demanding she wrap her hands around his cock because that's where he was the most feverish.

Yeah, he was definitely punchy.

Colt's cell phone vibrated. He checked the caller ID. Cam. "Hey. You out keepin' the peace?"

"Trying to. It'll be a challenge later since it's Saturday night. Got my fill of drunken cowboys fightin' last weekend."

"That part of your duty ain't gonna end anytime soon. Maybe you should've taken Dad up on his offer of workin' with us."

"Fuck off."

He smiled, regardless if Cam couldn't see it. Amused the hell out of him to tease his younger brother, just because he could.

"This is the thanks I get for keeping your humiliation under wraps?"

"Come on, Cam. Ranchin' with the family ain't that bad."

Cam snorted. "That's rich, coming from you. How you feelin'?"

"Sore."

"Could be worse."

"True. I could've been facin' forward and she could've shot

me in the dick."

"Ouch. Anyway, thought I'd give you a heads up. Blake will be there tonight."

"Be where?"

"In India's apartment."

"Why? Is he doin' some remodeling for her after hours?"

"No. They, ah, have a date."

The muscles in Colt's gut tightened. "Golden boy ain't pouring drafts tonight at the Rusty Spur?"

"Guess not."

"Where'd you hear this gossip? The diner?"

"I haven't been in the diner today."

"What the hell? You're in there like three times a day." Cam had a thing for sweet, shy Domini, the cook/waitress/hostess at Dewey's Delish Dish, the restaurant next door to the tattoo shop.

"There are other places in town I can get dirty looks with my morning coffee," Cam said without humor. "Anyway, I ran into Blake at the Super-Value. He was buying flowers, I asked him what for, and he mentioned his date with India."

Just what Colt didn't need, to hear Indy and Blake laughing, having a good old time, while he was hiding in the spare bedroom. Or worse, feeling like a pervert at hearing them squeaking the mattress springs.

"Why you tellin' me this?" Colt snapped.

A weighted pause hung. Finally, Cam sighed. "Colt, man, it's me. No bullshit between us, remember? I know you've got it bad for her. Probably have for years, huh? I just didn't want you to be caught off guard. Thought maybe you prefer to clear out."

Right then, Colt decided rather than let his imagination run wild about what Blake and Indy had done, he'd stay and learn what they were doing firsthand. "Thanks. I appreciate the warning, but I'll stick around."

"You sure that's the smartest choice?"

"No. But depending on what happens with them...it'll give me a reason to move on, either way. Time to fish or cut bait, know what I mean?"

"I hear ya. Just don't do anything stupid that'll bring me there in an official capacity tonight, okay?"

"Deal. And, uh, thanks."

"No prob. Think you'll feel up to working out this week?"

"As long as I ain't sittin' on a rowing machine, I oughta be good. Why? You ain't thinkin' of pussing out on me, are ya, *matey*?"

Cam laughed. "No chance, *rummy*. I can still whip your shot-up ass on the treadmill, even with a peg leg."

"Bring it." Colt hung up. He slowly rolled over and glanced at the clock. Roughly an hour before India closed up shop. Maybe if he was lucky he could get a little shut-eye.

The outer apartment door slammed ten minutes later, followed by the squeak of his door being opened. "Colt? You asleep?"

"Not any more."

"Sorry. Look, I think you need to—"

"Rest, yeah I know. You've barged in here like a hundred times today. You are single-handedly keeping me from getting any rest."

India blinked. "But, that's not what—"

"I'm sure Doc Monroe mentioned if I didn't have enough downtime there was a higher chance of infection and complications." Colt raked a hand over his stubbled jaw. "So soon as you feed me, I'd appreciate it if you piped down so I can conk out for a while."

"I have to come up with dinner for you? Tonight?"

"It ain't like I'm up to cookin'." Might make him a jerk, but Colt loved her wide-eyed expression of alarm. It wasn't his fault he was laid up; it was hers. And he had no intention of letting her off the hook so easily. Especially about Blake.

"Ah. I have plans tonight."

"Really? I hope you're makin' me something good to eat, because I'm starved."

She bit her lip. "No. I mean I have plans to go out."

"Out as in...out to grab us some food?"

"Umm...no. Out as in, out on a date."

He paused. "You have a date?"

"Yes, I have a date."

"Tonight?"

"Yes, tonight."

Colt laughed. He kept laughing.

"What's so damn funny?"

"You are. Whoa." He clutched his stomach. "You really had me goin' there for a sec."

"Had you going? What the hell is that supposed to mean?"

"Come on. Stop kiddin' around, Indy. It hurts when I laugh."

India actually stomped her foot. "You find the fact I have a date...*funny?*"

"Yep." He laughed harder.

"It's not funny!"

"Yes, sugar, it is."

"Stop laughing." India crossed her arms over her chest. "I'm single, I'm fun, and it's Saturday night. It is *not* that far out of the realm of possibility that some man would want to take me out and show me a good time."

Instantly Colt sobered. "Where's this mystery man takin' you for the rip-roarin' good time in the Sundance metro area?"

She shrugged. "Out."

"Out...where? Not out dancin', 'cause you don't dance. Not out drinkin', 'cause you don't drink."

"There are lots of other places we can go."

"Really? Name one."

Her mouth opened. And closed. Opened and closed again. She looked like an air-starved trout, not that he'd voice the comparison out loud.

"Wasn't it you, complaining to me, just last Saturday night, that there was nothin' to do in this town?"

"So?"

"So, I'm curious as to what's changed in seven days."

Those beautiful sapphire eyes sparked danger. "Why? What's it matter to you?"

Colt reined in his temper. Barely. "Two reasons. One, because damn near every Saturday night for the last two and a half years, I've heard you whine about the lack of entertainment options. I've offered to take you to rodeos, church socials, tractor pulls, community dances, demolition derbys, casinos, on horseback rides, fishin', campin', huntin' and concerts. What have we ended up doin' nearly every Saturday night?"

She kept her mulish mouth shut.

"Watchin' movies or playin' cards or cooking dinner. So yeah, maybe I *am* interested in what kind of fun and games this guy has offered you that I haven't."

India glared at him.

"I'm waitin'."

"Fine. He's cooking me dinner and then we're watching a movie at his place."

He grinned even when he considered what a rat bastard his cousin Blake was and how much he'd like to kick his ass.

"Oh, wipe that smile off your face, McKay. You said there were two reasons. What's the other reason you're being so damn snoopy about my personal life?"

"You think I'm snoopy?"

"Either that or you're living vicariously through me."

Colt opened his mouth to protest, then clamped his teeth together, choosing to glower at her.

"What's the matter? Did I hit too close to home?"

"Forget it."

She stalked closer. "No. You thought it was so damn funny that a man would actually want to spend time with me—"

"What exactly have I been doin' with you every weekend for the last two and a half years, huh?" *Besides spinning my wheels?*

"Spending time with me, but it's not the same thing."

"Why not?"

"Because we are not dating." She lifted both pierced eyebrows, drawing his attention to the sexy silver hoops. "Omigod, Colt. All this time, you haven't thought we were—"

"No, I ain't that stupid," he retorted. "I just find it ironic that after *you* shot me in the ass, and I'm layin' here in *your* house, in pain, you've got no problem leavin' me here while you're flitting off to go on a damn date."

India did her trout impression again.

Jesus. Way to sound like a needy, bitter bastard, McKay.

"Look, I didn't think—"

"No, you didn't think, which is typical behavior for you, Miz Impulsive, so I'm not surprised."

"Colt—"

"Just go. I'm tired." Colt shut his eyes and rolled to his side, giving her his back.

"But..."

"Just go," he repeated. "Shut the door on your way out. Oh,

and have a freakin' awesome time on your date."

He heard her shallow breathing as she debated on berating him or leaving him.

Guess which one she chose?

The door snicked softly as she let herself out.

Colt felt neither vindicated nor relieved.

Damn him. Her first real date in forever and Colt McKay had sucked all the fun out of it before she'd even left the house.

India threw the hairbrush in the sink. She snatched the gel from the cabinet and squirted the orange goo in her palms, rubbing it vigorously into her hair. Bah. It didn't help. She still looked like a porcupine who'd lost a fight with a weed whacker. Plus, she needed to recolor the tips. The fuchsia was fading into a hideous bubblegum pink.

What the hell did it matter what her hair looked like? It wasn't like they were going to be in public.

She froze. Was that why Blake wanted to cook for her at his place? Because the colorful tats and piercings were what most folks noticed and he was embarrassed by it?

Not Colt.

Why had everything circled back around to him?

Because you hurt him. And not just from shooting him in the butt with the nail gun.

That stupid voice in her head was mistaken. She had not hurt Colt McKay's feelings by agreeing to a date with Blake. She and Colt were friends. That was it.

Right?

Wrong. Colt's been more to you than just a friend, no matter how you slice it. And he deserves better than you running off for a date—a date you didn't want in the first place—with his cousin.

Blast it. Why had India said yes to Blake West? Sure, he was cute, golden curls, a brawny build and a bright white smile. He reminded her of the shaggy-haired surfers she'd grown up with in California. Blake was a cheerful guy, happy to help out his cousins Chet and Remy West whenever they were shorthanded in their construction business. Blake was sweet. He didn't have a horndog reputation. He was low-key, just the type of guy India wanted.

With one teensy-tiny little problem: when Blake West wasn't tending his sheep, he tended bar.

India avoided bars and nightclubs even eight years into her sobriety, so hooking up with bartender Blake wasn't a smart move. Plus, she had a sneaking suspicion as laid-back as Blake appeared, he wouldn't go for a casual relationship. He was the kind of guy who'd want exclusivity and promises, promises she couldn't give him or any man.

Could you give those promises to Colt?

Yes.

No.

Dammit! She was not listening to the voices arguing in her head. Colt was her friend. And she was *not* going to cancel her date because of one ornery cowboy who was being a pain in her butt. He was a guest in her house. Her house, her rules, she could do whatever the hell she wanted.

She picked up her cell phone and dialed Blake's number. "Hey, Blake. No, Alfredo sauce sounds great. Look. I just wondered...if you wanted to come over here after dinner? Why? Well..." India laughed. "You busted me. That'd be great. I've even got a fresh batch of apple dumplings from the diner." She hoped she still had time to pop downstairs and raid the pie case before Domini sold out. "I might be a little late, just wanted to warn you. Good. I'm looking forward to it too. Bye."

India grabbed her purse and raced down to the diner to pick up dumplings. She might as well grab dinner for Colt.

Four dumplings, one quart of chicken and wild rice soup, a grilled tomato and cheese sandwich later, India booked it back to her apartment.

She burst into the guest bedroom, startling Colt out of sleep.

"Christ, India. Do you have to scare the livin' hell out of me every goddamn time you open the door?"

"Sorry. I just wanted to get the food to you while it was still hot." She set everything on the dresser and spun around to give him a once-over. "Soup is kinda hard to eat laying down. Let me help you up."

"I don't need you—"

"Yes, you do. Just hold on." Threading her fingers through his, she pulled him to a sitting position. "There. That wasn't so bad. Let's get you to the chair. Stand up on three. Ready? One.

Two. Three." India jerked, hoping to take some of the strain. But she jerked too hard and he crashed into her.

"Shit. Too fast. I—"

"Hang on." Oh, he was a substantial guy. She braced her legs and smashed her face into his chest while maintaining a death grip on his upper back.

"Why'm I so dizzy?"

"Low blood sugar. It's okay. I've got you."

Colt's hands reluctantly landed on her hips. Almost against his will, he allowed her to hold him up.

As India's nose brushed Colt's pecs and her hands were spread across that incredibly muscular back, she felt his fingers squeezing her hipbones. A powerful sense of...longing overtook her. He was so solid and warm and he smelled all musky good like a man should and she absolutely did not want to let him go. Ever.

"Indy?" he said her name in a husky whisper.

"Mmm?"

"I think I can make it to the chair now."

"Oh. Right." She released him and settled him in the seat. "Do you need an extra pillow for your butt?"

"Nah."

"I'll grab the TV tray and be right back." After she'd arranged the soup and sandwich and refilled his water, she felt him staring at her. "What?"

"You didn't have to do all this."

Her pulse raced when she gazed into his compelling blue eyes. "I wanted to. I'm sorry about leaving you here alone tonight. I should've cancelled the date—"

"I'm the one who oughta be apologizing. I was a total dick. Who you date and what you do on your dates ain't any of my business." He gave her a head to toe inspection. "You look great, by the way. I've always loved that shirt on you. Brings out the color of your eyes." He smiled. "And sometimes, it matches the color of your hair."

She self-consciously adjusted the vivid blue satin strap on her baby doll blouse. "Uh. Thanks. I thought I might dye the ends blue tomorrow."

"That's my favorite." Colt stirred his soup and blew on a spoonful before popping it in his mouth.

Favorite what? Color on her hair? Or kind of soup? Soup, probably. "Would you like crackers?"

He shook his head.

"Do you need ketchup for your sandwich?"

"Eww." He shuddered. "You've been cookin' for Eliza again?"

"Yeah, and we both know grilled cheese is about the extent of my culinary expertise."

"Quit hovering and get goin'. You don't wanna be late."

Lightly, she said, "Seems like you're trying to get rid of me."

His laser-sharp gaze pierced hers again. "Never."

They stared at each other and the air crackled with energy.

Colt cleared his throat. "Just so you know, I probably won't be around in the mornin' if you choose to, ah, not come back here. You don't have to worry about me blabbing your personal business and I'll lock up for you since I already have a key."

India's jaw dropped. "Omigod. You don't think I'm going to sleep with Blake on the first date, do you?"

Pause. His eyes tapered to fine points. "You're goin' out with *Blake*? As in my cousin Blake? As in the guy whose nail gun took a chunk out of my ass?"

She winced. Crap, she'd forgotten to tell him that. "Yes."

"Did you agree before or after his machinery maimed me?"

"Before. Look, he asked me while he was putting up shelves in the shop. I've cancelled on him two times already, so that's why I can't back out tonight."

"You don't have to explain to me."

"But I do. He's interested in getting a tattoo on his—"

Colt held up his hand. "I don't wanna know where you're tattooing him, to be real honest."

Dammit.

"You go on and have fun. Much as I complain about him, Blake is a really good guy. He'll treat you right."

She was tempted to snap off, *how nice that I have your approval*, but that'd be bitchy and she'd acted bitchy enough. And truthfully, she didn't want his approval. She much preferred his smartass disapproval or his...jealousy.

"Don't wait up," she said half-jokingly.

"Don't worry. With you gone for a few hours, I'll probably finally sleep like the dead. I won't notice if you do come home in the middle of the night."

Six hours later, India slammed the door a little harder than necessary when she and Blake returned to her apartment.

They finished off the caramel apple dumplings at her dinette table. Coldplay drifted from the stereo. A sharply scented lemon verbena candle filled the air.

"I appreciate you taking a look at it, Blake."

"Be my pleasure." Blake scraped his fork across the empty plate. "Although, I'd hoped the invitation into your bedroom would be extended in a different context, India."

She grinned. "I imagine you did. But I'm not looking—"

"For a relationship, yeah, yeah, yeah."

"How'd you know that's what I was going to say?"

Blake looked at her from beneath incredibly long black eyelashes. "Because it's the same old tune, you're just a different singer."

"You run into this problem a lot?"

"Yep."

"So if I said, 'Blake, baby, let's burn up the sheets for just one night?'"

He stood so fast his chair crashed to the floor.

India laughed.

"What? You think I'd turn you down?"

"No. But I'll admit you don't seem like a one-night stand kind of guy."

"Wrong. I totally *am* that guy, it's just the ladies don't give me a chance. I must look like a 'relationship guy' to women instead of a 'one-night wild fuck' kind of stud," he grumbled.

"There are worse things."

"Yeah? Name one."

Shoot. Her brain wasn't crafting reassurances very quickly. "Women thinking you're a player."

"At my age, player behavior in a bar is considered a rite of passage." He waggled his eyebrows.

"How old are you?"

"Twenty-six. How old are you?" He shook his finger at her. "And don't pull that 'never ask a woman her age' crap."

"I'm thirty...something."

"And yet, you don't look a day over twenty."

"Did you attend the same cowboy charm school as your cousin Colt? Or is it inbred?"

"Cowboy charm is part of our DNA, darlin'. None of us can help it." Blake's smile faded. "Speaking of Colt...can I ask you something?"

"Sure," she lied.

"Why haven't you two dated? I mean, you are together all the time."

All the time was stretching it...wasn't it? "We're just friends."

"Might sound like I'm pandering to you, bein's we're on a date and all, but that's probably a good thing you're staying just friends."

That got her back up. "Why?"

"Stubborn people like you two would kill each other." He smiled. "Colt's a good guy. He's a great friend, actually, but I'm sure I don't have to tell you that."

No, she already knew. India smiled and changed the subject. "So how do you want to do this? I've got all the stuff in my bedroom."

"Good, let's get to it."

Chapter Four

Bang. Bang. Bang.

Quiet.

Bang. Bang. Bang. Then, "Fuck!"

A feminine giggle.

Bang. Bang. Bang.

Murmured voices.

Bang. Bang. Bang.

Colt closed his eyes and tried to block out the images of India and Blake. Naked. On the other side of the wall. Naked. Right behind his head. Naked. Rolling around together on the bed. Naked. India and Blake going at it like animals. Naked.

Fuck. *Think of something else. Think of water rippling in your favorite fishing hole.*

Bang. Bang. Bang.

Thinking quiet, serene thoughts didn't work. Maybe he should imagine chaos.

Think of bawling calves and the frantic momma cows answering moos during branding.

Bang. Bang. Bang.

Nope. That didn't do the trick either.

Think of how India's sweat-slicked skin would feel sliding beneath yours, her heels digging into your ass as you ride her hard enough to break the damn headboard, not just rattle it.

Yeah. That was helping. *Not.*

Bang. Bang. Bang.

He didn't know how much more of this he could take. He should've left when he had the chance, now it was too late. It'd been too late when he'd heard the apartment door slam. When he'd heard the bass tones of Blake's voice mixed with India's laughter. When he'd heard the seductive notes from the CD player. When he'd caught a whiff of the candle burning in the living room. When he'd heard India's bedroom door slam.

Bang. Bang. Bang. Bang. Bang. Bang.

Jesus.

The headboard banging had gotten progressively louder for the last twenty minutes. Twenty very long, very loud minutes.

It appeared his little cousin was quite the stud.

Yeah? Then how come you don't hear India shrieking with orgasmic pleasure? She would be if you were in her bed.

For Christsake. He'd gone from perverted to pathetic. And the sad thing was, he wasn't only thinking about tonight. He was thinking about all the nights, over the last few years he'd been pining over a woman who'd never see him as anything but a drunk on the lifelong road to recovery. Or worse, her good friend.

Enough was enough.

Wincing, Colt rolled to his feet and snagged his iPod from the dresser. He cranked it to high and lowered onto the bed, placing his feet by the headboard. Nine Inch Nails drowned out everything and he was able to sleep.

Early the next morning, Colt stumbled out of his room. Despite his intent to crawl in his truck and head home, a shower was a necessity.

As he crossed the living area, he noticed India's bedroom door was ajar. He peered through the crack and saw India sprawled in the middle of the bed. Alone. Alone and apparently buck-assed nekkid. Red satin sheets were twisted around her long legs and long arms, covering her torso, but hinting at the curves beneath.

Colt didn't gawk at her body to see if she was, in fact, pierced everywhere she'd hinted at being pierced. A man could only stand so much temptation. He backtracked to the bathroom.

The hot water lasted all of five minutes. And did the woman own every blasted lotion and potion known to mankind? He counted fourteen different health and beauty product bottles—after he'd knocked them all into the tub. Twice.

Still, he felt a million times better after an ice shower. His injury itched, so he took that as a sign of recovery.

He needed his caffeine fix and didn't want to stop at the Conoco and chance running into a member of his family. He plugged in India's fancy coffeemaker and dumped a capful of coffee beans into the grinder. While that machine whirred, he washed the glass coffee pot and the plastic filter basket. It took four cupboards before he found where India had moved the box of paper coffee filters. He filled the water reservoir, reassembled the various parts and hit start.

Colt picked up the trash in his prison room while he waited for the coffee to brew. When he returned to the kitchen, India stormed out of her bedroom.

Pity she'd put on a robe.

"The one day I get to sleep in and you're up at the butt crack of dawn making enough noise to wake the dead?"

"Oh, I see. It's different when *you're* disturbed out of your beauty sleep. Sucks, huh?"

"Funny."

"Besides, all I did was make coffee."

"Then explain what you were doing in the shower? 'Cause it sure as hell sounded like you were throwing rocks."

"If I didn't know better, I'd think your poor head was hurtin' and it was a hangover talkin'." Colt clucked his tongue. "Maybe you oughta get to bed earlier if you're so cranky in the mornin'."

"How do you know what time I went to bed?"

"I dunno, maybe it was the slamming door at midnight that tipped me off. Or maybe it was your headboard banging against my wall until the wee hours. I got tired of it around one a.m. and listened to my iPod."

"But Blake finished—"

"Huh-uh. I don't wanna know about Blake's big finish because I had enough of the pre-game." Colt sidestepped her.

"You think I slept with him."

He shrugged, determined not to let it show how much her horizontal mattress mambo with his cousin bothered him.

"Hey." Her hand circled his wrist and India yanked him

around to face her.

Colt looked into her angry eyes. "What?"

"You are a judgmental jerk, Colt McKay."

"Me? I didn't pass judgment. I just pointed out the obvious."

"Obvious?"

"Hell, I didn't even mention the candles and soft music and the laughter that preceded all the bedroom noises."

"Magnanimous of you."

"I thought so."

"Hah! You thought wrong." India's finger drilled him in the chest. "And it pisses me off that you think so...lowly of me."

"What else am I supposed to think?"

"That there's a logical explanation."

He laughed. "For havin' a man in your bedroom? After midnight? With the bed slamming against the wall? Sugar, sex isn't the logical answer, it's the *only* answer."

"Not all men have sex on the brain twenty-four hours a day."

Tired of her baiting him, Colt crowded her. "Any man with half a fucking brain, who is lucky enough to be in your bedroom at any time, ain't thinkin' about nothin' but how perfect it'd feel to have your hot little body under his. Or on top of his. Or in front of his. Over and over. And if it'd been me? Twenty-four hours would be the minimum amount of time I'd keep you in my bed."

India stared at him. "Is that what you were thinking about, Colt? Us having sex?"

Yes. Goddammit, that was all he could think about. Why in the hell couldn't she see it?

When he didn't answer, she blurted, "I didn't have sex with Blake last night, or any other night. Those banging noises you heard? Was him hammering—"

He actually heard himself growl.

"—my headboard back together. The last time I moved my bedroom furniture, the bed frame snapped from the headboard base and I asked him to fix it—"

Colt pushed her against the wall and smashed his mouth down on hers, taking the hot, wet kiss that he'd been dying for.

God. The softness of her lips. The feel of her fingers twining in his damp hair. The taste of her was as potent and intoxicating as he'd imagined. The warm wetness of her mouth, the eager touch of her tongue to his was like a drug. Colt was half-afraid to open his eyes and find this was a damn dream.

India wrapped her arms around his neck and pulled him closer, opening her mouth for total access.

His hands moved from her shoulders to caress her neck. He feathered his thumbs along the length of her jaw, still kissing her senseless, sucking her soft, sexy moans into his lungs like air. His cock was already straining at the waistband of his sweatpants and he'd barely begun.

She placed her hands on top of his, breaking the kiss to say, "Touch me. God, put your hands all over me."

Colt was captivated by the sight of her smaller hands guiding his bigger hands down her body. When the base of his palms reached the barrier of her robe, India slid her fingers beneath the lapels and ripped it open.

Sweet Jesus, her nipples were pierced. With little silver hoops that accentuated the rose-colored tips. His mouth watered. His cock twitched. He groaned and bent his head to taste, helpless to resist.

"Oh. Yes." India arched into him, her hands dropping to squeeze his hips.

Her skin had warmed the metal. He traced the tiny ring with the very tip of his tongue, then drew the beaded nipple into his mouth. With his each rhythmic suck, she dug her fingernails deeper into his skin.

As Colt kept nuzzling her breasts, kissing a line up her bared throat, using his teeth and his tongue and his lips, somehow one of India's hands had moved to his groin.

His breath stalled and he groaned.

She took that as a positive sign and she went from rubbing the length of his shaft, to curling her fingers around the base and stroking upward.

The softness of the fleece beneath the heated grip of her palm felt good, too damn good, because it'd been too damn long since he'd experienced a woman's touch. She had to stop.

Colt attempted to knock her hand free, but she'd latched onto his hip with her other hand and held him in place.

That tingling sensation started and his balls tightened.

No, no, no, no. Too soon. He couldn't blow this fast. He couldn't embarrass himself by shooting within a minute of her hand touching his cock.

Before Colt so much as said her name, he began to come.

Hot spurts shot out the end of his dick, soaking the waistband of his sweatpants. He froze, mortified by being so quick on the trigger. He didn't even enjoy the first orgasm he'd had in years that hadn't been brought about by his own hand.

Luckily it didn't last long. Colt jerked away from her, ignoring the pain in his ass as he spun around.

Fuck. Way to be a loser.

"Colt?"

He didn't respond, just kept walking toward the door.

"Where are you going?"

"Home."

"Why? Are you sorry—"

"That I came in the blink of an eye? Yeah, I'm really goddamned sorry."

"That's not what I was going to say."

"Doesn't matter."

"But—"

"Save it." He struggled to slip on his right boot without bending over, by bracing his hand on the wall.

Then India was in his face. "Don't do this."

"What? Embarrass you and myself? Too fuckin' late."

"Do I look embarrassed?"

Colt's gaze traveled the length of her body and back up to her face. "No, you look beautiful. Jesus, you always look so beautiful."

Her eyes softened. "Talk to me."

He shook his head. He should've been hanging his stupid head in shame. Somehow he'd managed to get one boot on. He switched his stance, trying to block her out.

But India wasn't about to be deterred. She ducked under his arm so she was closer than before. His determination to ignore her was temporarily sidelined when he noticed the gap in her robe had widened, granting him an even better view of those exquisitely pierced nipples.

"Fine, you're embarrassed. So I've got nothing to lose by asking you to tell me the truth."

"Indy—"

"How long has it been since you've had sex?"

Thump. His heel hit the floor as he got the left boot on.

"A year?"

Colt laughed.

"Two years?"

"Try three years."

India stared at him with confusion, then understanding dawned. "You mean, you haven't—"

"Had sex since I went through treatment? Nope. I've been celibate as long as I've been sober."

"By choice?"

How the hell was he supposed to answer that? "I hardly remember the last time I had sex. I was drunk. Or high. Or both. So I guess you can say I hardly remember what sex is like or what I'm supposed to do besides come in my pants like a teenage boy."

"Why haven't you talked about this at meetings?"

"Because it's not anyone's goddamned business but mine."

"Okay. But you could've talked to me. One on one. We're friends."

Colt laughed again, but it held a bitter edge.

"That wasn't meant to be funny!"

"Which is why it is." He grabbed the plastic grocery bag that held his toothbrush, iPod, extra clothes and started downstairs.

"You're just leaving?"

Was that a regretful note in her voice? He didn't turn around until he reached the landing at the bottom. "Do you want me to stay and finish what we started?"

India actually backed up a step. A look of surprise—or was it horror?—crossed her face.

Enough. Her expression told him everything he needed to know: it was time for him to move on, much as it pained him.

"But you could stay and we could talk about it."

"Nothin' left to say. See you around."

Halfway home Colt realized he never did get a cup of coffee. That harsh dose of reality had been enough to kick start his day.

Thursday evening in the gym, Colt and Cam were sweating and grunting, trying to outdo each other. The best five-mile running time went to Colt, but he admitted there was little victory in beating a man with half his leg gone.

Cam out bench-pressed Colt by almost fifty pounds. Their sets of crunches were declared a tie, by the Kewpie-doll manning the desk, who couldn't keep her jailbait eyes off either of them.

As was their post-workout ritual, they'd toweled off and sat on the wooden bench in the locker room. Colt downed half his water bottle in one gulp. "So, anything interesting happen in the world of law enforcement today?"

"Nope. How about in the world of the McKay gas baron?"

"Fuck you. No one's ever gonna let me live that down."

"Why would you want to? Christ, Colt, you're the one makin' the rest of 'em look dumb."

Colt mopped the sweat from his forehead. "Yeah, well it was pretty much dumb luck."

Years ago Colt had purchased a small tract of land from a little old ranch widow. At the time it'd taken all his money and some fancy talking to the banker to fund what his family called his "pity" venture. He figured he'd hold onto the acreage and figure out if improvements would make it suitable for grazing, if not, he'd sell it.

A few years passed and a surveyor approached him about testing for methane gas. Colt agreed only because it cost him nothing and he'd managed to retain all mineral rights from the original seller, that sweet old lady, who'd since passed away.

The surveyor made a startling discovery. Methane gas, in a place where methane gas was not supposed to be. So Colt signed off for a hefty chunk of the profits, and let the company set up a drilling site.

They hit Wyoming gold.

After his initial bragging about his cash windfall, and faced with his family's resentment that the land wasn't part of the McKay Ranch, hence they got no cut of the profits, he'd taken great pains to downplay his income. Within six years of purchasing the crappy land no one had wanted, Colt earned enough money to survive on his own without his portion of the

McKay Ranch or the earnings from it.

Round about that time, his brother Colby returned to Wyoming after a rodeo career-ending injury. At first, Colt was excited to have his brother back helping with the ranch. But that excitement dimmed when their father gave Colby a large chunk of the responsibilities that'd belonged to Colt.

Rather than see it as an easing of his workload, Colt saw it as an indictment of his abilities. He began to spend more time in the local honky-tonks. Drinking, chasing women, trying to build a reputation to rival his brother's and cousin's.

It worked, but not in a good way. Colt couldn't remember exactly when things had spiraled out of control. The year between his younger brother Carter's wedding, and his cousin Dag's death, Colt had alienated his family. He worked on the ranch when he felt like it, because he didn't need the money or the hassle. He drank, started doing drugs, and slept with whoever offered.

What did his loving brothers do when he'd started that downward spiral? Not a damn thing. Part of him wondered if they wanted him to die—because he was worth far more to them dead than alive.

The weight machine clanged in the other room, drawing his attention back to Cam who was saying, "...ain't been in town."

"Sorry. I spaced out. What'd you say?"

"Wondered what was keeping you busy at your place because you ain't been in town all week." Cam wiped the sweat dotting his neck. "India mentioned you missed the Tuesday night meeting."

Unreal. He'd been sober three years and missed one meeting in the last two and a half. "And here I thought that was supposed to be confidential information."

"It is. She told me you're not returning her phone calls."

"So? She ain't my keeper."

"She's worried about you."

"She drop any hints on whether you knew if I'd fallen off the wagon or not?"

"Nope."

"That's good. Where'd you see her? At the diner?"

"I haven't been in the diner since Friday night."

"Why? They stop givin' law enforcement officers free coffee

or something?"

"Or something," Cam muttered.

"What's up?"

Cam braced his elbows on his knees and pointed his face to the floor. "Evidently Domini saw me giving Doc Monroe a ride home Friday night after your unplanned piercing. The arctic princess blasts me with an icy glare if I so much as step foot on the welcome mat in Dewey's. Then she starts cursing at me in Ukrainian and stomps off."

"Huh. I didn't realize you and Domini were datin'."

"That's the thing; we're not. I'm not dating the good doc either. She and I are just friends."

"So Domini is jealous?"

"Hell if I know. Meantime, I've been forced to drink the black sludge from the Conoco station."

Colt fiddled with the cap on his water bottle. "You could remedy the jealousy situation and ask Domini out."

Cam laughed. "Right."

"I'm serious."

"So am I."

"What about her has you runnin' scared?"

"Everything. She deserves better than half a man."

Colt widened his eyes in mock shock. "Did part of your dick get shot off at the same time as your leg and your hand?"

The look on Cam's face was hilarious. "No!"

"Then you ain't half a man."

"What do I have to offer her? A soft, sweet, beautiful girl like her don't wanna get mixed up with a fucked-up man like me, guaranteed." The plastic bottle crumpled in his big hand. "I have dark edges she couldn't handle."

"Don't we all?"

"Not like mine." Cam's eyes narrowed. "Maybe you oughta take your own advice."

"You want me to ask Domini out?"

"Fuck off. Maybe you should quit mooning around India and do something about it."

Colt chugged the last of his water. "I have done something about it."

"What?"

"Given up."

"Are you kidding me?"

"Nope. I realized India ain't ever gonna see me beyond a drunk she's counseled or her best bud, so I asked someone else to the community dance Saturday night."

"Who?"

"Fallon Jacobson."

Cam's jaw dropped. "No fucking way."

"What makes you say that?"

"Because she's so not your type. She's..."

Irritably, Colt said, "She's what?"

"Nice. Normal. Quiet." He sipped his water. "Kinda plain."

"And that's bad?"

"Hell no. That's just not the type of woman you've chased after in the past."

"It's been so long since I've done any chasin' I figured my tastes have changed."

"How'd you hook up with her?"

"She was in the hardware store Monday mornin'. We got to talkin' and the next thing I knew I was askin' her out." His determination to move on had happened far quicker than Colt planned. "Maybe you should ask Domini and we can make it a double date."

Cam scowled. "Yeah. I'm a one-legged dancing machine these days. Thanks, but I'll pass from that public humiliation."

"You can run five miles but you won't two-step? That's sad, man. Lemme know if you change your mind." Colt stood. "I'm gonna hit the shower."

"Me too. Later." Cam grabbed his duffel and headed for the exit—the opposite direction of the showers. He never took off his prosthetic in public.

When Colt climbed into his pickup, his cell phone buzzed in the seat. He didn't have to pick it up to know who'd called him. Three times.

India.

Seeing her name—and no one else's—pop up on the screen, strengthened his resolve to put physical and emotional distance between them.

Chapter Five

"Come on, come on, come on, pick up," India muttered as she paced in her kitchen.

"The number you've reached is unavailable. At the tone, please record your message. *Beep.*"

"Hi, Colt. It's India. But you knew that. Anyway, I-umm, hope you're okay. We missed you at the meeting Tuesday night, and I'm...well, I'm worried about you. I've been trying to reach you since Monday." *Stupid, India, he knows that, courtesy of the twenty increasingly paranoid messages you've left him.*

"*Beep.* End of message."

"Fuck!" India hit redial and waited for it to kick over to voice mail. She half-listened to the same canned response. Finally, the beep sounded.

"Look. I understand that you're embarrassed about what happened Sunday morning. But I don't see where you get off blowing three years worth of our friendship just because *you're* embarrassed. We've always been able to talk through anything, and this shouldn't be an exception. You're making this so hard on—" Dammit. Should she have said *hard-on*? Should she have said *blowing*? Shit shit shit. Think back. Did she say *come*? Or *get off*? At any point?

"*Beep.* End of message."

"Fuck!" Infuriated, she pressed redial. This time she was ready for the beep.

"Quit being such a dickhead, McKay. Call me." She snapped the phone shut. Hah! That'll get his attention.

But hours passed and still no word from Colt.

India crawled in bed and stared at the shimmery silver canopy. For the hundredth time, she wondered how everything had spun out of control. Sure, she understood his anger at her accidentally shooting him in the butt and his frustration at being stuck in her apartment. India even understood him being pissed off about her going out on a date with his cousin and how he could've jumped to conclusions when Blake was hammering her headboard with such vigor.

What she couldn't understand? Why sexy-as-sin, charm-the-panties-off-any-woman-with-a-pulse Colt McKay hadn't gotten laid in three years. That boggled her mind.

The McKay men were all notoriously good-looking. Every. Single. One. Since her sister, Skylar, was married to one of those hunky McKay men, and those cowboy beefcakes congregated on a regular basis, India had plenty of room to judge. In her eyes, Colt was the best looking of all of them. Period.

Not only was Colt a shining example of masculinity, he was sweet. Smart too, but he preferred to hide his brainpower under beguiling smiles and cajoling words. He was fun to be around, thoughtful, insightful...so it made zero sense he wasn't getting any.

Neither are you.

And when had smokin' hot bad cowboy Colt started leveling his intense I-wanna-fuck-you-now stare...on her? And using a seductive masculine growl instead of words?

Why wasn't she put off by the changes?

Because it seems right. Natural. And about goddamn time.

India closed her eyes and relived the brief interlude in the kitchen. Her hand rubbing on his cock empowered her. She never remembered feeling such a thrill at a man's loss of control. Wanting to see how he could take control of her. To see how far he could push her before she lost it.

Hell, she'd been tempted to drag him into her bedroom and see how wild they could be together. But she'd backed off. Partially out of guilt for his injury, partially out of self-preservation, fearing a spontaneous tumble would irreparably damage their friendship—a friendship she valued above all others.

And look what that self-preservation had gotten her...the man had cut off all communication anyway. She could've had a mind-bending orgasm or twenty and ended up with the same result.

Frustrated, India covered her head with a pillow and tried to sleep. She'd definitely get in touch with him tomorrow.

*

India hadn't seen or talked to Colt for six days, which sucked, but not as bad as the impending humiliation sucked. She sighed. Loudly.

"Stop it," Domini said.

"But I don't want to go to this stupid dance."

"Tough. You are always making me do things I don't want to do."

India cocked an eyebrow at her. "Like what?"

"Things." Domini waved her off distractedly. "Anyway, you have to put in an appearance. This is a fundraiser for the community and you need to show your support."

"By donating a free tattoo to the highest bidder?"

"Better that than a week's worth of cooking lessons."

India knew who'd submit the winning bid for the private lessons, no matter how much it cost, even if he had to rig the results. "Just promise you won't ditch me. I probably won't know many people." The folks she knew through A.A. were an odd lot, she wasn't sure they'd admit to knowing her outside the meetings.

"You'll know everyone," Domini said. "Isn't your sister going to be there?"

"No. Sky Blue just donated a gift basket to the auction. Skylar and Kade don't have time to turn around since the twins came along."

"Ah. Then you are welcome to hang out with me."

"You and who else? Because if Cat is going to be there? No thanks, I'll pass." Domini's boss was a real piece of work.

"Cat is out of town on another trip to Denver, remember?" Domini sniffed. "It's Nadia, Anton and me. With him I'm guaranteed a dance partner."

"Until he hits the sugar crash stage from too much Kool-Aid." India turned sideways in the mirror. The skinny jeans looked good, but the shirt? No way. "I don't know which one of us is more pathetic, Dom. You, for having a six-year-old boy as a date, or me, for even trying to cover up my tattoos with this long-sleeved blouse."

Domini moved in behind her. Man, the woman was tall. In bare feet she towered over India's five-foot-four by a good six inches. "Why would you cover your skin in tattoos and then freak out about people looking at them? Show them off."

"Good point." India unbuttoned the plain white blouse and tossed it on the bed. She rummaged through her closet until she found her favorite sleeveless shirt, a delicate silk, covered with a bold oriental floral pattern. As she pulled it on over her head, she noticed Domini looking at her chest. "What?"

"This may be none of my business, but did it hurt when you umm...pierced your...?"

"My what?"

A blush stole across Domini's cheeks, turning her icy blue eyes even more vivid. "Your nipples."

"Oh. I don't remember, it's been so long. Why? You thinking of having it done?"

"No! I mean, I don't know. I would like to know if it makes...things more pleasurable?"

"Things...meaning sex?"

Domini nodded, blushing harder.

"It's an added bonus if your breasts are sensitive. Especially if you have a lover who knows what he's doing. Who understands your balance point between pleasure and pain."

"I've never had a lover give me what I really want." She looked away.

India waited, hoping Domini would say something else. When she didn't, India let it drop. "Are we ready?"

"I am."

They opted to drive to the community center. Upon seeing all the trucks and cars spilling out into the street and filling up the parking lot of St. Winifred's Catholic Church, they figured they might've been better off walking.

The band had set up in the back. Tables along the near wall were piled with cookies and bars; on the far wall the tables were crammed with auction items.

Nadia waved and Domini headed to the table. India hung back, her eyes scanning the crowd for a familiar face.

No, for *the* familiar face.

Lots of dark-haired men, but not the one she was looking

for.

She bulled her way through the crowd, smiling at the folks she knew, ignoring the pointed stares of the ones she didn't. She finally saw a face she recognized. Buck McKay, her sister's brother-in-law.

Sometimes India forgot Buck and Kade were identical twins because their personalities were so different. Heck, to her, they didn't even look that much alike. In the last year, Buck had grown a soul patch and shaved his hair to stubble. Good thing the man had a gorgeous skull. He had a gorgeous everything.

Not as gorgeous as Colt.

Dammit. She was trying not to obsess about him.

Buck opened his arms in welcome and she hugged him. "I didn't expect to see you here, Buck."

"Same goes. Normally, it's not my thing. But I promised Hayden if he helped me fix fence for two weeks without complainin', we'd bid on the fly-fishin' weekend. He upheld his end of the deal, so I'm upholding mine." He set his hand on the slender shoulder of the boy beside him. The kid's slight build and fair complexion made him look about seven, but his eyes behind thick glasses were wise for such a young age.

"This is my buddy Hayden. Hayden, this is India Ellison. She's Skylar's sister."

"Nice to meet you, Hayden."

"You own India's Ink, right?"

"Yep."

"When I'm eighteen, I'm going to get a tattoo just like Buck's." He gave Buck a look of absolute adoration.

India smiled. "It's never too early to start thinking about the perfect design. I'll look forward to seeing you in a few years."

"Why don't you grab us each a cup of punch before the band gets started?" Buck suggested. Hayden took off like a shot.

"What a cutie. He seems like a nice kid."

"He's great." Buck's gaze followed the boy across the room. "It's one of the best things I've ever done. Don't know if I ever said thank you for givin' me a dose of tough love."

"You're welcome. I'm just glad to see it's working out." A few months back, during a dinner at Sky and Kade's place, Buck had spent the evening whining. His twin was happily married. His cousin Colt had built a new place and sold the Boars Nest to Cam. Poor Buck was left homeless and lonely—a fact he'd bitched about until India snapped. If he was so damn lonely, there were plenty of boys in the Little Buddies program who needed time and attention from an adult male. It'd shocked her a few weeks later when Kade mentioned Buck had taken her advice and signed up for the program.

"I didn't expect to see you here either."

"Domini's idea. But I'd hoped to run into Colt. Have you seen him?"

Buck's eyes avoided hers. "Uh. Yeah."

"Where?"

"He's around."

When he stayed mum, India demanded, "What's going on?"

"You tell me. I figured you and Colt must've had a fight or something."

"Why?"

"Because he's here with a date."

A sucker punch couldn't have hurt worse. "What?"

Pause. "That motherfucker." Buck looked at her. "You didn't know?"

India shook her head.

"Just say the word and I'll kick his ass." Buck swore and wrapped his arm around her shoulder. "Ah, honey, I'm sorry."

"No wonder he's been dodging my phone calls all week."

"Stupid bastard."

That caused a small smile. For the hundredth time India wished she could fall in love with Buck McKay. He wanted the same thing she did—what Kade and Skylar had—true love, mutual respect, great sex, a real home, sweet kids, the whole shebang. Buck looked out for her, treating her like a little sister, which was the problem. It'd feel incestuous if they became more than friends.

It should feel incestuous with Colt too, since they'd been friends longer, but somehow...it didn't.

She pulled back in mind and body. "Thanks."

Hayden bounded up. Refusing his gentlemanly offer of his punch, India retreated to the shadows by the bathroom.

Her eyes continually scanned the crowd for Colt. Finally she caught sight of him on the dance floor. God. He was stunning. Absolutely freakin' stunning. He spun the woman in his arms around twice and kept zipping along the outskirts so she didn't get a good look at his date's face.

Why does it matter what she looks like?

It just did.

When they performed the forward turn, India scrutinized her. The woman was tall. Sturdy. Blonde, with a wide smile that almost hid her horse face. She was maybe five or six years younger than Colt. She dressed in the style of a ranch woman, dark jeans, a brightly colored blouse dotted with geometric shapes and rhinestone snaps. Well-worn ropers the same turquoise as her shirt.

Sad thing was, if Colt married her, local people would assume Colt had settled, especially in light of his reputation of preferring good-looking, wild women—of which this prim and proper lady was neither.

Oh, Ms. Horse Woman would pop out a couple of halfway cute kids, be the perfect FFA mom, she'd help Colt run the ranch at top efficiency. She'd...fit in, in ways India never would. It made India sick, because she figured Colt would be back on the booze within six months of committing his life to such a lackluster woman.

Colt needed someone like India in his life.

Right. He'll be dropping on bended knee after you called him a dickhead.

A fake smile creased Colt's face as he danced the woman backward and the couple disappeared into the crowd.

When the song finished, the lights clicked on and the auctioneer randomly selected prizes for bidding. First, a massage package donated by AJ McKay, of Healing Touch Massage, which earned a respectable bid of two hundred dollars. The band kicked off another song. As soon as it ended, the auctioneer took the stage. And so it went for three more tunes.

Skylar's basket sold for three hundred bucks. The private cooking lessons with Domini, head cook at Dewey's Delish Dish, fetched fifteen hundred dollars from an anonymous bidder. Domini was clearly flustered by the attention, but extremely pleased.

Buck placed the winning bid on the fly-fishing trip. He and Hayden waved to her as they claimed their prize and headed out.

After a snappy rendition of "Oh Lonesome Me" the moment India dreaded arrived. She kept to the back of the room, hidden in the alcove by the drinking fountain.

The auctioneer snapped the paper in his hand. "Well, I'll be. This is an interesting prize, a one of a kind tattoo, courtesy of India's Ink. Who'll start the bidding?"

Silence.

India wanted to throw up.

"Come on, folks, this is for a good cause. Shall we start the bidding at one hundred dollars?"

More silence.

"How about fifty dollars?"

She had to force her feet to stay in place and not run out the back door in sheer mortification.

"I'll give ya twenty," some guy shouted from the front row and the whole room erupted into laughter.

"Seriously, folks. Minimum bid is fifty dollars. Do I hear fifty dollars?"

Then, "I'll bid one thousand dollars."

A collective gasp rippled through the crowd.

The auctioneer pointed. "I have a bid of one thousand dollars. Going once. Going twice." *Crack.* The gavel landed on the podium. "Sold to the artistically minded gentleman in the black hat, for the sum of one thousand dollars."

A smattering of applause broke out.

And rather than rejoicing, India seethed.

Colt McKay was a dead man.

Chapter Six

As India headed for the punch table, she formulated a plan of attack. She didn't know whether to confront him here, or put the anger whammy on him when he least expected it. Her temper was a vile thing. Letting it fly was always a last resort, especially in public, since she usually picked up the nearest heavy object and let it fly too.

Colt snatched the choice away when he snuck up behind her and drawled, "I didn't think dances were your thing, India."

"You don't know everything about me." She whirled around. "Where's your date?"

"Where's yours?" he countered.

"I'm here by myself because no one asked me."

"I'm sure my cousin Blake would've been happy to escort you. Or aren't there any headboards here that he needs to fix?"

"You're hilarious, McKay."

Colt flashed his teeth. "I try."

"I expected better from you."

People around them were starting to stare.

"Meaning what?"

Through clenched teeth she said, "Meaning, I don't need your fucking pity."

"Why would I feel sorry for you?"

"Because no one else bid on my prize, and you're throwing cash around like—"

"It's my money and I can do what I want with it."

"Were you buying the tattoo package as a gift for your date?"

He scowled.

"She's not exactly the tattoo type, is she? And God forbid anyone else in this town would admit in public they'd pay to cavort with a low-class ink slinger like me."

Fury darkened his eyes. "Watch it."

She gave him an innocent look. "Did I insult her?"

"It ain't my date you're insulting, it's yourself, and that pisses me off worse, so knock it the hell off. I expected better from you, sugar."

"Don't you *sugar* me, Colt McKay." India tugged her wallet out of her back jeans pocket and unclipped the chain. "How about if I write you a check for a thousand bucks and we'll call it even."

"Put your money away."

"I won't be beholden to you for anything."

"Too fuckin' late and you're treading on thin ice, India."

She got right in his face. "So? I feel like stomping all over that ice, Colt, with sharp, pointy crampons to see who falls through the cracks first."

"It looks like you're the one who's cracking up."

"It's your fault."

"My fault? How do you figure?"

India smacked him in the chest with her wallet. "Because I've been trying to get in touch with you all week."

"Why?"

Because I missed you, you clueless jerk. "Because you missed Tuesday night's meeting."

Colt stared at her with belligerence. "So? I've been busy."

"You were too busy to come to a meeting?"

"Cut me some slack. I've missed one meeting in two and a half years."

"I left you a bajillion messages."

"I particularly liked the one where you called me a dickhead."

That brought a small smile. "If the shitkicker fits..."

"Don't fuck with me, India. I'm not in the mood."

"Well, gee, I wouldn't want anything to ruin your 'mood', especially since you have a hot date." India bit her cheek to keep from lashing out further. "You know what? Forget it. All of it. Have a lovely evening with your horse-faced honey."

Colt laughed and said, "Oh, no you don't," as he snatched

her elbow. "We ain't close to done with this conversation."

"We are. Just leave me alone."

"Like hell."

Stupid tears flooded her eyes. She couldn't blink them away fast enough and the stupid jerk saw she was about to bawl like a stupid baby.

"Sweet Jesus, are you cryin'?"

"No." She jammed her wallet in her back pocket and attempted to flee.

"Dammit. Don't you walk away like this."

"Haven't you humiliated me enough tonight?" India dodged people congregating in the hallways, fully aware they were gawking at her. And him. And them.

"Come back here."

Burning gazes of strangers raked her inked skin as deeply as if they were wielding tattoo needles. Disgusted glances at her piercings pricked her as sharply as if they were holding a piercing gun. Normally she could give a rip about the stares, but tonight she had a hard time holding her head up, which pissed her off.

She didn't get far before Colt clamped his fingers around her biceps. "Let me go."

"Not a chance."

"Where's your date?"

"Shut up, Indy."

"I hate you."

"No, sugar, you don't."

More tears surfaced.

He dragged her downstairs. Smart people scattered at seeing the intent on Colt's face and the fury in his every movement.

Taking a quick look around, he pulled her into a closet in the middle of the hallway. Then he stepped in front of the door, blocking her exit. "Start talkin'."

India mimed zipping her lip and tossing away the key.

"You are the most annoying woman I've ever met." Colt advanced on her. "For the record? There are lots of things I feel for you, but pity ain't one of them."

Her shoulders hit a wall.

"Still ain't talkin' to me?"

She shook her head.

Colt was a breath away. "I've got an idea on how you can put that smart mouth of yours to better use."

Her lips parted. In protest or invitation? Dammit. Lately whenever they got within kissing distance all she could think about was locking lips with him. For hours. Days maybe.

"Well?"

"Fine. If you wanna talk so bad, why don't you tell me one of the things you feel for me?"

"You couldn't handle it right now because you're mad and confused."

"Mad? Yes. Confused? Where do you get off—"

"Look, at yourself. Why are you pushin' me away with one hand, and pullin' me closer with the other?"

"I'm not." Then she noticed her right palm was flat against his chest shoving, while her left hand was bunched in his T-shirt pulling. "Nice try at changing the subject, but I know the real reason you won't tell me."

"What's that?"

"In your dating...*void* over the last few years, your silver tongue has tarnished and you aren't very good with words."

"Is that so?" His eyes never left hers. "I wish you weren't bein' so damn difficult because we both know the real reason you're fightin' with me."

"Wish granted." She sidestepped him.

A hand clamped on her shoulder. He used the momentum to spin her against the wall again.

"Let me go. You've made it clear—"

"No, I haven't." His hands braceleted her wrists and he held them firmly by her sides. Colt eliminated the gap between their bodies and nestled his cheek against hers. Whiskers scraped her jaw, his soft lips brushed the side of her neck, his hot breath skittered across her damp skin with every exhalation.

"This'll make it a damn sight clearer of what I feel for you. I wanna touch you, Indy. Right here. With your back up to the wall. I wanna suck your nipples through your flimsy shirt. Taste how anger changes the sweet flavor of your skin. When that ain't enough contact, I'll lift up your shirt so I can pull those pretty pink nipples in my mouth, rollin' my tongue around the hoops. I'll suck hard, suck deep, suck for a good, long time."

Colt's words set her blood on fire.

"That ain't all. I wanna go down on you. Yank off your jeans. Rip aside your panties and finger you until you're nice and wet. Then I'll drop to my knees and taste you. Gently at first. Lick a path from the top down to where you're weepin' for me."

India's knees threatened to buckle as he tormented her with erotic images.

"I'll swirl the tip of my tongue around your opening, never going higher, sometimes slipping just a little too far back. Nipping that tasty tender flesh between your thighs with my lips and teeth. Then I'll jam my tongue as deeply inside you as it'll go. I'll do it again and again and again. Licking you from the inside out. But I'd stop."

"No," she whispered hoarsely.

"*Yes.* I'll pull back and cool you down." He blew a stream of air across her neck. Chills beaded her skin. "Can't you feel it? My breath blowing on the hottest part of you?"

"Colt—"

"When you can't stand it, when you're grinding your wet sex against my face, demanding release, then I'll give you what you crave. My thumbs will spread you wide. I'll set my mouth on you and I'll suck until you explode on my tongue. And I'll lap up your sweet juices like candy."

India panted. She clenched her thighs together, hoping the pulsing tremors would break free into a full-fledged orgasm.

He dragged openmouthed kisses across her throat to her ear and whispered, "You still thinkin' I ain't good with words?"

She glimpsed fire burning in his eyes before he crushed her lips beneath his and kissed her until she thought her head would explode from the sheer hedonistic pleasure of it.

Eventually she recovered her sanity. "Is this some kind of game to see if you can get me hot and bothered?"

"You ain't the only one who's hot and bothered." Colt released her right hand and placed it over his fly.

India felt his hardness straining against the zipper of his Wranglers. She stroked him until air hissed through his teeth. "Colt. What are we doing here?"

"Goin' straight to hell."

"Then why doesn't this feel wrong?"

"It isn't. Stop." Colt pushed back, putting a few feet between them. "I can't do this again."

"Do what?"

"Want you when I can't have you and be miserable because I can't stay away from you. I've tried. And what's the first thing I do when I see you? Run the other direction? No. I haul you off and maul you."

While India stared at him, he stared at the cement floor.

"I don't want you to stay away from me, Colt."

"Sayin' stuff like that is not helpin' this situation."

"What will help?"

"I don't know." Colt left without another word.

India's urge to cry was almost as strong as the one to run. Her fingers had circled the door handle to chase after him, when she heard a lilting voice say, "Colt?" on the other side of the door.

"Hey, Fallon. I was just comin' to find you."

"Really? Because I've been looking all over for you."

Fallon? His date was named after a character on *Dynasty*? Seriously?

"Sorry, I didn't mean to run off."

"But you did." Pause. "What were you doing in that closet?"

Crap. They were so busted.

"Because someone told me they saw you and that tattooed woman sneaking in there together."

That tattooed woman.

"Who told you that?"

"About half a dozen different people. Are you denying it?"

"Who's to say those people might've been mistaken about what they'd seen, or what they thought they'd seen?" he countered.

Not exactly a lie on Colt's part.

"Tell me the truth. Were you in there alone?"

The tension crackled through the wooden door slats and India held her breath.

"No."

"That's what I thought. You were in there with her. When you were supposed to be on a date with me. People warned me about you, 'Don't go out with Colt McKay, he's a womanizer and a player of the worst sort' but did I listen to them? No."

India's stomach churned.

"Did you honestly believe no one would see you taking her into a supply closet for a quickie? Are you that much of a sex maniac? Good Lord. You have to know I am not the kind of woman who does that sort of thing on the first date."

Tell her you haven't been on a date in your sober state. Tell her you haven't had sex in three years.

He stayed mum.

"I cannot believe I thought you'd changed."

"Live and learn, I guess," Colt said bitterly. "You ready for me to take you home?"

She laughed. Cruelly. "Right. Like I'd be seen with you again. It's probably just as well I caught you cheating right away, rather than finding out later what kind of sneaky man you are. And if she's the kind of woman who lets you screw her in public? Then you two deserve each other."

Her angry bootsteps faded down the hallway.

Colt didn't call after her.

Poor Colt. India really had no idea what to do.

You could've defended him.

Yeah, popping out of the closet with her lips swollen from his hard kisses would've been a sure-fire way to defend Colt's honor.

When India finally found the guts to open the door, Colt was long gone.

Chapter Seven

"I cannot believe I thought you'd changed."

Story of his life in recent years.

Colt chinked his glass of Diet Coke to his reflection in the sliding glass door as a sarcastic self-toast. Well done. He wasn't surprised Fallon had lashed out. He'd hurt her; her natural instinct was to strike back.

His natural instinct was to hole up with a bottle.

Not possible, but his body still craved a drink so badly his teeth hurt.

He'd tried to get out of an unhealthy situation with India, only to find himself defending her at the first opportunity.

The silence in the community center after the auctioneer announced India's prize package tied Colt's guts in knots. India might act tough, but beneath that hard outer shell was a softie trying to find her place within a community that didn't easily welcome strangers.

Or didn't readily believe long-time citizens could change.

They were both screwed. No wonder they'd been together these last few years. And Fallon, while trying to make it an insult, had it exactly right: they did deserve each other.

How could he convince India that statement was true?

The high point of the night had been the ten minutes of heaven he and India carved out in the supply closet. Nothing else mattered but the need pulsing between them. Each kiss, each touch, awakened the sexual beast sleeping inside him.

Maybe that's why he'd been content living a celibate life. He'd needed to learn who he was as a man, not a male who only thought with his dick.

So what now that the beast was fully awake?

Sate it. With lots and lots of sex.

Colt knew if he drove back into town and trolled the bars he could have a woman in his bed within an hour. But there was only one woman he wanted in his bed.

India.

Avoiding her had only produced a sharper ache. Lining up a date with another woman only proved he'd compare every female to the tattooed smart mouth who'd stolen his heart. Goddamn, she could piss him off one second and fire his blood with lust the next.

Drown your sorrows. You deserve to cut loose and try and forget about her.

Nights like this were the worst, being unsure and frustrated only increased his cravings for alcohol.

So booze was out. Sex was out. Sleep was a lost cause. That left one thing.

Colt changed into workout shorts. In the spare bedroom, he slipped on his boxing gloves and beat the stuffing out of the punching bag until he was sweaty and too exhausted to think.

The next morning the phone rang as Colt came inside from stacking wood. Only three people called him before eight on Sunday. India, his cousin Chassie, and his mother. Lately Chassie didn't bother phoning first, she barged right into his house. He didn't need to look at the caller ID today. "Hey, Ma."

"Good morning!"

Carolyn West McKay was the cheeriest morning person on the planet. He poured the last of the coffee in his mug and listened to her chatter like a chipmunk. She'd get to the point of the call eventually. But she had this perverted sixth sense—if she thought you were trying to speed her along, she'd find irrelevant things to yammer on about.

"...just wanted to double-check that you were coming for an early family supper tonight."

Finally. "How early?"

"Four o'clock."

"Sure, I'll be there."

"Good. Cam is coming when he gets off shift. Wish Carter and Macie and their boys could be here. Keely too. It's been a long time since we've had a family dinner." Her weighted pause actually caused Colt to hold his breath. "Is there a chance you'll be bringing a date?"

Shit. He wasn't surprised word of his date with Fallon—and the fiasco afterward—had already fueled the gossip channels. Still, that was fast, even by Sundance standards. "Nope. No date. Sorry to disappoint you."

"Oh. No, son, I'm not disappointed. I'm looking forward to catching up. You're not around as much since you built that house out in the middle of nowhere."

"Everywhere in Wyoming is out in the middle of nowhere," he said dryly. "Besides, it's only thirty miles."

"Seems like you're three thousand miles away," she murmured.

Sometimes I wish I was.

As he hung up, he couldn't remember the last time he'd looked forward to Sunday dinner with the family, instead of feeling a sense of dread.

The McKay house was complete chaos. Kids running around, babies crying, his mother and his sisters-in-law jabbering like they hadn't seen each other in months.

He'd been hanging out with his nephews in the family room, when he realized he was the only male adult in the room. He tracked his brothers and his father outside, lounging against the split rail fence running along the front of the house, drinking beer and shooting the shit. Even after three years of sobriety, they weren't comfortable popping a top or two around him. Which was just another reason Colt only stayed long enough to be polite. Not that he contributed much to any conversation.

Carson said, "I don't know what the hell Charlie was thinkin'."

"Why didn't Quinn and Bennett say something?" Colby asked.

"'Cause I don't think they knew."

Cord tipped his long neck beer bottle toward Colby. "I'll bet you fifty bucks Aunt Vi had something to do with it."

"You're on."

They chinked bottles.

Colt shifted his stance and dropped his water bottle, reminding Cord, Colby and his father he was not part of the fence.

"What do you think about it?" Carson McKay demanded.

"So they bought a pair of llamas, big deal," Colt said. "I don't see how it affects us. Besides givin' us ample opportunity to razz our cousins to no end with the question: Is your mama a llama?"

Laughter broke out. Cord's son Kyler's obsession with that book as a toddler meant they'd all been forced to read it until they could recite the thing from memory. That'd been a happy period in Colt's life, one of the memories of that time not tainted by alcohol.

"Seems Ky's reading skills will come in handy with the new baby."

All gazes zoomed to Cord.

He grinned like a loon. "AJ's pregnant. She wanted to wait until she's past the first trimester to tell folks, bein's it's her first baby and all, but I can't help it."

Carson clapped Cord on the back. Colby said, "Congrats. Man, must be something in the water. Channing, Macie and AJ are all pregnant at the same time."

"Least they're not all gonna pop durin' calvin' season," Carson said.

If both his brothers' wives were pregnant during the busiest time of the year, it meant Colt would shoulder a bigger chunk of the responsibility.

Big surprise. Didn't it just figure everyone in the family assumed he'd be around to pick up the slack? Hell, when push came to shove, only Cam and Carter owned less of the McKay herd than he did. They both had other jobs. Colt's sullen side silently retorted that no one expected *them* to do more than their fair share. In fact, with Cam's war injury he couldn't do much. And Carter split his time between here and his in-laws' place in Canyon River.

"Colt?"

He shoved aside his sour thoughts and focused his attention on Colby. "Yeah?"

"Carter told me to tell you that you could stay at his and Macie's place durin' calvin' so you don't have to drive so far."

Would it be petty to point out neither Colby nor Cord offered up their places for him to crash?

Yes.

Jesus. He was stuck in "feel sorry for me mode" tonight. It'd be best to smile and suck it up, rather than point out neither of them had to give up their comfy beds for a month. Every year.

"If you don't wanna do that, I'm sure Cam'll let you bunk with him for the duration."

Cam wouldn't look him in the eye.

And right then, Colt had enough. "I appreciate it, but it ain't gonna be necessary."

Cord frowned. "That's a long damn drive. Especially with the weather bein' shitty that time of year."

"I'm sure you guys'll handle the weather and the calvin' just fine without me."

Shocked silence. Then, Colby said, "Without you? What do you mean?"

"I ain't gonna be here."

"Where you gonna be?"

"I'll be in Hawaii."

His dad demanded, "For how long?"

"For a month."

"What are you doin' over there for a month?"

"Sittin' on the beach, whale watchin', surfing. Maybe I'll learn to scuba dive. Or golf. Whatever people do when they're on vacation."

"Very fuckin' funny," Cord said.

"Might be if I was kiddin'."

They all stared at him.

"You can't just schedule a damn vacation durin' the most important time of the year in the cattle business."

Colt shrugged. Maybe it was childish, but he felt the need to push them. See if anyone would voice the questions and contempt he saw in their eyes. If he'd ever truly be forgiven or if they were waiting for the other boot to drop. Or for him to revert to his formerly destructive behavior.

Cam scratched at the label on his beer bottle.

Colby spoke first. "That's just great, Colt. Once again you'll be off fuckin' around while the rest of us are bustin' our asses."

"Man, I thought you'd changed," Cord said. "But we're back to the same old bullshit."

There it was. The word that damned him either way—change. If he did change, it was wrong. If he didn't change, it was wrong.

"Why's it such a big deal for you to stay with Cam or at Carter's? It ain't like you've got a family to go home to every night."

A beer bottle flew and crashed into the side of the barn, shattering the illusion of stillness.

All eyes zoomed to Cam.

"I'm so sick and tired of the 'holier than thou' attitude in this family. So Colt screwed up. Every one of us has screwed up at one time or another. How long are you gonna make him pay for it? Jesus, he hit the skids over four years ago. He's been on the straight and narrow for the last three. During which time, he's been busting his ass on this ranch, despite having to listen to you berate him and complain about him, or ignore him, or belittle him. None of you have ever been lily white and you've got no business judging him."

"You weren't here, Cam."

Cam whirled on Colby. "Guess what? Neither were you! You were off rodeoin' and playin' cowboy while Colt was here, actually *being* a goddamn cowboy, day in, day out, for twelve fuckin' years. Don't forget you couldn't do shit for months while you recovered from your rodeo injury—months in which, once again, Colt had to do not only his work, but your work."

Holy shit. Colt had never seen Cam so furious.

But Cam wasn't finished. He turned his ire on Cord. "Didja forget you got pissed off at Dad and left for a coupla years? Who picked up the slack then? It sure as fuck wasn't Colby the rodeo king, or Carter the college boy, or Keely the baby girl or me."

Without moving his angry gaze from Cord, Cam pointed at Colt. "It was him. But you forgot that little factoid, didn't you? And isn't it convenient that you all expect Colt to stick around, year in, year out, and do every shit job you don't want to, because he doesn't have a...family?" Cam faced Colby again.

"That 'you don't have a family' comment is the single shittiest thing I've ever heard anyone say. Ever. *You're* supposed to be his family. So are you." He pointed to Cord. "And you," he said to Carson. "And me. But when Colt really needed his family to support him and help him? Were any of you there? No. The only person who gave a shit about him...was Kade."

"That's enough," Carson said.

"How could you all rally around me, offering me support, when you didn't do the same thing for Colt? When he was hurting just as bad? When he's the one who's always deserved it way more than I ever did. Because he had no choice but to stick around and live this life, when I had the luxury of leaving it behind."

Colt's eyes burned. Leave it to the one-legged man to make a stand for him when no one else in his family ever did.

Ugly, thick silence lingered.

"I'm not surprised you've got nothin' to say. You oughta be hanging your heads in shame. I'm outta here." Fabric snapped as Cam jerked his coat off the fence. He limped to his truck. After he opened the door he looked at Colt. "Sorry, bro, I know you didn't ask for this, but it needed to be said. It needed to come from someone with an outsider's perspective."

"You're not an outsider, Cameron. You might've been gone for a few years, but you've always been part of this family."

All eyes turned to Carolyn McKay. No one had heard her come out onto the porch.

Cam shook his head. "Thanks for the invite to supper, Ma, but I've lost my appetite."

She twisted a dishtowel in her hands, tears streaming down her face as she watched Cam drive away.

Great, his mother would probably blame him too.

Colt didn't make eye contact with anyone as he climbed in his pickup and started the long, lonely drive home.

Chapter Eight

He'd hit the outskirts of Sundance, when his cell phone vibrated. He had half a mind to let it go to voice mail. Another confrontation today would do him in but he checked the caller ID anyway. Kade and Skylar's home number. "Hello?"

"Colt? Omigod, I'm so glad you answered. I was afraid you were still avoiding me, and—Eliza Belle! Get down right now!"

"Indy? Why are you callin' from Kade's house?"

"Sky and Kade planned a romantic getaway and Grama Kimi caught the flu. And rather than let them cancel their first trip alone since the twins were born, I said I'd watch the girls. Only they're screaming, all three at the same time—" an ear-piercing shriek echoed in the background, "—and I can't do this by myself! This is insane. How can anyone take care of a two and a half year old and six-month-old twins? Can you please please please come and help me? I'll pay you, I promise I'll do anything—"

"Anything?"

"Yes—No! Eliza, do *not* put that in your mouth!"

Colt grinned for the first time in hours. "Take a deep breath, sugar, I'll be there in thirty minutes."

"Oh. Thank you, thank you, thank you, I owe you. Big time."

Dial tone.

"Yes, Miz India Blue, you surely do owe me."

He spent the remainder of the drive figuring out all sorts of inventive ways India could pay off her debt.

*

"I wanna cookie."

"No."

"I wanna cookie...please?"

"No way, Eliza, the last thing you need is more sugar." India had Shannie cocked on her left hip and Peyton screamed from her high chair.

A mulish look settled on Eliza's face. "Mama—"

"Mama is not here." *Please, Colt, hurry.* Surely it'd been longer than a half hour. She had no idea why her sweet nieces had morphed into monsters.

"I gonna call her," Eliza announced.

"No!" India snatched the cordless receiver and put it on top of the refrigerator next to the other cordless receivers she'd confiscated. Eliza had already tried to throw India's cell phone in the toilet in the guise of "washing" it.

Right. Eliza's devilish smile belied her innocent baby blues. The girl was the spitting image of her father in looks and her mother in temperament.

Peyton continued to scream. Shannie kept trying to pull out India's earrings. Eliza stood on her booster seat and hoisted herself on the table, crawling toward the package of animal crackers.

"Oh, no you don't, missy." India scooped her up and set her on the floor. "No more. I mean it."

Startled by India's unusually stern tone, Eliza began to cry, which made Shannie start bawling.

Wonderful.

"I heard there was a party goin' on in here with four wild girls. To be honest, I expected some of ya'll to be wearin' less clothes."

India spun around and saw Colt leaning against the doorjamb. She wanted to smack him for looking so damn good when she looked like a train wreck. She wanted to burst into tears for his good humor when hers was gone. Mostly, she wanted to kiss him for showing up and saving her sanity when she had no one else to call.

"Unka Cole!" Eliza jumped from the chair and ran toward him full bore. He barely managed to keep her from racking him.

"Hey, short stuff." He picked her up and propped her on his hip. "Why the tears?"

Eliza, that shameless charmer, laid her head on Colt's chest and sighed. "I hungry."

Lord have mercy. The man was about four seconds from melting.

"Don't fall for it," India warned. "She is a c-o-o-k-i-e monster today."

"Huh-uh, I not a monser," Eliza said. "I jus' lub cookies."

Colt grinned. "She's a smart cookie too." He looked from Shannie to Peyton, who'd both gone quiet. "Seems you've got it all under control now."

"A temporary delusion."

"Have they had supper?"

"Miz Eliza has if you count the box of sugary disks she's stuffed in her sweet face like a rabid squirrel. I was about to heat up the twins' baby food, when I lost complete control of the situation and called you."

"That's your first mistake. Never show 'em fear." Colt gave Eliza a smacking kiss on her cheek and she giggled. "You wanna color at the table while Auntie Indy and me feed your sisters?"

"Yay!"

He looked at India over Eliza's head. "The coloring books are...?"

"All over the floor in the living room. There's some on the stairs I think."

Colt swung Eliza around for a piggyback to the living room and she squealed with delight.

India tried to put Shannie in her high chair, but Shannie arched her back and held tighter to the big hoop earrings in India's ear. The kid was part crow; mesmerized by shiny objects. India took out two jars of pureed green beans and two jars of carrots and put them in a shallow pan of water already on the stove.

"Okay, Eliza, here you go. Your colors and your favorite 'My Little Pony' coloring book. Make me something purty as you."

India turned and Colt was right there. In her face. Close enough to kiss.

He cringed when he saw Shannie's death grip. "Holy crap—"

"Holy crap," Eliza repeated.

"She's got hold of your earrings good, doesn't she?"

"Usually I don't wear jewelry around the girls, but I forgot today until it was too late. Eliza's the reason I let my lip piercing grow shut."

"I'd wondered about that. Damn shame. It was sexy as hell. I spent lots of hours wondering what it'd be like to kiss you with that." He held out his hands. "Hey, baby girl. Come see your uncle." Shannie flashed a gummy grin, let go of India's earrings, and practically dove at him.

"Do all females fall into your arms so easily?"

"Not all." Colt granted her a molten look. "Some take a little more coaxing. And that's when the fall is so much sweeter."

Now India didn't know which was worse; dealing with three screaming kids, or one scheming man.

But damn, what a man. If she pressed her lips together, she could still feel the surety of his mouth on hers as he'd leveled her with a steamy kiss last night.

"Need a bib?"

Crap. Was she...drooling? Her back snapped straight. "Why in the hell would I need a bib?"

"The hell," Eliza mimicked.

"Not a bib for you, for Peyton."

"Oh."

Colt smiled and popped Shannie in her high chair. He chatted at both baby girls, as well as Eliza. His ease with the kids didn't surprise India; that was why she'd called him.

Bibs on, food warmed, India grabbed the rubber-coated baby spoons from the dishrack. "Which one do you want?"

Without looking away, Colt said, "Eliza, does Shannie still spit her food everywhere?"

"Uh-huh."

"Then I'll feed Peyton."

"Chicken," India taunted.

"A chicken says, bawk bawk," Eliza offered.

India and Colt both laughed.

Shannie managed to eat half her jar of beans, the rest she sprayed all over India. But Peyton wasn't a picnic; she cried and rubbed carrots in her eyes, which made her scream.

"I'll give Peyton a quick bath if you watch Shannie and Eliza."

"Deal."

By the time India undressed the fussy baby, ran the bath water, scrubbed her, rinsed her, dried her, diapered her, clothed her and returned to the kitchen, half an hour had passed and Shannie was crying in her high chair.

India said, "Trade ya," handing Peyton to Colt and lifting Shannie out. She shot a look at an entirely too quiet Eliza...who blinked at her impishly as she bit into a cookie. In fact, Eliza had a whole stack of cookies in front of her.

"Colt! Where did Eliza get—"

"We were counting them, and since she's bein' so good and such a helpful big sister, entertaining Shannie Banannie, I let her have a couple extras, right, cookie monster?"

Eliza giggled.

"You are a s-u-c-k-e-r, Colt McKay."

"Mmm. Totally when it comes to these darlin' girls." He rubbed his cheek over Peyton's head. "Babies smell so great after a bath, don't they?"

Seeing Colt's softer side always made her melt a little. Where else did he show such sweetness?

He shows it with you all the time.

"What now?" he said.

"Will you heat up two bottles while I bathe Shannie?"

"Sure."

Thud. Eliza stood in front of her, cookie crumbs all over her face and clothes. "Innie?"

"What, sweetie?"

"I wanna baf with Shannie."

"Okay. But no splashing."

Serious contemplation occurred before Eliza grudgingly said, "Okay," and flounced up the stairs.

Bathing two kids took twice as long, especially when the older one insisted on "helping". The living room was quiet when the three of them trooped back downstairs.

The TV was on low. Peyton's bottle was empty. She was sound asleep and drooling on Colt's shoulder. Colt didn't mind. He wore a look of contentment India had never seen, nor expected to see. The thought *he'd make a terrific father* flashed through her mind, and she tamped down envy for the lucky woman who bore his children because he'd make a terrific husband too.

Eliza bounded over and jumped next to him on the couch. Right next to him.

Peyton stirred and Colt gently rubbed her back.

"You want me to put her down?"

"Nah. I'll do it. Shannie's bottle is in the pan." He stood and Eliza immediately scooted into his spot. "I'll read you a bedtime story when I get back if you pick a book, cookie monster."

"Huh-uh. I not sleepy."

But Eliza didn't last long. Both she and Shannie conked out at the same time. Colt tucked her in while India laid Shannie in her crib and grabbed the baby monitor.

India flopped on the couch and closed her eyes. A few minutes later the floorboards creaked. "Man, this parenting stuff has me whupped."

The couch cushions moved slightly as Colt sat beside her. "How long did you sign on for?"

"Today and tomorrow. Sky and Kade will be back late tomorrow night." She sighed. "It's weird. I see the girls for a couple of hours every week and I think they're all sweet smiles and cute clothes. But then, I see what it really takes to take care of them every day..."

"And what? It seems like too much work?"

"No. The exact opposite. It seems like the only kind of work that's worthwhile."

Neither one spoke, but it wasn't an awkward silence.

Finally, Colt said, "You see yourself havin' kids some day?"

"Sometimes I think I'm ready now if I find the right man, but yeah, definitely some day. A couple. Or more." Pause. "How about you?"

"I can't wait to have kids. I feel like I'm finally at the time and place in my life where I'm ready for them."

"Is that why you asked Fallon out? Because she's wife and mother material?"

Colt didn't say a word.

"Look. I'm sorry. None of my business who you date."

"Maybe it should be your business."

A funny tingle started in her chest but she still didn't open her eyes.

"I'm sorry I dragged you into a pile of shit last night. I

swear to God I didn't bid that high to embarrass you."

"Why did you?"

"Because people in this town have no fuckin' idea how talented you are. It pissed me off."

A beat passed. "That's sweet, but since you have so much credit with me, that means I'm going to be pushing for the starburst nipple design."

He laughed softly.

India wasn't about to let him off the hook. "As far as Fallon?"

"She was a mistake."

"Then why'd you ask her out?"

"I don't know."

"Come on, Colt, that's crap. Why'd you ask her to the community center dance where everyone could see you two were on a date?"

"Because she wasn't like you."

"Gee. Thanks."

"You took that the wrong way."

"How else am I supposed to take it?"

"Listen, I thought if I was with someone who wasn't like you in any way, I wouldn't...compare."

That hurt. She might've actually winced. Then she felt him move next to her and his breath fanned her cheek.

"Dammit. I'm doin' this all wrong. Look at me."

She turned her head and opened her eyes.

Colt was right there, with his head next to hers on the couch. "Every single woman comes up short when I compare them to you. And before you ask, I ain't talkin' about you bein' short in stature."

"You know me so well."

"I do. And that's what this crazy week has proven to me. I don't want to watch you datin' other guys. I don't want you to watch me datin' other women. I don't want to have to drag you into a supply closet to kiss you and then apologize for doin' it."

"Colt—"

"I don't want to be just your friend any more, Indy."

"Why not?"

"Because I think we can be so much more."

Her heart beat a mile a minute. She took a chance and

blurted, "I want that too."

"You do?" Colt's eyes searched her face. "Since when?"

"Since that night I shot you with the nail gun."

He smiled. "So I guess I can quit bitchin' about that, huh?"

They stayed like that for a long time, not touching, just looking at each other, and just breathing the same air.

"So what do we do now?" she asked.

"We start dating. Official like."

"Dating? Like you pick me up at my place, hold the door for me and take me out for dinner?"

"Something like that." Colt paused. "How long has it been since you dated?"

Would Colt be pleased or pissed if she told him the last relationship she'd been in was purely sexual? When India thought about it...had she ever really just "dated" a man?

No. She'd had sex with plenty of guys, hooked up with more than her fair share, but flowers, dinner, and moonlit walks? Not so much a priority in her younger years when she was drunk or high. Since she'd cleaned up, fixing herself was more a priority than getting fixed up with some man. And in the three years since she'd starting hanging out with Colt, she'd been content to be with just him. She hadn't needed or wanted any other man.

So what did that say about their friendship?

It's always been more than just a simple friendship and you were too stubborn to admit it.

"Indy?"

"Sorry. I don't think I've done the dating thing since I was a teen."

"Funny, I was about to say the same thing."

"Really? We're a pair, huh?"

Colt eased back. "Which makes it all the more important that we do this right. Goin' on dates. Takin' it one step at a time. I've screwed up everything that matters in my life in some way or another, India. Our...relationship is too important to throw away on a quick tumble."

"To me too."

"So you agree to go slow?"

"Go slow, as in..."

"Just dating. No sex."

Chapter Nine

"You're joking."

"I've never been more serious in my life."

"But..."

India stared at him with such confusion he almost laughed. "To answer the question I see in your eyes, yes, I wanna get nekkid with you. I can't wait to get nekkid with you. We are so gonna set the mattress on fire when we do get nekkid."

"But?"

"But for the past three years you've thought of me as Colt, your buddy. Or your Saturday night movie pal. Or the alcoholic you've counseled. Or the tattoo guinea pig. Or the guy you call when you need help with your sister's kids. Or Colt, the cowboy." He touched her face. "I am all of those, but I want you to see me as a man first."

"Never any doubt in my mind you're all man, Colt McKay."

He cupped her face with one hand and kissed her.

India's lips parted, but he didn't delve into temptation. Instead, he feathered his lips across her trembling mouth, as if gauging the best way their lips fit together for a soft exploratory kiss. Or for an openmouthed, tongue clashing, passionate kiss. Or for a playful, biting kiss.

Her breath stuttered when he finally slid his tongue into her mouth. He stroked and licked and tasted without hurry. Without mercy. As if kissing her were the end-all, not just the means to the end.

Colt kissed the corners of her smile, outlining the shape of her upper lip and lower swell with an insistent swipe of his tongue. He nipped and nuzzled and seduced, and yet his hands never moved from her jawbone.

"More. Please."

"Wantin' more ain't a bad thing," he whispered. "That's why we oughta take it slow."

"It's never been like this for me."

"Like what?" He moved back slightly, keeping his cheek pressed into the cushion.

"Real."

Silence.

India chewed her lip. Indecision warred in her eyes.

"Sugar, you know you can tell me anything and I ain't gonna judge you."

"I know. I just..." She inhaled. Exhaled. "We've talked about some of this stuff in meetings. How so many activities and events in our former lives as users were tied to booze." A long pause ensued as India struggled to keep going.

Colt reached for her hand. "No hurry. We don't have to talk about this now."

"But we do. And I'm relieved to finally be talking about it, to be honest because I've never been able to tell a man the truth about my past. Some of the things I've done."

He waited.

"Just like you, I've had no real relationships in my sobriety, Colt. I've held back...because I'm ashamed."

"Who you were then, ain't who you are now, Indy."

"I can tell myself that, and you can tell me that, because we've walked in those shoes. But we both know that's not always the case with other people in our day-to-day lives. Even people who supposedly care about us."

His thoughts flashed to his family and their continued skepticism of him.

"And if you share that humiliation, there's the chance the person will use it against you at the first opportunity. Or they'll cut you out of their life entirely. So how do you ever trust someone? Without giving them the power to destroy you?"

Colt knew exactly what she meant. Part of him realized it was a trust issue everyone had on some level. But a larger part of him understood addicts harbored dark secrets that would shock and sicken some people who'd never had to deal with an inner demon hell bent on self-destruction.

Twelve-step meetings were a safe haven, a place to talk to

folks who'd also hit rock bottom. But in some ways, those meetings provided attendees a false sense of security. If you're in a roomful of drunks and addicts, and they're accepting of your sordid history, well, then maybe there's a chance others will accept you as you are now, and not judge you on what you'd done in the past.

Wrong. It didn't work that way.

Colt saw India's chest rising and falling as if she'd run a race. He let his thumb drift over the back of her knuckles. "Breathe. Slow and steady."

After a few minutes, she'd calmed down.

"Better?"

"Yeah. Thanks."

"That's what I'm here for."

A soft laugh. "So the question of the day is…will you still be here after I make my confession?"

"Yep. I told you, Indy, I ain't goin' anywhere."

She locked her gaze to his. "If we're going through with this crazy dating idea of yours, then this is something you should hear. You should also know I've never told this to anyone I care about."

Rather than let loose a whoop because she admitted she cared about him, he said, "Skylar doesn't know?"

"No. Just a couple of detox counselors in California and…the other people involved, but I doubt they remember and they were just as stoned out of their gourds as I was."

Then Colt knew her impending confession would be ugly. He didn't say a word. He just held her hand, and her gaze and hoped it'd be enough.

"During my using years, I traded sex for drugs. And a couple of times when we couldn't make rent, I charged for sex."

"Oh, sugar. That had to've been rough."

The wariness didn't leave her eyes. "It's kind of a blur. I've never been sure if it's because I blocked it out, or if it was because of the drugs and booze."

"Probably some of both. How'd it happen?"

"The guy I was with at the time, Larry, a loser I'd hooked up with in art school, was a small time dealer. We'd get high on whatever product wasn't selling. His boss would come around to collect the money, and usually we'd snorted or smoked or shot up more than Larry's cut. So, the boss would take the difference out on trade. Since Larry didn't have shit, I was the commodity."

"How long did this go on?"

"A couple of months. Then I OD'd. I don't really know how I made it to the hospital, but when I woke up, Skylar was there and Larry was long gone. She sent me to detox. By some miracle I hadn't contracted AIDS or hepatitis or an STD during my blackout sexual hi-jinks. She took me in for a while. I stayed clean, but I got a job at a bar and started drinking. Heavily. And you pretty much know the rest of the story."

In and out of jail. In and out of treatment programs. Another OD. When they'd met three years ago, she'd been clean and sober for five years.

It amazed him, how India turned her life around. She'd taken her passion for art and turned it into a career. After her mother died, she'd moved away and started over thousands of miles away.

Colt didn't have the balls to do that. His life had taken a downward spiral for a year or two, but he'd never contemplated shucking it all and starting over out of Wyoming.

"You're awful quiet, McKay."

"Just thinkin' about how brave you are."

"For telling you my dirty little secret?"

"Maybe. But mostly because you haven't let your past experiences paralyze you." He studied her, wondering if he'd overstep his bounds if he voiced the issue on his mind.

"Just ask me the question I see in your eyes, *sugar*."

Colt gave her half a head butt. "Smartass woman, makin' fun of a poor, dumb cowboy like me."

"Last thing you are, Colt, is dumb. So ask."

"You are okay with sex now? No guilt, no—"

"—feelings of shame that make it impossible for me to enjoy sex? I love everything about sex. I'm just a lot choosier about who I have sex with. Why?"

"In the years I've known you, I don't recall you ever talkin' about a specific man, or a relationship, or sex and I wondered if this thing with your past might've affected it."

"Only in that no one knows. After I first moved here, I kept a long distance, fuck buddy type thing with a guy from Denver for a while. But it didn't last."

Jealousy tightened his gut. "How come I never knew?"

She shrugged. "It's easier all around if I keep my personal life out of the meetings. When we were together at A.A., especially in the beginning, I was focused on keeping you sober. It was important you saw me as a survivor, not as a woman."

"I might've been a drunk, Indy, but I ain't never been blind to the fact you're all woman."

"Sweet-talkin' cowboy. There's been no one since."

"No one? Not even a one-nighter?"

"Nope. To be crude, I've been getting off with BOB, my battery operated boyfriend, or my own hand." She gave him the same questioning look he'd given her. "What about you?"

"I'm well acquainted with my own hand."

"Been dating Rosy Palm, have you?"

He laughed. "Exclusively."

"But I'm talking about when it comes to sex with a person. You've made no bones about the fact you were a serious horndog with a bad reputation *before* you had a drinking problem."

"I was. I didn't particularly care which woman I ended up fucking at the end of the night, just as long as I got laid. Just as long as I satisfied her to the point she'd tell every other chick in four counties what a stud Colt McKay was, so I wouldn't have to work at all to coax any woman I wanted into my bed."

"Whoa."

"Yeah. And it worked. For years. Might sound cocky as shit, but I barely had to wink at a woman and I could have her on her knees or on her back in no time flat."

"Didn't the easy pickin's get old?"

He grinned at her. "Are you kiddin' me?"

India whapped him on the arm. "I'm serious."

"Yeah, I guess it did. It all changed when my brothers started pairing off. I was jealous, but rather than try to settle down, I got wilder. In my way of thinkin', if one woman was good, two would be even better. I'd make them jealous of *my* lifestyle. I'd be the Hugh Hefner of the notorious McKay clan, charming, sexy, with a rocket in my pocket ready to blow at the first spark and a legion of women lined up to light that match."

"So what happened?"

"Besides getting hooked on all the booze I had to drink to maintain the illusion?"

She nodded.

"I woke up in the middle of a pile of nekkid bodies. Not all of them female."

Silence.

He closed his eyes. *Way to toss that embarrassing fact out there like a rotten fish, McKay.*

A cool hand touched his cheek. "No judgment, remember?"

"Good thing, because I don't remember a damn thing. I could've had sex with any one of those guys, or all of them. I blacked out."

"Was that the first time you'd blacked out?"

"I wish. So, I was totally hungover, I couldn't find my clothes, had no fuckin' clue where I even was. I managed to hit a familiar road outside of Wheatland, more than a hundred miles from my house—with no memory of how I'd gotten there. When I got home, I found out my mother and my aunt spent the day cleaning my house.

"We're talkin' bags of beer bottles and cans. Bags of liquor bottles. Empty condom wrappers, empty condom boxes. Hell, we even left used condoms all over the whole house. Even though it was a pigsty, I was livid. Probably out of embarrassment, but at the time, it felt like a total breach of privacy."

"Why?"

"Because I wasn't some fifteen-year-old kid. I was a thirty-year-old man, who owned a house and held a job that required more responsibility than I ever wanted. I was a landowner in my own right, outside of the McKay Ranch, with money in the bank, and a brand new truck. I had the adoration of women and the envy of men. Who the fuck was my mommy to stick her big goddamn nose into my business?"

"Oh Colt."

"I called her up and said all that shit to her. Really let her have it. And by that time of day, I'd sobered up some, which upset her even more, which pissed my father and my brothers off and they all but kicked me out of the damn family."

"Then what happened?"

"My cousin Dag basically killed himself in a stupid fuckin'

accident. But it was almost like...he'd wanted to die. I figured it'd be the best thing for me—and everyone else in my family—if I followed his lead. It wasn't the cold bucket of water Kade dumped on me that woke me up. It was the truth that Kade seemed to be the only person who cared whether I lived or died, when he should've hated me for fucking up things with Skylar.

"Might sound sappy as shit, but I wanted to be the kind of man Kade was. A stand-up guy. He and Keely and our cousin Nick West got me into rehab. A month later I came back here and met you."

They stared at each other in silence for several long minutes.

"Talk about spilling our guts, huh?" she said with a laugh.

"Yeah. Mine hurt a little, to tell you the truth."

"Regrets?"

"No." Pause. "You?"

She shook her head.

"So the question is...you still up for datin' me?"

"Uh-huh. But no sex? Seriously?"

"Nope. To start with, just havin' you in my arms all night tonight would be good enough."

"It has been a while since you've had sex, if you think cuddling is a good substitute for it."

Colt laughed.

"Would there be kissing?"

"Some."

"Touching?"

"Some. Only over our clothes, not on bare skin."

India's mouth dropped open. "We're going to have our clothes on?"

"Yep."

"All our clothes?"

"Well, you can take your socks off as long as you don't put your cold feet on me."

Her surprised look morphed into a shrewd one. "Fine. I'll literally only sleep with you tonight. On one condition."

"What's that?"

"We have an end date for the moratorium on sex."

He considered it. "Two weeks. From last night. That sound fair?"

India rolled her eyes. "I was hoping for two days."

"Be glad I didn't go with my original plan of two months."

"That's just cruel, McKay."

"I've—we've—waited this long, a couple of weeks will be a snap." He ran his knuckles down the side of her neck.

India leaned forward and kissed him. "I'm gonna so love tempting you into giving in before the official time is up."

"You can try. But I can be damn stubborn."

A cry sounded from the baby monitor. Then silence. When he looked back at her, she was yawning.

"Let's call it a night. How about you check on the girls, I'll set the alarm system and track down blankets and pillows?"

"Sounds like a plan." India popped up off the couch like a jack in the box.

Less than five minutes later, they looked at the couch and then at each other. "What now?"

"Now we do what parents with little kids do. We fall into bed, exhausted, with thoughts of raunchy, hot sex the furthest thing from our minds."

"That'll work. But if you snore, I'm punching you in the nose."

Colt tumbled them onto the couch, wrapped her in his arms and felt at home for the first time in years.

$$*$$

"But I really am a princess," India read. She covered her hand with her mouth and yawned.

The book jiggled and an impatient Eliza said, "Innie. Read."

"Eliza, we've read this book twice already. It's boring me. Can't we read something else?" Headlights swept across the living room windows. "Hey. I think your mom and dad are home."

The book flew and Eliza slid off the couch. She ran to the foyer and jumped up and down in front of the window.

The door opened and Eliza launched herself at the first person through the doorway.

"Daddy!"

Kade dropped the overnight bag and scooped Eliza into his arms. "Whatcha doin' up, girly? It's past your bedtime." He kissed her cheeks and her forehead and the crown of her head.

Lord. He was so wrapped around her finger it wasn't funny.

"I miss you, Daddy."

"Missed you too, princess. Let's move outta the way so Mama can get in."

The second Skylar came in Eliza wiggled to be let down and threw herself at Sky. "Mama!"

"Whoa." She lifted Eliza and the little girl clung to her neck. "It's good to be missed."

India hung back while Eliza chattered away at her amused parents.

"...an' unka Cole an' me frowed rocks."

Kade looked at India. "Colt was here?"

"He came by to help out."

"Did the girls give you enough trouble so you had to call in reinforcements?"

"Yes. My God, at one point I think we all were crying at the same time."

Skylar laughed. "Not as easy as it looks, is it?"

"I never said it was, Sis."

"Shannie and Peyton asleep?" Kade asked.

"I put them down about an hour ago."

"We've got a couple hours before they're up again," Sky said. "Thanks for pinch hitting, India. We really appreciate it."

"So you guys had a good time?"

Kade grinned. "Oh yeah."

Skylar blushed and handed Eliza to India. "Give your Auntie Indy a bye-bye kiss and Daddy will tuck you in."

"Unka Cole kiss Innie bye-bye too."

India whispered, "You are a traitor, Eliza Belle. See if you get cookies from me again." Then she blew a raspberry on her neck.

Eliza giggled and held her arms out to Skylar. "Mama tuck me."

"I'll be up in a minute," Kade said to Skylar's back.

"Well, I'm pooped. I don't know how you guys do it."

"Take it day by day. Sometimes hour by hour."

Almost word for word on how to deal with addiction, but India doubted Kade would appreciate the comparison.

"Twins were a surprise, that's for damn sure. Not that I'm complainin'." He smiled. "Much as I love our girls, I love spendin' time alone with my wife, so thanks."

"You guys deserve it." She picked up her overnight bag. "And you're welcome. See you later."

"Huh-uh, not so fast. Tell me about this goodbye kiss Uncle Colt laid on you that impressed Eliza."

Dammit. "It was no big deal."

"So, it ain't gonna bother Colt if I tell him you said that kiss wasn't a big deal?"

India spun around. "Don't say that to him."

"Your words, not mine."

"Fine. It was a big deal, okay? A very, very big deal. And while I'm confessing, you should know he spent the night here too."

Kade's eyes narrowed. "Were you two havin' wild monkey sex while you were supposed to be watchin' our kids?"

"No! Colt and I aren't having sex, which is why the kiss was such a big deal." She took a deep breath. "Colt and I have had our...issues come to a head in the last two weeks. We've been friends for so long that it shocked both of us to figure out we don't want to be friends anymore...ah hell, we're dating, okay?"

"Since when?"

"Since last night. He came over and helped me with the girls, because I was stressed. After they were in bed, we ended up talking for hours. Which was different than all the other times he and I have talked for hours. Then this morning, he played outside with Eliza while the twins napped. But he did lay a sloppy, wet kiss on me before he left and Little Miss Tattle-Tale saw it."

Kade didn't utter a word, which bothered India worse than if he would've chewed her out. "I don't know how to say this."

Not good. "Just spit it out, Kade."

"You're family, Colt is family. There's more at stake here for everyone than the two of you datin' for a while and then callin' it quits. I'm as close to him as I am to Buck. I don't wanna see him get hurt. He's been hurt enough."

India looked away.

Kade put his finger under her chin and lifted her face back up. "But I don't wanna see you get hurt either. You've had your share of hurts too, Indy."

"What are you getting at?"

"I don't know. Just be careful, okay? Be mindful. And just so you know, I'm gonna tell him the same thing. Even if it pisses him off. Ever since he sobered up, he's wary of family getting into his personal business."

Yeah. She'd figured that out before he'd shared some of his backstory with her.

She opened her mouth. Closed it. But ultimately blurted, "Colt was involved in a big fight with his family last night before he came over."

"Ah hell. What happened?"

"I don't know. He said something to his dad, Colby and Cord said something back, and then Cam jumped in."

"Shit."

"Yeah. Evidently Cam told everyone off. Then he took off. Colt wasn't real anxious to get to the ranch today."

"I can imagine. Is that why he was hanging around, teaching Eliza to throw rocks?"

"Teaching her? That kid is a deadeye. She was teaching him."

Kade grinned. "That's my girl."

"You might give him a call tomorrow to see if he's all right. And remind him of our date." She winked. "It wouldn't hurt my feelings at all if you hinted around to him that I'd liked to be romanced. Flowers, poetry, expensive chocolate, hand holding at the movies, walks in the park, fine dining...you know, normal, traditional dating stuff."

"That ain't you at all, Indy," he scoffed.

"Maybe that's who I'd like to be with him."

The dumbfounded look on Kade's face was priceless.

Chapter Ten

Dating Week One

The back door opened. India craned her neck and her stomach performed a loop-de-loop when Colt sauntered inside.

The man simply didn't play fair. He wore a pair of faded Levis that hugged his every thigh muscle. Her gaze followed the contours of the black long sleeved T-shirt molded to his broad chest and wide shoulders, giving him the appearance of a sleek, black panther. He exuded confidence, sexiness and raw magnetism.

And she wasn't supposed to sleep with him? For two weeks?

Right.

Be interesting to see which one of them broke first.

When he grinned and stalked her, India felt kinship with prey and fought against taking cover. "You're early."

"Just anxious." He grabbed her hand and brought her fingers to his lips, in a gesture both corny and sweet. "Are you ready?"

"Yeah. Where are we going?"

"The Pizza Barn in Moorcroft."

Why were they going out of Sundance? Was Colt embarrassed to be seen with her?

He must've seen the questions in her eyes. "Have you been there?"

"No."

"Good. I wanted to take you someplace neither one of us have been for our first date."

"You're determined we're really gonna do this dating thing?"

"Yep."

"Have I mentioned I suck at dating?"

"But, you haven't dated me."

"I've known you for three years. What's so different about dating you?"

"I'll be a perfect gentleman."

"Then no way do I want to date you, McKay."

"I'll be a gentleman for two weeks, then all bets are off."

"If I refuse?"

"Too late. You already agreed to my terms."

"I was under duress."

"Good to know my kisses fluster you that much." He smooched her nose. "Let's go."

The Pizza Barn didn't exactly drip romance. The square table was standard, covered with a red and white checked tablecloth. Plastic flowers jammed in a Perrier bottle coated with dripped wax was centered between a shaker of Parmesan cheese and crushed hot peppers.

"Do you know what you want?"

India batted her lashes and cooed, "Guess."

When the waitress came by, Colt offered India a smug smile and recited their usual pizza order. "A large pepperoni with green olives and two mugs of rootbeer."

After she'd dropped off their drinks, she'd warned them it'd take at least an hour to get their pizza. India said, "Why do you think the wait is so long? There's hardly anyone in here."

"Because they want customers blowing tokens in the arcade. Which is a great idea." He scooted out of the booth. "Come on, let's check out the games."

Colt dragged her to the arcade and bought twenty bucks worth of tokens. She watched as he played every game from simulated golf to shooting hoops. Damn man made every shot. He was probably a helluva basketball player in his day.

When he hopped into a virtual NASCAR machine, complete with padded seat, steering wheel, goggles and gearshift, she allowed a weary sigh to escape.

"Don't you wanna play?" Colt indicated the empty machine next to his. "Or are you afraid I'll beat you?"

"I know you'll beat me," she retorted as she slid into the seat. "I suck at this kind of stuff."

"Didn't you play video games in high school?"

"Not really. Unless you count the time my boyfriend dragged me out of the fall festival and down the street so he could challenge the high score on Pac-Man at Burger King."

"Seriously?"

She crossed her hand over her heart. "No kidding. I never fully recovered."

"I'll bet the game was the only place he scored that night."

"You got that right." Well, they'd scored some premium grass right after that, but it wasn't something she wanted to confess to Colt. She blew out an impatient breath after struggling with the mass of wires attached to the goggles.

"Here, lemme help you." Colt brushed her hair from her face; his touch lingered on the curve of her neck. India held perfectly still, hoping he'd kiss her. But he only eased the helmet on with a friendly pat on her helmeted head. "Ready?"

"No."

He dropped four tokens in the slots anyway. The racetrack roared to life inside her goggles and she was lost to everything but the thrill of the chase.

It wasn't much of a contest. Colt won every game. Evidently gentlemanly behavior didn't include allowing your date to win even *one* race.

India ripped off the goggles with mock disgust. "I give. Now can we play a game that I might have a chance at beating you?"

"Like what?"

She spied the skee-ball racks in the corner and grabbed his hand. "Like that one."

"Sugar, have you ever played?"

"No. But how hard can it be? Bowling with croquet balls?" She preened a bit. "I rock at croquet. Bet I can kick your butt."

"What are you willin' to bet?"

"That's just an expression Colt, don't be so literal."

His answering chuckle was low and sexy. "Just as I suspected."

"What?"

"You ain't willin' to put your money where your sexy mouth is."

He thought she had a sexy mouth? "And you are?"

"Yep."

"Okay, Mr. Moneybags, you're on."

"Name your bet."

"One dollar."

"Nope."

"Fine. *Two* dollars."

He shook his head. "Not what I want."

"What do you want?"

"How about a kiss?"

Her midsection tightened and blood rushed into all the places blood wasn't supposed to rush on a first date. "Three dollars?"

"A slow kiss," he said, acting like he hadn't heard her.

"Five bucks."

He erased the gap between them, forcing her to meet his twinkling eyes. "One slow, deep, wet, kiss, for as long as I want. That's my final offer."

"Do I get to pick where you kiss me, slow and long and deep?"

"Ornery woman. You're hell on my intention of bein' a gentleman."

"If I preferred a gentleman, I'd be dating your cousin Blake." Shit. That was the wrong thing to say. "I'm sorry, I didn't—"

"Think? Yeah, I get that a lot from you. Just forget it." He scowled, shoving a hand through his hair. "Let's just play the damn game and have some damn fun."

For the next ten minutes, India watched him from the corner of her eye. Didn't seem like he was having fun. At all. He cursed every time the ball landed in the lowly five-point hole, which was a lot.

She had to do something to make up for her bout of bitchiness. She could be fun. Playful.

As Colt was about to toss the ball, she tickled his left side, from his hip to his ribs. He faced her with a look of utter disbelief, forgetting about the forward motion of the ball. It flew from his hand and bounced off the top of the metal cage, rebounding toward them.

India yelled, "Duck!" and jerked him down, keeping an eye on the ball as it bounced on the red carpet and narrowly missed smashing his foot.

"What the hell were you doin'?"

"Saving you from the run-away ball." Why wasn't he pleased by her quick thinking?

"You were *saving* me?" he echoed. "It was your fault that the damn thing got away from me in the first place. Were you hopin' to distract me so you'd win by default?"

"No. I was trying to be spontaneous and fun. Jesus. Now do you believe me that I suck at this dating stuff?"

A beat passed. Colt bestowed that bad boy grin that wreaked havoc on her at the most basic level. "Well, if the datin' stuff doesn't work then we can go to plan 'B'."

"Which is?"

"Lots and lots of kinky, wild sex."

"Have I mentioned I'm an alternative plan kind of chick?"

He laughed. "Thought that might spur your interest. Let's stick with plan 'A' for now. Maybe we'd better sit down."

As Colt led her back to the table, they passed a walled-off area she hadn't noticed. Apparently he hadn't noticed either because when he did, he almost dislocated her arm dragging her inside the small space. "Holy crap. I haven't seen one of them in years."

India wasn't sure what he was gawking at. "What?"

"*The Eight Ball Express.* It's a classic pinball machine." He dropped her hand, staring at the machine with reverence. "Just one game."

When Colt plugged the tokens into the slot, his eyes lit up as brightly as the lights on the machine. His concentration through the *cachink cachink* of the metal ball, the buzzers, the trilling bells and constant flipper action was impressive. But after ten minutes, India was bored. She sighed heavily.

He glanced at her for all of one second. "Ain't this great?"

"Yeah, it's hard, holding in all my excitement."

The machine beeped some kind of tinny, victorious sound. He punched the air and said, "High score!"

He grinned in the boyish way that had her returning his smile without hesitation. "I see that. Does that mean you're finished?"

Colt latched onto her hips and thrust her in front of him. "Uh-huh. Now it's your turn."

"But I don't know how to play."

"I'll help you." Colt guided her fingers to the circular buttons on either side of the machine, snuggling his body behind hers. "These are flippers, they keep your ball in play." He pressed her fingers and the small mechanical arms moved. "See? Now get ready." He pulled back on the silver knob on the right side, which connected to a shiny spring.

India watched the metal ball travel up the canal and bounce around the posts at the top, before continuing down the middle and out of sight.

Not a good sign. "Sorry. Told you I was bad at this."

"It's okay, but next time, hit your flippers." Colt released the spring again, sending the next ball to the left side. India continually pushed the buttons.

He murmured, "Slow down. Not yet. Wait for it."

His husky voice sent a shiver up her spine. She completely forgot what she was doing until the flash of the silver ball caught her eye as it rolled down the center.

Colt groaned.

India groaned. "I did it again."

"It's all right." His warm breath fluttered over her neck. "Just takes practice." He flicked the ball high, murmuring encouraging comments in her ear.

Whoa. Tandem pinball had serious benefits. Colt did a little hip wiggle, positioning his hard body firmly into her backside and a blast of pure sexual heat rocketed through her. She closed her eyes to savor the moment.

Colt's disgruntled snort forced her eyes back open.

"What?"

"The key to this game is concentration. I know you can do it. I've seen you with a tattoo gun. Focus." His hands tightened over hers on the flippers.

She imagined his warm, rough palms sliding up her arms and across her chest. First he'd squeeze her breasts, then pluck her nipples between his fingertips. He'd keep smoothing those wicked hands down her stomach until they landed on her hips. His fingers would meet in the center of her body; one quick tug and the top button on her jeans would pop open—

"Are you even watchin'? Because you didn't use your flippers once—"

She spun around so quickly he staggered, grabbing onto

her shoulders for balance. "Actually, I wasn't paying attention. It's distracting when you're pressed against me."

"Sorry."

"Don't be. I liked it. A lot."

The scant space between them crackled with energy. Neither spoke, neither broke eye contact. Several long seconds passed before Colt lowered his mouth to hers.

India's head buzzed while his lips moved back and forth. Lightly. He kept the kiss soft, sensual. Rough thumbs caressed her cheekbones before his fingers tunneled into her hair.

He canted her head to his liking. Teased her with soft lips and sharp nips of his teeth and warm breath, sweet there-and-gone kisses. His hands began traveling down her body. He slicked the very tip of his tongue across the seam of her lips and her mouth opened to him.

India boldly thrust her tongue in further, hoping for a stronger, more complete flavor. He tasted faintly of root beer and toothpaste; with an underlying hint of spice she'd associated as uniquely his.

Colt gripped her hips and pressed his pelvis closer as he maneuvered her against the pinball machine.

A sharp pain jabbed her spine. "Ouch."

"Hang on," he muttered against her throat, hoisting her on top of the pinball machine. Urging her knees open, he positioned himself between her thighs and clamped his mouth over hers with renewed fervor.

Lights flashed, bells clanged and India knew it wasn't from the arcade games. His cunning hands and hot mouth unleashed a steel ball of desire and it broke free to ricochet wildly in her blood. She wanted the heat bubbling under her skin to ignite his. She let her head fall back as he trailed openmouthed kisses down her neck.

His hot breath scorched her. He yanked her shirt down, exposing more skin to run his tongue and his teeth over without impediments.

She shivered and squeezed her thighs tightly, trying to line up the wet, aching part of herself with his cock.

He circled his arousal against her, finding the perfect friction, and took the next kiss down to where she felt it in the very depths of her soul.

"Hey!" A gravelly voice barked. "I warned you kids once about messing around in here."

India opened her eyes and focused on Colt. She'd never seen such hunger on a man's face. Hunger for her.

The intruder shuffled closer and said, "Well, hell, you two aren't exactly kids."

"We're aware of that." Colt kept his gaze on India as he helped her slide off the machine.

She stood next to him on wobbly legs.

"You oughta act better than this. It's those damn teenagers I usually hafta worry about." The man's jowls shook. "Found a used condom behind that pinball machine. Had to close the place down to clean every horizontal surface."

He glared at the pinball machine behind India, looking like he expected her to pull out a bottle of Windex, a roll of paper towels and wipe her butt prints off the machine. His bulk shifted as he waited for an explanation for their behavior.

But India shot the man a flinty eyed stare. "So, we got carried away. I swear we weren't to the condom stage…"

Yet.

The unspoken word hung in the sexually charged air.

The fat man snarled, "Get out."

Two weeks would kill him. Hell, they hadn't passed the two-hour mark without mauling each other. In public. Getting kicked out of an arcade for lewd behavior. For Christsake, they were adults!

Yeah. He sucked at this dating stuff as much as India did. Which reinforced his determination to see it through. To the end. Twelve days. Two hundred and eighty eight hours.

Not that Colt was keeping track.

They returned to the table as their pizza arrived. For the next hour, the conversation wasn't different than the other times they'd gone out as friends.

With the exception they were holding hands.

With the exception they were making googly eyes at each other and lacing their banter with sexual innuendos.

With the exception Colt's cock was as hard as a hockey stick.

Nah. That wasn't anything new.

On the way back to Sundance, India scooted next to him on the bench seat. She fiddled with the radio. The temperature. The position of the air vents.

She was nervous. Interesting.

Colt pulled up to the back of the building.

India said, "Is this where you tell me you had a great time and you'll call me?"

"No."

"You didn't have a great time?"

"I had a fantastic time." He curled his hand around her jaw and turned her face to his. "I'd like nothin' better than to come in, but we both know it's better if I say goodnight here."

She kissed him with sweet regret. "I'll see you at the meeting tomorrow night?"

"Yep. And afterward, I want to do something with you."

"Not do something *to* me?" she teased.

"Hold that thought for another twelve days. How about if we go out for ice cream?"

A devious smile lit up her face. "With the no sex rule, you seriously think you can handle watching me lick an ice cream cone for more than thirty seconds?"

The reality of her pink tongue lapping. Her mouth sucking. Watching her throat muscles as she swallowed the creaminess. No way. "Point taken. How about a—"

"How about if you leave it up to me?"

Colt frowned.

"Innocent fun. I promise."

"No peeking, McKay."

"I can't see a damn thing."

"Good."

After the A.A. meeting, India had commandeered his truck and blindfolded him. She held his hands as she helped him out of the passenger side. She kept holding his hands as they walked up a small incline. They were outside, on grass, not gravel. He was trying like hell not to be freaked out. He was hoping like hell this wasn't some bizarre game of trust she'd concocted because he hadn't participated in the one at the meeting again.

"Ready? Keep your eyes closed."

The silken scarf slipped from his eyes, teasing him with the aroma of her perfume.

"Okay. You can open them."

His eyes blinked a couple times. He looked around. Two swing sets, a jungle gym, a sandbox and monkey bars. They were in City Park.

"A playground. You brought me to a playground?"

"Yep. Pull up a swing." India ran to the swing on the left and hopped on the rubber seat. She wrapped her hands around the chains and started to move, pumping her legs.

He ambled over and plopped next to her, straddling the swing so the chain followed the line of his spine and he could look at her.

"Aren't you gonna swing?"

"Nope. I'd rather watch you."

"Suit yourself." Each pass took her swing higher. The metal bars bounced and the chains squeaked.

India's movements hypnotized Colt. The wind ruffling her coal black hair, the ends colored a vivid blue, which emphasized the paleness of her skin. The scarf fluttered behind her in a jaunty wave as she swung forward.

His stomach fluttered. God. She was so beautiful. So happy in her own tattooed and pierced skin. So honest and thoughtful and crazy fun. So...India.

So mine.

She slowed and stopped by letting her combat boots drag in the shallow dent in the dirt, facing him in mirror position. "Don't you like to swing?"

"Been so long I don't remember." He grinned at her. "So...come here often?"

India returned his grin. "No. Sky won't let me bring Eliza yet."

"So you brought me instead?"

"Do you mind?"

"Nope, I just don't understand why."

"This might sound silly and sappy and stupid."

"I doubt it."

She poked her fingers through the chain links. "You know

all those romantic comedies where the man and woman end up in a park having a heart to heart on the swings? Or the swing set is their special meeting place from their childhood and they reconnect there as adults? Or where they had their first kiss?"

"I guess."

"I've never done anything like that."

Colt waited.

"My memories of schoolyards are mostly bad. Hanging around, looking for drugs, getting into trouble. I'd like to have a good memory. Something romantic like in the movies." She finally looked at him so earnestly his heart melted. "With you."

"Ah hell, sugar, c'mere," he managed over the lump in his throat. He scooted forward and yanked her chain, bringing her swing closer to his. "I'm not really romantic leading man material."

"You are to me," she said softly.

Colt touched the side of her face. "Know one of my favorite things about you? You live in the moment. Without apology. With gusto. It's a helluva thing to see."

She appeared poleaxed by his words.

When he leaned forward to kiss her, he urged, "Close your eyes."

Her dark lashes fanned her cheek.

He brushed his lips over hers. "Your mouth is so soft. Such a perfect fit for mine." At first, Colt kissed her with passion and promise, then he gentled the kiss into something wholly different. Sweetness. Tenderness.

India sighed in his mouth.

His smile broke their lips free. "So in any of these romantic comedies, do they end up doin' it on the swing?"

"Umm. No."

"Pity. That, I'd pay to see."

"Maybe we oughta jot that down on our kinky sex fantasy list to try, once we actually start having sex."

"You have a...list of that kinda stuff?"

"Uh-huh. Don't you?"

"No, but you can bet your sweet behind I'm startin' one right now."

She laughed.

They held hands as they walked back to the truck. "Thank

you for tonight."

"You're welcome. What are we doin' tomorrow night?"

"Nothing. We can't have a date every night of the week, Colt."

"Why the hell not?"

"Because I think I'm supposed to play coy, bat my lashes, and pretend to be 'busy' washing my hair for the next two nights to keep you interested."

He snorted. "The datin' handbook clearly states we spend as much time together as possible to keep me interested."

"There's a handbook?"

"Yep."

"Then you've got an advantage over me because I'm flying blind here, Colt." India gave him all-too brief a kiss before she hopped out of the cab.

He was damn tired of saying goodbye to her from the driver's seat of his truck. And it was only their second date.

Colt put India out of his mind during the hours he spent working on the ranch. She'd kept her tattoo shop open late some nights, so she'd bailed on him for a third date.

When he'd called after breakfast and asked her plans for the evening, she'd offered some half-assed excuse. He couldn't imagine she'd actually attempt the "playing hard to get" angle.

Instead of brooding and pacing in his empty house, he headed to the community center. He ran. Lifted weights. It helped if he focused on the pain of pushing himself to the limit and couldn't flash back to the way India felt in his arms. The sweet, addictive taste of her mouth. The intoxicating scent of her hair and her skin. Her soft, breathy moans when he kissed her. The husky, sexy timbre of her voice in his ear.

Think of something else or you're going to get a hard-on in the gym.

Workout complete, he looped a towel around his sweaty neck and cut through the main hallway to the men's locker room for a cold shower.

But it seemed as if those reminders were stuck on a continual mental loop. India's taste. Her scent. Her laugh. Her voice. Her instructions for everyone to sit down and listen up or no one would get a cookie.

Huh?

Colt shook his head. Pathetic. Hearing her phantom voice. Except...he took another step and heard it again.

"No, Ginny. Poke a hole in the cup first. Then put in the gravel."

His heart kicked harder than when he'd been running flat out on the treadmill. India was here? He followed the sound of her voice, coming from inside a small room. He hesitated outside the door, in case he was delusional and hearing things.

"Once you get the soil in the cup—Jeremy honey, only fill it halfway, no, don't pack it so tight—we'll put in the seeds."

"Oh, no, I spilled—" a girlish voice wailed.

"It's okay, Becca, don't cry. I've got lots more."

"But I wanted to take it home to my mommy tonight!"

"You still can. We have time, sweetie, don't worry. Go grab another cup and start over. I'll be right there to help you."

"India? Ruger threw a rock at Anton."

"Did not!"

"Did too."

"No throwing rocks, Ruger."

Colt poked his head in and saw...total chaos.

At least ten kids, a mix of boys and girls, around seven years old, were flinging dirt all over a long table. A few boys were throwing small marble-sized gravel at each other. One red-haired girl poured water on a pile of dirt while an Indian girl stirred it into mud. A bespectacled kid was methodically stacking empty Styrofoam cups in precise rows. Some youngsters were actually sitting still, awaiting additional instructions.

But India wasn't fazed. She stopped the rock fight, the mud-pie makers, and managed to get the cups back in the plastic bag, all while directing the kids in the next step of the project.

Colt was absolutely stunned. This was the woman who'd called him in a panic? About three kids? And she was juggling...ten? A disconcerting thought on its own, but not as confounding as why hadn't India just told him about this when he'd called her this morning?

"Whose daddy are you?"

India looked over at him and froze.

"I'm not anybody's daddy." He glanced down at the tow-headed boy. "I was just passing by and wondered what you guys were doin'. Looks like fun."

"We're planting flowers!" the mud-pie maker exclaimed, throwing her hands up, flinging mud everywhere.

"Cool. Can I watch?" He stepped inside, bracing himself for India's reaction.

She didn't growl or demand he leave, like he'd expected, she smiled the angelic smile that twisted his guts into a pretzel. "Sure. Come on in. You can even help."

The bespectacled boy asked, "What's your name?"

"Colt. What's yours?"

"Hayden." He gave Colt a thorough once-over. "Hey, are you Buck's cousin?"

"Yes. I am. Do you know him?"

"Uh-huh. He's my big buddy."

"Lucky for Buck. So, Hayden, think you can help me make one of these things?"

Hayden beamed. "Yes. It's quite logical, really."

The rest of the kids started talking all at once, offering suggestions. Crowding him, but he didn't mind.

India clapped her hands. "Okay, munchkins, listen up. Once everyone has soil in their cup, we'll move to the next step, the fun part; planting the seeds."

"Carrot seeds?"

"Eww. Gross. I hate carrots."

"No, Anton. Sunflower seeds."

Chatter rose again, but India focused her charges' attention to the task at hand. Colt labeled each child's name on their individual cups with masking tape.

After the seeds were planted, and another thin layer of soil sprinkled on top, and each cup was watered, the kids lined up at two sinks and washed up.

As India tried to get a handle on the mess, Colt handed out cookies.

During the brief lull, he managed to sidle closer to her.

She spoke before he did. "Surprised to see me?"

"Yeah. I didn't know you did this sort of thing."

"Normally, I don't."

"So how'd you end up doin' it?"

"Torture and bribery." She smiled. "Not true. I'm filling in for Domini. I usually help out during the fair and do face painting and airbrush tattoos. That's a little more one on one, rather than ten on one."

"Didn't seem like you had a problem. You're really good with kids, India."

Parents started showing up, whisking their children away. Colt got into a lengthy conversation with Hayden's mother in the doorway. When he returned to the empty room, India was stacking supplies in the corner cupboard. "Do you need help?"

"No. I've got it." For the next few minutes she ignored him completely.

Colt placed his hand on her arm. "India? What'd I do?"

"Nothing."

"Huh-uh. Tell me what's wrong."

She slammed the cupboard door. "Did you have fun showing your cowboy charm to that hot-looking redhead?"

"What? I was just talkin' to her."

"Fine. Forget it. See? It was nothing." She stomped to the sink in the corner and turned the water on full blast.

India was...jealous? It shouldn't make him grin, but it did.

India splashed cool water on her face, as close as she could get to a cold shower. The man set her blood on fire with a smoldering look. In a roomful of first graders. And did he have to spread that sexy sweetness all around? He'd just smiled at the hot mama and she'd practically fallen at his feet.

Not Colt's fault. You know he didn't do anything wrong beside stand there and look good.

Argh.

She'd be better off dating a toad instead of a prince.

Prince? Right. He's just a man. You've spent way too much time reading fairy tales to your nieces.

India reached for the bar of soap and the scent of musk and cotton surrounded her.

"Let me help you scrub up," he said over her shoulder.

"Colt—"

"Two hands are better than one. How about if you hold the

soap and I'll do all the dirty work?" His low, seductive voice whispered across her damp skin. Strong arms circled her waist and he tugged her to his chest, his hips tight against her backside. He nestled his chin in the slope where her shoulder met her neck and he removed the soap from her tentative grip.

She couldn't move. She didn't *want* to move.

When Colt's hands began creating suds, she forgot to breathe.

"Relax," he murmured.

His long, tanned fingers worked the hard bar of soap into creamy softness. The soft lather contrasted with the coarse edges of his fingers. He gathered her right hand inside his, scrubbing the thick soap into her palm, then slowly across her knuckles. He massaged the bubbles from her wrist to her fingertips, threading his fingers through hers, back and forth, his wide palm cradling the back of her hand.

With Colt's body heat scorching her, she barely noticed the soapy swirls spinning down the drain. How could such simple contact be so unbearably erotic? She sagged into him, her hand slipped from his grasp.

"India?" His husky voice sent a shiver zinging through her. "Do you want me to stop?"

She shook her head and her cheek scraped his scruffy beard.

Colt switched hands, repeating the process, with more excruciating slowness. Long, sensual strokes. Light. Then firm. Oh-so-painstakingly adept.

Desire swamped her, left dampness on her belly, her spine, between her legs. His breath crested over the wet spots beading on her neck.

After sluicing warm water from the ticklish bend in her elbows, to her fingertips, Colt ripped off a paper towel and dried her as thoroughly as he'd washed her.

She hissed at the abrasive feel of the towel's nap on her moist, over-sensitized skin.

He turned her around. "I missed you."

"It's been one day."

"One very long day."

His eyes were blue flames of pure desire. As he traced a rivulet of water trickling down her cheek, India was shocked the heat between them didn't evaporate the tiny droplet into steam.

Colt angled his head, slanting his mouth over hers.

India felt his breath on her lips. Anticipation hummed between them like an electric current. Her heart raced, her blood ran fast. Her lashes fluttered, her mouth parted slightly. She leaned in, a silent plea for him to close the distance.

He'd almost made contact; she'd nearly experienced the warmth of his tempting mouth, the flicker of his velvety tongue against hers, when Cam's booming voice echoed into the small space. "Colt! I thought that was you."

At the sound of Cam's voice, India jumped back and lost her balance. Rather than letting her smack her head into the bottom of the cabinet, Colt caught her, losing his footing in the process, and hitting his chin on the cupboard door.

"Fuck."

"Are you all right?"'

"Gives the phrase, 'taking it on the chin' new meaning."

She tried to get him to lift his face. When he finally did, she gasped, "Omigod Colt, you're bleeding." She handed him the paper towel. "Here."

"Lemme see it," Cam barked.

Colt whirled around. "It's just a scratch, leave it be. What the devil were you doin' sneakin' up on us like that anyway?"

"I wasn't sneaking. I didn't see India behind you. She's such a little bitty thing she gets lost in your shadow."

"Oh, bite me, McKay."

Cam and Colt said, "Gladly," in stereo. Then they laughed in stereo.

"Now I know you're fine if you can slip in a lewd comment. That's my cue to leave."

"Wait," Colt said.

"No, that's fine, I'll leave," Cam said.

"Wait, just a damn minute. Both of you." He faced Cam. "Why'd you barge in here in the first place?"

"I tracked you down to ask if you wanted to come over and watch ESPN tonight. The Broncos are playing. Kansas City."

Colt seemed torn.

India kissed his cheek. "You sure you're okay?"

He pulled the paper towel away. "See? It already stopped bleeding."

"Good. Thanks for your help tonight. Now go cheer on the Broncos."

Chapter Eleven

Dating Week Two

"Hey, India, can I talk to you for a second?"

She turned from her conversation with Bert Spotted Tail and smiled. "Sure. Almost done here."

"No hurry." What a lie. It took every ounce of control not to drag her away from the old coot who'd been monopolizing her time for the last twenty minutes.

If it wasn't for that coot, you wouldn't even know her.

Bert called out, "Heya, Colt, one of these days we're gonna get you to participate in the circle of trust."

"Don't count on it."

The circle of trust was an exercise where one person stood in the middle of a circle of people and fell back trusting someone in the circle would catch them. Colt didn't trust anyone so blindly. So while they'd been doing this exercise for the last few months, Colt stood on the sidelines. He took some crap about it, but he didn't care. No way was he taking some psychiatrist's version of the Nestea plunge.

"You playin' in the basketball game for at-risk youth tomorrow night?" Bert asked.

With this dating business, he'd forgotten. "Yeah. Thanks for the reminder."

"No sweat. You oughta bring India. In fact, if you promise to come, I'll save you a courtside seat, eh?"

"Sounds like you're asking me on a date, Bert."

A date? Like hell. Colt growled. India and Bert both gave him a strange look.

"*Shee.* I'm too old to be tryin' to win the tattooed hand of a wild thing like you. But back in my heyday...I was as rough and rowdy as a mustang. Sorta like McKay." Bert's contemplative gaze pinged back and forth between Colt and India. "Maybe you oughta be datin' him."

India lifted her pierced brows at Colt.

Rather than snap, *she is dating me*, Colt said, "I'm tame as a trail pony these days."

"Some of them docile lookin' ones still gotta lot of buck left in 'em, boy. You just hafta pick the right kinda rider to let the beast loose."

Colt couldn't help but laugh.

"I'll see you tomorrow night. And put on a good show, will ya? I bet twenty bucks on your team."

"So tell me about this charity basketball game," India said to Bert as Colt headed to the kitchen.

He rechecked the coffee pot he'd unplugged ten minutes ago. Although it'd been a short meeting, it seemed he waited for hours for the attendees to leave. From the moment they'd arrived. Might've made him selfish, but for the first time in years, Colt hadn't paid attention to what his fellow A.A. members discussed. His focus was on one thing.

India.

The outer door slammed, signaling Bert had left. He heard India moving closer, each combat booted footstep across the tile floor pulsed in his groin.

"What did you need?"

The second he got a whiff of her wildflower scent, he spun around and erased the distance between them in two steps. Curling his hands around her face, he pushed her against the pantry door, crushing her mouth beneath his.

The instant her lips parted, he canted his head and thrust his tongue deep, kissing her with all the pent-up passion, need and longing he'd held in for the last day.

As he filled his mouth with her taste, he rested his thumb in the arc of her throat where her heart raced. Stroking that sweet, sensitive section of skin in tiny circles, as if he had his hand on the sweet spot between her legs.

She twisted her mouth free. "Wow."

"I saw more of you when we weren't dating."

"Does that mean you want to stop dating me?"

"Screw that." Colt clamped his lips to hers again. He'd intended to seduce her with a sweeter kiss, but the heat between them expanded, burning hotter than his first attempt.

"Stop."

"Why? Damn, I love the way you taste right here." He placed his mouth beneath her ear and sucked.

"Colt McKay. Stop right now or I'm going to punch you."

That grabbed his attention. "What?"

"You're giving me a hickey in a church."

"So?"

"So you're the one who wanted to take this slow. Yet, you're mauling me at the first opportunity."

"There haven't been many opportunities. That's why I'm takin' advantage of it when I can."

"Prove it."

"Are you issuing a challenge?"

"Yep." India gave him a look that'd melt ice. She undid the first two buttons on her blouse.

Whoa. Was she wearing a bra?

By the fourth button, his answer to the bra question was a definite *no*. Damn.

He managed to ask, "What are you doin'?"

"Giving you an opportunity."

"For my balls to explode?"

She laughed. "Want me to keep going?"

Yes. "How far would you go?"

"I would say all the way, but that's not an option, is it?"

Hell yeah. No. Dammit. Say no. Colt rubbed the underside of his jaw. "Nope."

Up went the buttons. "You're a cock tease, McKay."

"Me?" he aped.

"Yes, you. Attacking me with all those hot kisses. Talking to me about your balls. I'm going home to take a cold shower."

"I'm coming with you."

"We'll both be coming if you and I are alone in a room with a bed after avoiding temptation for more than a week."

"India. For shame. Dirty talkin' me in a church. Maybe we'd better lock up before we get struck by lightning."

"At least I'd feel that sizzle of electricity before I died."

Outside, Colt led her to his truck. "I'll give you a ride."

"No, you won't. Not even if I beg you to ride me all night long."

"Lord, did you always have sex on the brain and I just never noticed?"

"Nope. You just bring out the beast in me."

"That's a plain mean thing to taunt a guy with who hasn't had sex in the last three years." He opened the truck door. "Get in."

"I think it'd be better if I walked."

"Like hell. You ain't walkin' alone at nine at night."

"It's Sundance. What can happen to me?"

"Nothin' if you're ridin' in my truck, now get in."

"Fine." India stepped up on the running board and crawled across the bench seat.

Hoping to lighten her mood, he said, "I wish you were wearin' a dress."

"I wish you were wearing a condom."

"Holy hell, India Blue Ellison, are you an ornery woman."

"A *horny* woman."

At the back of the building, Colt shut off the engine and looked at her. Her mood had changed in the two-minute drive, nothing new; India's moods were as unpredictable as the Wyoming weather. "Now what's wrong?"

"I don't know. Doesn't this feel...weird? Last week, I had a great time with you. I see you tonight at the meeting, expecting it to be the same. But it's different. Then Bert is trying to set us up on a date..."

He watched her fingers pinch the seam on the seat cover.

"And you don't even tell him we are dating," she finished in a rush.

Colt snatched her restless hand. "Is that what's bothering you? That we didn't come out and tell anyone at A.A. that everything has changed between us?"

"Maybe. Look, I know it's stupid."

"It's not stupid if you're upset. C'mere." He tugged her until she was practically in his lap. "I feel I've done something wrong. So I'll do anything to fix it."

"Like what?"

"I'm open to suggestions."

India swung her leg over his until they were matched groin-to-groin and chest-to-chest. "Okay. Let's mess around."

"That's a good idea."

She laughed. Then she kissed him. Her hands clutching his hair, her crotch grinding on his, her nipples rubbing with enough friction he swore her piercings scratched his chest through their clothing.

He'd gotten used to being the aggressor, so her dogged seduction was incredibly potent. Each teasing, tantalizing kiss destroyed his resolve to maintain a cool head, especially when the head in his Wranglers burned hot as a branding iron.

India's lips followed the slope of his jaw to his ear. "So strong. So smooth. Did you shave just for me?"

"Uh-huh."

"Mmm. You smell good too." She nuzzled his neck. "You know my favorite thing about you wearing aftershave?"

"Ah. No. I don't."

"Anticipating how it'll smell on my skin. After you've rubbed your face and mouth all over my chest. And my neck."

His cock twitched. Her little chuckle meant she knew it. Felt it. Sassy wench.

"Unbutton my blouse, Colt."

Good thing he was dexterous. All her rubbing and nuzzling could've distracted a lesser man.

Once her shirt was undone, she leaned back until her spine met the steering wheel. "If I ask nice, will you put your mouth on me?"

"Is that what you want, Indy?"

"Yes. God yes. Ever since that morning you sucked my nipples, I've been dying to feel your lips and tongue on them again."

Colt growled. He yanked the shirt open and jerked it down, immobilizing her arms.

Her complaint of, "Hey!" was lost the second his mouth enclosed the bared tip.

Her skin was so warm and silky under his callused hands. While he suckled the right nipple, the fingertips of his left hand stroked the underswell of her left breast. He'd always been a fan of big tits, but this handful of perfection was more than enough to satisfy him.

He slowly freed her nipple, tugging on the ring with his teeth, and watching her shadowed face to gauge her reaction.

"Colt."

"You're right, my aftershave does smell good on you." Colt rubbed his cheek and jaw across her chest, and used his chin to separate her cleavage, kissing the inside of each breast. "Kinda makes me wonder where else it'd smell good." He rained kisses, brushing his smoothly-shaven cheek over her arched neck. "Mmm. Here's another good spot."

India groaned. A shiver rippled through her.

"I'm bettin' the best place is that tender spot right between your thighs. Am I right?"

"Yes. You're welcome to test it out."

He trilled his lips to her left nipple. "I wish I hadn't shaved. I'd like you to feel my whiskers on your delicate skin as I'm markin' you with my scent."

"Please. I-I—"

Colt's tongue toyed with the nipple ring. He licked circles around her areola just to watch it pucker into a tight point. "Tell me what you want."

"To get off with you. Like this, fully clothed. With your mouth sucking my nipples as I'm rocking on you."

"It'd be the second time you've made me come in my pants."

"Then next time you can come in my hand. Or in my mouth. Or in my pussy. But damn you, Colt, I'm so wet and—"

He slammed his lips to hers to shut her up. Jesus. If she continued that tempting talk he'd come without her touching any part of his body. Keeping hold of her shoulders, he angled his pelvis so all their good parts rubbed together.

She arched in complete abandon. "Yes."

"Where do you want my mouth? Here?" Colt scraped his teeth down her neck. "Or here?" He latched onto her right nipple.

"There. Oh. Damn. Can I move my hips faster without smashing your cock?"

"Move as fast as you want. The faster, the better."

"Thank God."

The air in the cab seemed to increase by a thousand degrees. Heavy breathing distorted the stillness and steamed up the windows. Perspiration coated her skin as he feasted on her. When he felt her thighs tighten, and heard her soft gasp, he bit down on the captive nipple.

India came in a bucking, noisy explosion of heat and sound that sent Colt straight over the edge.

It'd taken him longer than a minute, but not by much.

She slumped forward, burying her face in his neck. "If you don't want to drive home in those sticky jeans, you're welcome to come in and take them off."

He laughed softly. "Generous of you."

"I thought so."

Colt pulled her sleeves back up, freeing her arms. He fed her a long, deep, wet kiss while he buttoned her shirt.

Looking as dazed as he was, he traced the outline of her bottom lip, while he stared into her eyes. When her saucy tongue darted out to lick the callused pad, his hand fell away.

She smirked.

"I know that look. You still think you can convince me to give in to your hot sexy body before the two weeks is up."

"I'm an optimist." She bestowed a smacking kiss square on his mouth. "See you tomorrow night at the basketball game."

India arrived at the high school parking lot to find it jam-packed. Inside, she saw Bert pointing to the empty space beside him in the front row of the bleachers.

"Thanks for saving me a spot," she said, squeezing the gnarled hand resting on his cane. "I had a late client. It hasn't started, has it?"

"Not yet."

India scanned the teams on opposite sides of the court. Her gaze zeroed in on the tall, dark-haired man, wearing an electric blue tank top and shorts. Talk about muscular legs. And arms. And chest. How much weight had he been lifting with Cam?

Colt sensed her gawking at him. He trotted over, the warmth in his eyes made her tingly all over. "Glad you made it."

Concentrate on his eyes and not his nearly nude body.

He grinned as if he'd read her thoughts.

The whistle blew and he scrambled toward his teammates.

India muttered, "I am in *way* over my head."

"He is too, if it's any consolation."

She faced Bert. "What's that supposed to mean?"

Bert clutched her hand on his cane. "I like you, India. That's why I sent Colt to you in the first place. He wouldn't open up to me the way he has with you. You were good for him."

"*Were?*"

"Ladies and gentlemen, let's get this event started!"

India half-listened to the opening remarks of the MC. After a precocious nine-year old girl warbled "The Star-Spangled Banner" they sat down. She tried to watch the action unfold, but ignoring Bert's curious stare proved impossible. "What?"

"As awkward as this might be, I'm recommending you terminate your role as Colt's sponsor."

"What?"

"Hear me out before your wicked glare singes what little hair I have left."

"Does he know you're doing this?"

"Yes, it was my idea after he called and told me you two were dating."

So Colt had listened to her concerns last night.

Why are you surprised? Colt always listens to you.

"You're important to the program, India. But you're also important to him."

She didn't know what to say.

"It'd be easier all around. You've been so busy taking care of others I'm worried you're not taking care of yourself."

"I'm fine, Bert."

"We've all said that, India. We've all been there, thinking we're 'cured' and trying to hide the difficulties from our peers. No one ever is cured. You remember that. And if it gets to the point you need help...my door and my ears are always open to you."

"Thanks."

Bert slammed his cane into the floor and pointed. "Hey! Will you look at that? Number thirty-six fouled him!"

She shifted her attention to the court.

The match was a charity event and the men were supposed to be playing for fun, but the taunts and cheap shots screamed the aggressive nature of the game. Colt was out there in the thick of it, sweating, grappling for the ball. His competitive streak had him jabbing his elbow in his opponent's ribs whenever the ref wasn't watching.

During a lull in the game, India studied the local people filling the bleachers. Kids munched popcorn and sipped soft drinks from red wax cups. Mothers bounced babies, holding conversations with other mothers who did the same. Men, young and old, shouted approval or dismay at the official's calls while teenagers ducked under the risers to steal a kiss away from prying parental eyes.

Odd, she didn't see any of Colt's family members in the stands. Why weren't they here rooting for him?

The third quarter ended. A pregnant woman waddled toward one of Colt's teammates. The man's face clouded with concern as he stroked her distended belly. Then he brushed her curls from her face and watched her holding the small of her back as she disappeared out the side door.

What would it be like to have a man look at her as if she hung the moon and stars? To have her belly round with his child? A burst of intense longing filled her.

"That's Dr. Brewer and his wife, Susie," Bert commented. "Nice couple. They just moved back to Wyoming last year. He's a veterinarian and she teaches at the reservation."

"Do you know everything about everyone in town?"

"No, but Jay—Dr. Brewer—and Colt have been friends and rivals since high school. Why they haven't killed each other is a mystery, because they both play rough and don't know the meaning of the word quit."

Like Bert needed to warn her about Colt's tenacity.

The buzzer sounded and the teams took the floor for the last quarter. India automatically zeroed in on Colt.

God, he epitomized the perfect male animal, all sweaty, scowling and masculine.

It was a five-point ballgame. The level of aggression on the court increased. One player from the opposing team fouled out and a scuffle erupted.

With seven minutes left to play, the score tied, and the other team in control of the ball, Colt leapt into the air to block a pass. The next thing happened in some kind of sick, slow motion.

An airborne Colt, still clutching the stolen ball, lost his

footing and sailed toward the announcer's stand. The back of his head clipped the corner of the long metal table and he slammed into the floor. He lay motionless as the entire gymnasium watched in horror.

The ball slowly rolled to the center of the floor. The referees blew the whistle, the time remaining on the scoreboard stopped ticking.

The crowd grew quiet.

Officials, teammates, and opposing players surrounded Colt. The only thing visible from their seats were the soles of his tennis shoes.

"Why is Colt still lying on the floor?" Bert demanded, his concern echoing hers.

"I don't know." She hopped up on her chair for a better view. "I can't see anything."

The man Bert pointed out as Jay Brewer trotted away from the team's chairs and disappeared back inside the circle of people.

She waited several agonizing seconds before scrambling down from the chair. "I'll see what's going on." India sidled between two very sweaty, tall men and one shorter, bald man in a shiny suit. She peered around a referee and watched Dr. Brewer shine a penlight into Colt's eyes.

Colt murmured something and shook his head.

That's when India noticed the red spots dotting the white linoleum. Her vision grayed and she bumped into the official standing in front of her.

"Hey! Who are you? You shouldn't be here."

She swallowed her panic, ignoring the red smears beneath Colt's head. "I'm his, umm...girlfriend."

Dr. Brewer glanced up at her admission and motioned her over. India dropped to her knees. "Is he okay?"

"Appears to be, but he won't let me call an ambulance. He's worried Cam will freak out when he hears the call go through dispatch."

"Make the call. Obviously he isn't thinking clearly."

"He," Colt ground out from his prone position on the floor, "is perfectly capable of makin' his own decisions. And I'm not goin' to any damn hospital." His eyes opened. "I'll be fine. I just need about three hundred aspirin and a good night's sleep."

"What about the blood? How bad is Mr. Tough Guy bleeding?"

Colt grimaced, squeezing his eyes shut again. "What blood?"

"Yeah, what blood?" Dr. Brewer echoed.

"There." She pointed to the red splotches on the floor. "That blood."

Dr. Brewer peered over the top of Colt's head. "That's not blood."

The bald man crouched down and admitted sheepishly, "That's my blackcherry Icee. He knocked it over when he hit the table."

India chose to feel relieved instead of stupid.

"McKay, sit up so I can see how bad it is. I'd be surprised anyone with a head as hard as yours can bleed at all."

One of Colt's teammates assisted the doctor in getting Colt upright. "In my opinion, he needs—"

"Then it's a good thing you're my veterinarian and not my doctor."

"You sort of are acting like a jackass."

The crowd around them snickered.

"Just help me up." Colt struggled to his feet.

Two teammates supported him and the crowd cheered at Colt's apparent recovery. He paused outside the locker room door.

The pain in his eyes nearly had her carrying him to the hospital. "I'm coming in there to make sure you don't pass out."

"I'll remind you this is the *men's* locker room."

"So?"

His breath tickled her ear and his voice dropped to a growl. "So, the first time you see me completely naked, ain't gonna be in front of a bunch of other guys."

"Good point."

Thirty minutes later, after the game ended and the crowd disappeared, India paced until Dr. Brewer ambled out. "Is he okay?"

"It's not as bad as I initially believed, but he insists he'll be better off with you than at the hospital."

"With me?"

Dr. Brewer measured her thoughtfully. "Are you up for taking care of him tonight? Because he's as grouchy as a grizzly with a sore paw. And we both know he won't take pain meds."

"How did I get elected as bear bait?"

"Ask Colt. He said that you..." Dr. Brewer looked around and lowered his voice. "You already played Nurse Ratchet when you shot him in the butt with a nail gun and you owe him big time."

"He *said* that? Haul him to the morgue. He'll need funeral arrangements, not medical care when I get finished with him."

The doctor chuckled and rummaged in his coat pocket for a sheet of paper. "My home phone number is at the top. Call me if you need anything."

"Your wife doesn't mind?"

"My wife is used to it, although human patients are a novelty. This late in her pregnancy she can't sleep. Which means I don't sleep."

"Thank you."

A freshly showered, but very slow moving Colt exited the locker room. He managed a half-smile before he sagged against the brick wall. "Did Jay talk to you?"

"You should be in the hospital, not having me play nursemaid—"

"Forget it." He closed his eyes. "I'll just go home alone and sleep it off. Ain't like it'd be the first time."

Guilt kicked in. "Colt. Look at me."

His eyes opened.

"I'm sorry. I'm just worried and I'm not qualified—"

"Don't matter if you're qualified, I just want you with me." He winced.

"Stay put. I'll get my car." India turned around as the side door slammed.

Cam strode toward them, an imposing figure in his khaki uniform. "What the hell happened?"

India froze. Even Colt snapped to at Cam's commanding tone.

"I lost my footing in the game and smacked into the table. No big deal, besides I've got a helluva headache."

When Cam moved, India noticed Domini was right behind

him.

"I heard about it on the scanner." Cam gave Colt a head to toe inspection. "You refused to go to the hospital. Big surprise. Although, I'm startin' to think maybe you're not the best thing for him, India. Every time I've seen you two together in the last two weeks, he ends up injured."

"Shut up," Colt snapped. "It has nothin' to do with her."

Cam put up his hands in mock surrender. "Sorry."

"You should be. Why are you here anyway?"

"I need to talk to India." Cam motioned Domini closer. "I wondered if she could stay with you tonight. That asshole ex-husband of Nadia's keeps calling to find out where she and Anton have gone. I'm afraid he'll show up at some point and I don't want her stayin' alone."

India looked at Domini. Tear tracks lined her face. She'd wrapped her arms around her stomach, but it didn't keep her body from shaking, even in Cam's enormous jacket. The poor woman was seriously freaked out and India didn't blame her. Nadia's ex was a bad guy. "Sure you can stay at my place. I'll get you set up before I leave—"

"Whoa. Leave? Where you goin'?"

"To Colt's house. I'm keeping an eye on him tonight. Dr. Brewer's instructions."

"Huh-uh. If she is stayin' in your apartment, I want you there with her. I don't want her to be alone anywhere."

"Then why doesn't she stay with you?"

Silence.

Domini dropped her chin to her chest and studied her feet.

Come on Cam, here's your chance, take it and run. Domini would rather be with you, not me. Why can't you see that?

"Because she's gotta work at the crack of dawn and your apartment is right above the restaurant, so that makes the most sense." Cam sighed. "Look. I'm about to get off shift. I'll take Colt home with me and keep an eye on him if you watch out for her."

"*Her? She?*" Domini said. "I have a name, Deputy McKay and if you insist on treating me like a child—"

Cam whispered something directly in her ear that shut her up.

"Colt? You okay staying with Cam?"

He looked at India and shrugged. "I'll be lousy company. It's just as well Cam has to deal with me rather than you."

"It's settled." Cam shifted his stance. "Miz Katzinski, would it be all right if I had a word with you? In private?"

Domini stomped away and Cam followed.

India stepped in front of Colt and placed her head on his chest. "I'm worried about you."

"I'll be good as new if I get some rest."

She kissed his chin. And his jaw. "Probably a good thing I won't be taking care of you tonight."

"Why? Because you always interrupt my sleep a billion times and then pick a fight with me so I'll kiss you?"

"No. I'd've tucked myself right in with you and there wouldn't have been a damn thing you could've done about it because it would've been on doctor's orders."

"You are ornery."

"And a little mean. Okay, a lot mean."

He shuddered. "Remind me not to piss you off."

Chapter Twelve

Stupid Colt McKay should've taken his own advice about not pissing her off, India thought for the millionth time as she slammed a box of essential oil in the middle of the showroom floor.

She and Skylar spent Saturday afternoon at Sky Blue doing quarterly inventory and India was glad for the busy work. It kept her mind off Colt.

That dickhead.

They'd had another fight. A doozy of a fight. A throwing-things-get-the-hell-out-I-don't-want-to-see-you-until-I-cool-down kind of fight.

Naturally, her sister brought up the elephant in the room when the last box of lotion had been tallied. "Don't you think you're acting unreasonable?"

India slammed the cupboard door. "Nope."

"It's been two days."

Two very long days. "So?"

Sky gestured to the enormous bouquet lined up on the counter. "Obviously Colt is sorry."

"He should be."

"Aren't you being hard on him?"

She whirled around. "What would you have done, if Kade had stormed into the factory, chewed you out for...something someone else had *supposedly* seen you do? Ripped you a new one in front of a customer? And then literally dragged you off to—" *Kiss you until you couldn't breathe, touch you so thoroughly you had to check your skin for branding iron marks. Turned you so dizzy with want and anger and fear you couldn't choose which feeling made you craziest so you acted out on all three? At the same time?*

"To what?" Sky prompted.

"To make your head explode. The man is infuriating."

"What is infuriating? That he wanted to talk to you because he was worried about your risky behavior?"

"Colt didn't talk; he yelled. And isn't there some legal confidentiality clause that Deputy Cam can't call him up and tattle that he thought I was driving my motorcycle too fast?"

Skylar wagged her finger in India's face. "Tough. You drive that deathtrap like Wyoming is the autobahn. I've been telling you that for years. And I wish Cam would've chased you down and given you a ticket."

"You're siding with him? With both of them?"

"Yes. Cam only told Colt because he knew it'd be better coming from him than from someone else in this gossipy town. And Colt confronting you on your dangerous activity is not surprising because he cares about you, Indy. He really, really cares about you."

"Yeah? Then how do you justify Mr. Caring barging in here and going all caveman on me, practically dragging me away by my hair, in front of a client?"

"Simple." Skylar smirked. "He's a McKay."

"That is not even close to funny, Sis."

"It wasn't meant to be. Chest thumping is part of Colt's genetic makeup and if you're going to be with him for the long haul, you'd better get used to it. Besides, wasn't the client just Colt's cousin, Blake?"

"So?"

"So, I doubt Colt would've acted so agitated if it'd been a stranger in your tattoo station."

"That is not the point! He acted totally inappropriate."

"You aren't exactly blameless, India. You reacted just as inappropriately." Skylar rolled her eyes. "Honestly. Did you have to throw a wrench at him?"

India's cheeks went hot with shame. "How'd you find out?"

"Colt told Kade. Kade is now blaming Eliza's tendency to throw things on my side of the family. A wrench for godsake. Why?"

"It was the closest thing I could find." And the tool belonged to Blake, so it'd seemed like karma at the time. Now it just seemed stupid, dangerous and childish. She sagged into a chair. "God. This is so screwed up."

"What's really going on? You have a nasty temper, but this knee-jerk 'anger and retreat' reaction is so unlike you."

"I know."

"Talk to me."

"I'm scared, Sky. I don't want to fuck this up. And I'm afraid I already have."

"So fix it."

"How?"

"Channel that anger into a more productive activity."

"Like what?"

Skylar slipped on her coat. "Do I really have to spell it out for you? Go out to his place, accept his apology, apologize yourself, and fuck his brains out until Monday morning."

"Which would be a brilliant idea, except Colt and I aren't having sex."

"Excuse me?"

Crap. "We're dating, not sleeping together."

Sky started laughing.

"It's not funny."

Her sister had to grip the counter she laughed so hard.

"I fail to see the humor in this."

"You've managed to hold Colt off for almost two weeks?"

"Huh-uh. He's held me off."

"Oh. That's even better." Skylar wiped her eyes. "I figured you guys would last about two days with the no sex rule."

India sniffed. "We aren't animals. We can control our baser instincts." Maybe. Kinda. Sorta. Not really. Okay, it was a fucking miracle they weren't balling each other's brains out at every opportunity. They definitely weren't lacking in the passion and chemistry department.

Skylar looked thoughtful. "Do you want to make the leap from friends to lovers?"

"Like you wouldn't believe. We're good at the friendship part. Actually, we're great at it. Colt is my best friend. He's been my best friend since six months after I met him. I trust him like no one else, I really like him, I can tell him anything and we have fun together. He makes me laugh. He gets me. He doesn't judge me. We have so much history...if we fuck this up, we lose so much more than I can even fathom. It's sort of paralyzing me, to tell you the truth."

"So don't fuck it up. You've got the friendship part down solid. Now it's time to concentrate on the lover's part. And in my experience the sex part is way easier."

"You think so?"

"I know so." Skylar grabbed India's hands and pulled her to her feet. "Make the jump by jumping him. Do it now before you chicken out."

India gave Skylar a quick hug. "Thanks, Sis."

"I owed you one for giving me a kick in the ass about Kade a few years ago." As India reached the back door, Skylar yelled, "But for God's sake, don't forget condoms."

✳

The universe fucking hated him.

At least it seemed as if the universe was conspiring to keep him from indulging in the most amazing sex in the history of the universe with the sexiest woman on the planet.

It was Saturday night. Two weeks had passed since he and India started dating. Technically, tonight could be *the* night.

So why wasn't his lover here in his arms, basking in the afterglow of smoking hot sex?

Because she was mad as a wet cat.

All due to a misunderstanding.

All due to you being a total dickhead.

Okay. Maybe he *had* acted like a dick, threatening to take her keys if he ever heard she'd ridden her motorcycle like a bat out of hell again.

Granted, he probably shouldn't have brought it up while she'd been at work. But that was the root of Colt's other problem: India had been working on Blake West. Namely, Blake's chest.

So maybe he'd gone a little psycho when he'd seen his shirtless cousin stretched out in the tattoo shop, with India bent over his naked torso, laughing. Maybe he shouldn't have dragged her away and laid a tonsil-scratching kiss on her. Maybe he shouldn't have demanded they end their two-week abstinence right then and there, with Blake in the other room.

Big mistake steering her in the backroom, where she had easy access to tools. Heavy tools. She'd thrown a wrench at his head, for Christsake.

Then she'd thrown him out of her tattoo studio.

He'd done everything right. Romanced her. He'd taken her out for dinner—sure, Dewey's wasn't on par with The Four Seasons. He whisked her to a show—sure, the movie theater in Wheatland wasn't a Broadway play. He'd taken her bowling. And to a rodeo. He'd toed the line of just kissing her.

Mostly. The hot incident in the truck notwithstanding.

His showing off at the basketball game hadn't turned out so well, yet...it'd given him a glimpse of India's caring side. A side she showed to her sister, Kade, her nieces, and to Domini, but rarely to him.

Wrong. She showed it to you after she shot you in the ass with the nail gun.

Well, she should have.

What about all those times over the last few years when she arrived on your doorstep with chicken noodle soup, tissues and Vicks VapoRub? Or with movies? Or with "a little something" for your house? Or when she's dropped everything to help you, even when you didn't ask? Or how she just always knows when you need her around?

India showed him her thoughtfulness every time they were together. The fact she showed him her bitchy, violent side, made him feel...special, because she trusted him enough not to hide it.

Enough stewing. Enough supposing. Buck up and act like a man. In other words...grovel.

He dug out his cell phone and called her.

She answered on the first ring. "I was just about to—"

"Let me say my piece first and then you'll get your chance."

Silence.

And then Colt couldn't think of a damn thing to say. Dammit. He used to be considered charming. What'd happened to his silver tongue? Or had he been delusional and the booze was responsible for his sweet-talking ability?

"Colt? I'm waiting."

"Sorry I acted like a jerk."

"Go on."

"You deserve better from me."

"Keep going."

"I was an asshole, especially in front of Blake."

"Yes, you were."

"I saw your hands on him and I..."

"What?"

"All I could think about was I wanted your hands on me like that. I wanted to make it crystal fuckin' clear to him that you'd never ever put your hands on him like that in private. Never. Because that privilege was all mine."

"I tattoo people for a living, Colt. I'm going to have my hands on a lot of men. On some interesting places on men."

"I don't think it would've bothered me if it'd been anyone besides him."

India sighed. "Well, your message to your cousin couldn't have been clearer. I half expected you to whip out your dick and pee on me as you snarled at him and marked your territory."

"Jesus." Colt winced. "I'm sorry. Really sorry, India. You have to believe me."

"I know you are. And as long as we're apologizing, I'm sorry I threw the wrench at you."

"I'm glad Eliza didn't get her rock throwing abilities from you, as I would've had another head injury to deal with."

"How is your head?"

"Evidently I'm a lot more hard-headed than I realized."

"And yet, you sound so surprised by that statement, McKay." A slight pause. "How's your ass?"

"You expectin' me to say I'm a dumbass?"

"Or a smartass. Or you behaved like a jackass...take your pick."

He smiled. "I've missed you like crazy the last forty-nine hours."

"You've kept track of how long it's been since you've seen me?"

I always do. "Uh. Yeah. Does that make me a pathetic loser?"

"No, it's very sweet, in a stalkerish sort of way."

"Indy—"

"So you really missed me?"

Colt rested his hot forehead against the cool glass of the sliding glass door. "Like you wouldn't believe."

"You have a funny way of showing it."

"You mean fighting with you in public? Or groping you in public?"

"Both, I guess."

"I'm hopin' you preferred one way over the other."

"I did."

"You gonna tell me which one?"

"Nope." She let loose a husky laugh. "But I might be convinced to show you."

"I wish you were here."

The doorbell rang.

"Hang on, someone's at the door." By the time he reached the foyer, he prayed his suspicion was right.

India stood on his steps. "I was on my way over to check on you before you called."

"Why?"

"I thought I might've scared you away for good. I wanted to make sure you were all right."

"All right as in...you wanted to check if I'd swung by the package liquor store?"

"No. I'm not here as your sponsor." She frowned. "Especially since I'm no longer your sponsor."

"Then why are you here?"

India locked her eyes to his. "Because I missed you."

"And?" The moment of truth. Of intent. His heart raced. His body went on full alert.

"And you *do* realize our two weeks of strictly dating are up, right?"

Colt decided doing a victory lap would be a little over the top. "Yes."

"Can I come in?"

He set his phone on the library table. "As long as you understand the instant you cross that threshold, India Ellison, I'm gonna be all over you."

Giving him a cocky grin, she stepped into the foyer.

He had India in his arms before her other foot met the tile. His mouth was on hers as he carried her into the living room.

Between frantic kisses, he whispered, "I need—"

"I know, Colt, me too."

"No foreplay."

"Fine." She kissed him. "Good." She kissed him again. "Whatever. We've had two weeks worth of foreplay."

"Hell, woman, we've had three fuckin' *years* of foreplay," he growled. "In my bed. Now."

"No. No more waiting." India trapped his face in her hands. "Right here."

"Where? Against the wall? On the couch? Over the chair?"

"On the white rug. Move the coffee table."

"Done." He set her down and dragged the iron and glass table out of the way as if it weighed nothing. Then he reached for her again.

The kiss was explosive. She tasted of mint and coffee. She fought him for control, her tongue dueling, then coy and teasing.

Colt could kiss her for days. And he would, right after he fucked her. At least twice. "I wanna see you. All of you. Clothes off."

India whipped her shirt over her head. Unhooked her satin bra and tossed it aside.

He groaned. "Those pierced nipples are about the sexiest things I've ever seen."

"Oh, trust me, you ain't seen nothin' yet." She peeled the black denim down her legs and kicked it by the couch. A funny smile twitched the corners of her lips. Wearing just a teeny pair of dark blue panties, she raised her arms above her head, performing a whole body shimmy.

When she spun around, his mouth watered. The fact India wore a thong didn't surprise him. The sun and moon tattoos, one inked on each of her perfectly round ass cheeks—now those surprised him. "Goddamn, I cannot wait to trace those designs with my tongue."

"Come closer. I want you to take my thong off."

"With pleasure." Colt dropped to his knees and hooked his fingers into the elastic running across her hips. He paused to kiss the jewel dangling from her belly button. Keeping his hungry gaze on hers, he slid the thong until it reached the tops of her feet. He allowed his eyes to gorge on her as they descend the length of her body, taking in the beautifully long sweep of her neck, her delicate collarbones, the gentle swell of her chest. Her compact ribcage, the muscles of her torso and the body jewelry winking at him from the sexy indent of her navel.

His gaze moved to the rise of her mound. Her completely hairless mound. He grinned. "Sugar, I should've guessed you'd be a Brazilian kind of gal."

"You approve?"

"Mmm-hmm." Colt placed his mouth on the top of her pubis and brushed his lips back and forth across the bare skin. So soft. Closing his eyes, he let his tongue follow the sweet cleft leading straight to paradise. At least, he'd intended to, but his tongue ran into a barrier. A metal barrier. He opened his eyes.

Holy shit. A thin bar stretched above her clitoris, piercing the skin above it.

"Surprise."

"Sweet Jesus. And I thought the nipple rings were sexy." He closed his mouth over the piercing and her clit and sucked. Once. Twice. Three times. He groaned at the sweet, musky, slightly metallic taste and the way her hands tightened in his hair.

"Colt—"

"I wanna spend hours with my mouth between your legs. Sucking. Licking. Biting. Makin' you come all over my face, drivin' you to the point you won't even know your own damn name."

"God. Yes."

He gave her one last lingering suck before he pushed to his feet. "Look at me."

India locked her eyes to his.

With one hand he pulled at the edge of his shirt until the snaps popped. "Touch yourself as you're watchin' me get undressed. But don't come. There'll be hell to pay if you come before I'm inside you."

"Oh. Umm. Are you always this...?"

"Demanding when it comes to sex?"

She nodded.

"More than this. Is that gonna be an issue for you?"

She shook her head. Her eyes roamed over his chest. His abs. His arms. Back to his pecs.

"Indy," he said sharply. "Are you supposed to be doin'

123

something for me?"

"Uh. Yeah."

"So what's the problem?"

Her gaze finally made it to his face. "No problem. I've seen you with your shirt off, Colt. But it's like this is the first time I'm really seeing you. You're amazing. All golden skin and delineated musculature. I want to run my hands all over your chest and belly. I want to trace every muscle and vein with my tongue until your skin is shiny wet with my saliva. I want to suck on your nipples. And while I'm sucking on them, I'll imagine how it'd be to tattoo such perfect skin."

"Enough." Colt unbuckled his belt, wincing at how hard his cock was. "Get to it."

"I totally forgot what I was supposed to be doing."

He smiled wickedly. "Touchin' yourself."

"But, I don't know—"

"Need a little direction?"

"Please."

"I like it when you say please. I'd like it even better if I heard you beg. Put your finger in your mouth. That's it. Now get it nice and wet." While watching her, he unzipped his jeans. "Put it on your clit. Show me how you get yourself off when you're alone."

India moaned softly as she rubbed the skin beneath the piercing.

"Do you pinch your nipples?"

"Sometimes."

"Show me."

She stilled. "Not until I see your cock."

Colt raised his eyebrows at her demand.

"Please."

He gave her his back as he removed his jeans. Before he could turn around, her hot, naked flesh pressed to his.

"I'll finger myself to orgasm and let you watch another time, but right now... I want you so bad." She brushed openmouthed kisses across the center of his spine. "Please."

No way could he deny her or himself another second. "I'll grab a condom and be right back."

"I bought a box on the way over. They're in my purse."

His cock twitched so hard it slapped his belly. "Get one.

Now."

The sound of cardboard ripping. Plastic crinkling. Then India stood in front of him holding a purple square. "Can I put it on you?"

"Nope." Colt snatched it out of her hand, ripped the package open. While he sheathed himself, he lowered his head and kissed her. He hadn't meant for the kiss to be lazy and languorous, but it was. Sweet and perfect. "Indy. I need to fuck you before I lose my ever lovin' mind."

"Yes."

They fell to the rug in a tangle of arms and legs. He rose above her, his cock poised at her entrance, his gaze holding steady, his breathing ragged, fear and anticipation warred inside him.

"Colt?"

"I'm here. Where I've wanted to be for too damn long." Pinning her wrists above her head, his gentleness vanished. He snapped his hips, slamming home with one deep thrust.

Fuck. Fuck. Fuck. Fuck. If he came at the touch of her hand, what were the chances he's last beyond three or four more strokes as her pussy sucked at his cock like a hungry mouth?

None. Zero. Zilch. Nada.

Colt rubbed his mouth over her ear, letting the studs and piercings catch on the inside of his lower lip. "This is gonna be short and sweet."

"Thank God. Because I'm already close. Been a long time for me."

"How long?"

"Not as long as you." She slapped his butt. "Move your fine ass, cowboy."

A snarl escaped as he pulled out and thrust in. seven, eight, nine times. "Tighter. Squeeze me tighter. Like that. Oh fuck yeah, exactly like that."

India's nipple rings rasped over Colt's chest as their upper bodies thrust and retreat. Tingles broke out across his skin. When that zippy feeling burned down his spine, and electrified his balls, he knew he'd reached the end.

Colt threw his head back, groaning, letting the sensations overtake him. Hot pulses. Pounding blood. That rush of endorphins. Three years. Three excruciatingly long, lonely years he'd gone without this feeling of euphoria. Of connectedness.

He didn't remember sex ever being this astoundingly good.

A sexy moan escaped from India and Colt raised his head to watch pleasure wash over her. After her soft, sated sigh, Colt kissed her. He rested his forehead to hers.

"Was it worth the wait?"

Yes, it was perfect. But he couldn't seem to find his voice.

"You aren't one of those narcoleptic guys who immediately start snoring afterward, are you?"

"No. Why would you—" He hid his face in her neck and pretended to snore. Loudly. Great big gulps of air that vibrated against her throat with each exhalation.

India giggled and squirmed. "Hey, stop. That tickles."

God. He loved the sound of her girlish giggles. "I'll stop on one condition. Spend the night with me. All night. In my bed."

"If I say no?"

"I'll tie you to the headboard and keep you here as my sex slave for as long as I want anyway."

"Ah. Is this where you remind me you're wicked good with ropes?"

"Don't insult me by limiting it to ropes. I'm wicked good with anything that can be hooked, tied or fastened together."

"Then I guess you leave me with no choice."

Colt raised his head to study her. "I was kiddin'. You don't have to stay."

"I didn't mean that the way it sounded. I'm here because I want to be here. There's nowhere else I'd rather be." She smoothed a section of hair from his forehead and he resisted purring like a contented cat. "Although I don't have any idea what we do now."

"Me neither. I guess we'll have to wing it. I think we oughta move someplace more comfortable."

She stretched. "Mmm. I've always wondered what it'd be like to lie on this rug naked. I thought it might be scratchy."

"I never would've tried to stop you from testing that theory."

"How about if next time you're on the bottom?"

"Deal." Colt smooched her forehead. "Lemme ditch this condom and I'll meet you in the bedroom."

Chapter Thirteen

India picked up the box of condoms and headed down the hallway to Colt's room. She switched on the overhead light and cast a quick glance around. Earth tones prevailed. The walls were deep hunter green, the fabrics a mix of browns, tans and golds, the carpet a sandy beige.

The frame of the four-poster California king-sized bed was constructed from logs. Nightstands crafted out of the same honey-colored pine book-ended the enormous bed. A matching dresser spanned the far wall. A buffalo-skin leather chair and ottoman were set at a jaunty angle beside it. The door to the walk-in closet was closed, but the door to the master bathroom was ajar. She caught a glimpse of the oversized shower and the tile floor.

It was weird to think she'd helped choose the furnishings for Colt's room, from the color palette to the bedding. And now she'd be sliding around naked with him on those striped cotton sheets?

Weird indeed.

His muffled footsteps stopped behind her. He was close enough his body heat burned her naked back, but he didn't touch her. "What are you thinkin' about right now?"

"I remember when we went to Cheyenne and picked out the bedding. How you insisted on nothing too 'girlie'. Heck, I remember picking out the bed. Bouncing on the mattress and laughing, trying to freak out the salespeople by pretending we were having sex. I never imagined you and I would actually be..."

"Didn't you? Didn't you really? It never once crossed your mind that you'd be in my bed?"

India couldn't answer, mostly because she didn't know the right answer.

Colt's lips landed on the nape of her neck. "Lemme show you all the things I thought about doin' to you in my bed."

Tingles raced down her spine.

He took her hand and tugged her behind him. He tossed the pillows to the floor and yanked back the coverlet. Facing her with a wicked grin, he patted the mattress. "Hop up. Get in the middle."

A bout of nerves hit her as she set the box of condoms up in the corner and lay flat.

Then Colt was hanging above her. Kissing her with fire and sweetness. "Indy—" he said her name between kisses, "—put your arms straight out so I can see you. All of you."

She did.

He nuzzled her neck, nipped at her jaw. "Tell me about your tattoos."

"Which one?"

"All of them on the front." His callused finger traced the designs on her right arm, from the ball of her shoulder down to her wrist. "Why'd you go with a sleeve on one arm and not the other?"

Colt's mouth on her skin was beyond divine, but it was hell on her concentration. "It wasn't intentional. I wanted a cool snake curling up my arm, with the tail on my wrist and the head on my biceps. I had no idea my buddy GG planned to ink a flesh-colored snake until it was done."

"It really is unique."

"Then I knew the skin around it needed to be brightly colored with geometric shapes and abstract images so I designed those."

"It's sexy as hell." Colt bent his head and licked, from the tail of the snake up to the fangs.

"Oh. Wow. That's the first time..."

"The first time what?"

Any man has paid homage to my tats with his tongue. "You've said anything about my tattoos."

"Really? I love them. All of them. Especially the twisted barbed wire circling this biceps. It looks so real. The drops of blood on the tips of the barbs are a realistic touch."

"Is that why you had me do one on you?" She traced the thick black lines on Colt's biceps. His tat was a far better design than hers. She'd killed herself drawing it, and spent extra time inking him, desperate for Colt to be proud to have it on his arm.

"Yep. If I had the guts, I'd have you continue all the way down to my wrist so it looks like my arm is trapped in barbed wire."

India's head started spinning. That would actually make a kick-ass tattoo.

"And this one?" He pressed his lips to the black scorpion tattoo on the upper swell of her left breast.

She refocused. "I thought it'd be funny to have a deadly insect crawling out of my bra."

"What about this one?" He traced the large blue starburst pattern surrounding her belly button.

"I designed it when Skylar decided to leave the rat race in California and turn her hobby into a business." Her belly rippled when his thumb brushed over the design and the jewel dangling from her navel.

"Seems odd that you'd celebrate her success by inking yourself."

"It was supposed to be for her, but she chickened out. I liked the design too much to let it go to waste. My friend Brett in Las Vegas did it."

"Another good decision." Colt lowered his head, allowing his hair to tease her skin before his mouth descended to lick the outline of the tattoo. Repeatedly. Thoroughly.

"Any other questions?"

"Not right now." He dragged his tongue down the center of her body. Slowly. "God, you're so soft." Colt nuzzled her mound. "You smell so good. I wanna bury my face here. Let your scent mark me. Feel your sweet juices flowing down the back of my throat."

"If that's what you want, Colt, I won't stop you."

He looked at her across the expanse of her body. Those blue eyes were dark with intent. "Oh, I want."

"Are you going to make me wait?"

"No. I've been starvin' for a taste of you for too long. Spread your legs." He traced the metal bar with his tongue. "Did it hurt to get pierced?"

"A little."

"Why'd you do it?"

"I lost a bet."

Colt looked up. "Seriously?"

"Uh-huh. Since I lose all the time I should probably give up betting, huh?"

He chuckled. "I don't mind when you lose to me, sugar."

"After I had it in for a while...I liked it."

"I like it too. A lot." Then he pulled the piercing and her clit into his mouth and sucked.

Her pelvis shot up.

He clamped his hands around her hips and held them down. Again, no foreplay, no teasing, no fingers stroking the inside walls of her pussy, just a relentless rhythmic sucking.

"Your mouth is so...God, do you know how to use your mouth."

A hum of approval vibrated up her core. He backed off and blew across her flesh, wet from his mouth and her own arousal. "Give it to me. I wanna feel you come." He refocused all that suctioning power on her clit.

That's all it took. The orgasm pulsed through her so fast she barely squeaked a sound as her sex throbbed beneath his dancing tongue.

Damn. Talk about quick.

After Colt released her tender flesh, he kissed the inside of her thigh. "You okay?"

"Mmm." The crinkle of a condom wrapper forced her to open her eyes.

"Now that we finished the speed round..."

Heat stained her cheeks. "Sorry."

"Don't be. I am still the undisputed winner for the first time you put your hand on me at your apartment."

"I'm not sorry I touched you."

"Me either, to tell you the truth, since it finally brought us to this point."

Then Colt was on her, belly-to-belly, chest-to-chest, his shaft thick and hot on her sex, acting all predatory male. He shoved into her in one quick movement. "Sweet baby Jesus you feel so fine, Indy. So damn fine."

"You ain't so bad yourself, cowboy." Colt did some hip

wiggle maneuver as he withdrew and plunged back in and she gasped.

"What? Did I hurt you?"

"No. Just surprised me."

"Maybe I oughta slow down."

"Maybe." India let her hands flow over his arms, loving the flex of the hard, carved muscles. Loving the look of concern and awe on his handsome face. Damn, he was beautiful. She knew he wouldn't appreciate her saying so. It caused her to wonder what he saw when he looked at her. Like this. Naked, in body and soul. Face to face. As close as two people could possibly be.

"Sugar, you have the oddest look. Am I doin' something wrong?"

She shook her head. "It's just...you're so...and being here with you like this...being turned on and happy and scared and not knowing if you feel the same."

"I feel the same, do I ever." Colt kissed her. Soul-kissed her with such warmth, passion and precision her toes curled. He threaded his fingers through hers and stretched their joined hands above her by the headboard. In this position, it seemed as if their bodies were closer. His pelvis rocked, his cock tunneled in and out of her wet and welcoming sex, not in a fast movement. Languidly. But no less potently. No less erotically.

His damp skin sliding across hers. Melting hot and lazy kisses. Each grinding glide of his pelvis to hers built her higher. So close, if she could just... She hooked her feet on the outside of Colt's ankles, trying to free herself to grab his butt.

Colt squeezed her hands and pulled back to look at her. "Something you need?"

"A handful of your ass would be great."

"Huh-uh. Right now I'm makin' love to you this way."

"What way's that?"

His lips brushed the sensitive section of skin in front of her ear and she shivered. "My way. Maybe if you're a good girl, I'll let you pick the next way."

"Colt—"

"Every inch of you against every inch of me, India. Skin to skin. That's the way I've always wanted to take you the first time in my bed. Come with me like this. I'll get you there if you'll let me."

His words, his intent, his smoldering kisses sent India spiraling into the unknown. She'd always been in charge in the bedroom. Not a crop-wielding dominatrix, but she always felt her orgasms were her responsibility. How freeing would it be to pass that responsibility to him?

Like heaven.

When Colt stretched her arms higher and whispered, "Let go," she did.

She fell even as she soared. Her hips pumped and met his thrust for thrust. Her gasps cut through the sex-scented air, mixing with Colt's grunts of satisfaction as he let go right along with her.

This time when India tried to break his grip on her hands, he didn't protest. She touched him everywhere, running her palms down those fabulously sculpted muscular arms. Her fingertips danced across his broad chest, her thumbs strummed his nipples. His answering hiss meant she'd definitely spend more playtime there.

Colt lifted his face from where he'd buried it in her neck.

India pecked him on the mouth. "Ding ding ding! I declare round three a tie."

He grinned. "Yeah?"

"Mmm-hmm. Thank you. That was incredible. So now what?"

"You already eyeballing round four?"

"Of course, since you said I get to pick the next way."

"You think so?"

"I know so."

"Maybe there's something else you oughta know about me."

Beyond you're spectacular in the sack?

If the man could wring three orgasms from her in less than three hours, when he hadn't practiced the fine art of lovemaking in the last three years, what would it be like when he did return to his former sexual glory?

Magnificent.

Her pussy clenched around his cock just thinking about the delicious ways he'd prove his prowess.

"Do that again."

"What?"

"Tighten around me."

Grinning, she did.

He hissed. "That feels good."

India kissed the sexy dent in his chin. "Mmm. You must've forgotten how good sex is in your sexual sabbatical."

"No. It's never felt like this. And I don't believe it's because I was wasted some of the other times."

Her heart leapt.

"But there is one thing I remember."

"What's that?"

Colt clasped both her wrists in one hand and pinned them above her head. "I am in charge. I ain't the 'Would it be okay if I did this, honey?' kind of lover. I'm demandin'. Greedy. And I prefer a little kink."

She'd heard rumors of some of that kink, but Colt had never confirmed nor denied. "Should I be worried?"

"That I'm gonna have your sweet little body every which way I've fantasized about? Absolutely. That I'm make you forget any other man who's ever touched you? Without apology. That I'm gonna cause your body to sing and sigh and weep with pleasure? Guaranteed. That I'd ever hurt you? No. That I'd ever share you? Bring another lover into our bed? Hell no. *Fuck* no." His lips were a whisper away; his eyes flashed a dangerous glint. "You're only ever *mine. My* hands on you. *My* mouth on you. *My* cock in you. Understood?"

The annoyed feeling India expected never surfaced. This side of Colt wasn't as alarming as it was...arousing. The position of his body, the set of his mouth, the heat in his eyes all bespoke of his domination.

Since her relationship with Larry, she'd avoided domineering men. Since she'd been clean, she'd avoided men from twelve-step programs. Since she'd moved to Wyoming, she'd avoided cowboys.

The irony that Colt was all three wasn't lost on her.

"Indy?"

"Sorry. Just thinking."

"About?"

"About how glad I am that you only wanna be with me. Just us, doing all the kinky things you've been stockpiling in your years of sexual deprivation."

His slow, sure grin was a thing of beauty. "Oh, you don't

know the half of it." Without releasing her hands, he destroyed her with a kiss so blistering hot she suspected her lips were smoking when he finally pulled back.

"So what do we do now?"

"Now we do the normal date thing. Pop some popcorn. Put in a movie, neck on the couch and see where it takes us."

"You know exactly where it's gonna take us, Colt McKay. Straight back to bed."

"That's what I'm hopin' for."

India settled on his couch, wearing his button-down shirt, looking unbelievably sexy, balancing the enormous popcorn bowl on her lap.

After Colt plopped beside her, he clicked start. He'd cued up the movie, skipping the *wawka wawka* music and telling previews.

"What're we watching?"

"A comedy."

India laid her head on his shoulder. *Crunch crunch.* "This is nice."

"We do this damn near every Saturday night."

"But not like this. Snuggled close in the afterglow of amazingly perfect hot sex."

"True. Quit hoggin' the popcorn. That's something else you always do. And crunch it as loud as humanly possible."

"Sorry." She laid a buttery, salty kiss on him and held the bowl closer.

The sex flick started as so many of them did. A hot woman, yakking on the phone to her friend about her lousy dating life. How she'd love to get some action but her prospects were thin. The doorbell rings. She hangs up in such a hurry to answer the door that she forgets to put a robe on over her negligee. Standing on the other side of the door is a repairman.

"I don't recognize any of these actors."

"Really?"

India knew something was up when the repairman bent over to "fix" the knob on the stove and the woman came up behind him, spinning him around to bump and grind on his tool.

"Colt, is this porn?"

"Yep. Keep watchin'. It gets better."

"I cannot believe we're watching porn after we just had sex two times."

"Three if you count oral." He tossed a couple kernels in the air and caught them in his mouth. "I'll bet we have sex again before the movie ends."

"What do you want to bet?"

"Don't be so literal, India. We don't have to bet on everything," he teased.

She faced him. "No, seriously. Put your money where your sexy mouth is, McKay. What's the bet?"

"One dollar."

"Nope."

"Two dollars."

"Nope, not what I want."

"What do you want, Miz Moneybags?"

"One kiss. One deep, slow, wet kiss."

Colt pretended to consider it. "No deal. When I win, I wanna nail you from behind while we're watching the scene where she's being fucked by three guys and one chick."

Her eyes flashed interest. "How does that work?"

"You'll see." Colt leaned over and licked the salt from her lips with a flirty kiss. "I dare you not to get turned on by that scene."

"I'm gonna lose, aren't I?"

"But that's the beauty of bettin' against me, sugar. Neither of us really loses."

As the movie progressed, Colt knew India was getting turned on. She squirmed, even when her legs were primly pressed together. She bit her lip. Her face was flushed. Her breathing choppy. But mostly he could tell because of the scent of the warm, sweet cream drifting up from between her thighs.

His dick tented his boxers but India was taking great pains not to notice.

Colt curled his hand around her knee. "Here's the scene."

The main character returned home and found her best friend in bed with the repairman. She was livid. Her idea of punishment was having her friend lick her pussy while the repairman sucked her tits. The camera shots consisted of the brunette going to town between the blonde's thighs, licking her slit over and over with long sweeps of her tongue. Or vigorously rubbing the blonde's clit with a sharp-tipped red nail as they both moaned in ecstasy.

Meanwhile the bad repairman was devoting all his attention to the woman's breasts. More sucking and tongue curls around the rigid tip as the woman writhed on the bed between them. She climaxed with gusto.

As she came down from her sexual high, the doorbell rang. Too tired to answer it, she dispatched her best friend to see who was at the door. The best friend came back to the bedroom with two new repairmen, who were sent to find out what happened to their male coworker. Their clothes flew, and they joined in the fun.

From the corner of his eye, Colt saw India was almost holding her breath.

Back on the screen, one of the new guys was spread out on the bed with at least twelve inches of thick cock sticking straight up. The woman straddled him and impaled herself. Before she could arch back, the first repairman grabbed her hair, turning her head and shoving his dick into her mouth. She noisily sucked him off. The third man watched as her best friend licked a line up the woman's butt crack, from where her pussy was already stuffed with dick. She licked and tongue fucked that beige pucker until the man pushed her aside and rammed all ten inches of his cock into that tight asshole.

The woman went ballistic. Cock in her mouth, cock in her pussy, cock in her ass. She allowed the men to set the pace, but they all fucked her hard. When the moment of truth came, one at a time, they pulled out and sprayed her body with come. The blowjob guy came on her face. The ass fucker came on her butt crack. The pussy fucker blew all over her bouncing tits.

The best friend took that as her cue to jump back in the fray. She rubbed in the come dotted across her friend's nipples. She licked the come off her friend's face. Then she shoved two fingers up her friend's pussy as she sucked her friend's tits and brought forth yet another orgasm from her horny friend.

Colt hit pause. "You okay?"

India shook her head.

"What's wrong?"

"I hate losing a bet." Then she attacked him. The popcorn

bowl hit the floor. She bounced on his lap, kissing and biting and scratching like a wildcat.

He loved every fucking second of it.

"Hang on, lemme get this shirt off."

"Hurry. Hurry, hurry, hurry."

Somehow between India's frantic kisses, he got rid of his boxers. Luckily he'd remembered to bring a couple condoms and he was suited up in no time.

"Fuck me, Colt, please."

"Oh, I'm gonna fuck you. It ain't gonna be sweet and easy."

Colt turned her toward the TV. "Spread your legs. Grab onto the coffee table. Yeah, Indy, that's sexy as hell." The second his cock touched the slippery core of her, he hissed.

He clicked back to the beginning of the scene and hit play. Then he lifted her slightly and plunged in.

She pushed her hips back at him. "Again."

Colt obliged her, keeping a relentless pounding rhythm. He looked up at the screen. The brunette was busy eating pussy. "Does girl-on-girl turn you on?"

"Not usually. This scene is hot, but not as hot as the one where they're all fucking her. Three men at once. I wonder what that—"

"As long as you're with me, you'll never know." Colt released her hip so he could grip her hair and pull her ear back to his mouth. "You and me, India. No one else. If you wanna know what it's like to have every hole filled, I'll stick a dildo in your ass and one in your cunt while my cock is in your throat."

India whimpered.

"Would you like that?"

She whimpered again.

He pulled her hair a little harder. "Answer me."

"Yes, all right? I want to feel you in me everywhere, just you."

He growled. "Do you want me touchin' your clit or your nipples?"

"My clit. Please. Rub on it like that woman is."

Colt stroked in the identical rhythm on the big screen as he snapped his hips. "More?"

"I'm about to... Yes! That's it." She squealed and slammed back into Colt's tunneling cock with enough force the couch cushions shook.

The hot grip of her pussy muscles around his cock, milking him, sucking at him, and the throbbing cadence of her pulse beneath his stroking finger, all proved too much.

Colt threw his head back and came with a primal roar.

When he returned from that otherworldly place where he existed only as pure sensation, he realized he'd clutched her hard enough to bruise her skin.

Not that she seemed to mind. India pushed up, dislodging his softening sex before she spun around and kissed him. A melding sweetness of raw emotion. She touched him, soothed him, and proved he hadn't been wrong to fall for her because there was so much more to her than what met the eye. She was everything. *Everything.* And finally, she was his.

"Indy—"

"Colt," she whispered, tugging on his earlobe with her teeth. "Don't get serious on me. This night, heck, the last two weeks, have been too amazing to ruin by dissection. We're both guilty of doing it out of habit because of A.A. Just let it be, okay?"

"Okay. For now."

Bad porn music played in the background.

She eased back to look into his eyes, stifling a yawn. "I'm tired. Can we just crawl in your big comfy bed, snuggle up and go to sleep?"

There'd be no more confessions or revelations tonight. Truthfully, that was probably for the best.

"Come on then, sleepyhead. Let's get you a pair of socks, 'cause no way in hell are you puttin' them cold feet on me."

Chapter Fourteen

The front door slammed. A feminine voice called out, "I brought caramel rolls. They're still warm. They have extra, extra caramel, just like you like 'em. And I'm hopin' because I'm hand delivering your favorite breakfast sweet that you'll sneak me some of that high octane coffee I smell brewing." Chassie Glanzer screeched to a stop. "Holy crap. India? What're you doin' half-naked in Colt's kitchen?"

"Hi Chassie."

"I mean, wow, nice to see you. You caught me by surprise."

"I sorta figured that."

"Guess I oughta knock before I barge in next time. Not that it's never mattered before since you're the first woman I've seen in my cousin's house for an overnight...ah hell, I'm makin' a mess of this, aren't I?"

"Forget it." Although, India was secretly glad to see she wasn't the only one who babbled from nerves.

"Where's Colt?"

"In bed. I lost a bet so I had to get up and make coffee." She'd sworn she couldn't come from just the vibration of the water jets on her clit, but Colt had proven her wrong. Twice. Early morning shower sex, with the oscillating water spray aimed just so...oh, what a way to lose.

"Colt is always up at the crack of nothin', hard at work," Chassie said.

Was he ever *up*. And *hard*. Dammit, talk about a continual loop of sex on the brain. "He's tired."

"I'm glad."

"You're glad?"

"Yep. He's been alone a long time." Chassie set the metal, foil-covered pan on the counter. She turned and gave India a once-over, taking in Colt's long-sleeved button-up shirt, her bare legs, and her mussed hair. "He needs someone like you."

India resisted jerking the lapels closed, even when chances were good whisker burns and love bites decorated her skin alongside her tattoos. "Someone like me...meaning?"

"A woman who really knows him. And really likes him. And believes in him. And makes him happy. You do all that for him."

"I do?"

"Come on, you had to have known how crazy he's always been about you, India."

"I swear I didn't."

"Well, then, you were the only one."

Had she really been so blind?

"I suppose you're wondering why I'm here at nine in the mornin'."

"I hope our activities last night weren't loud enough to wake up the neighbors and you're coming to complain."

"Nope. You'll never hear me complaining about loud sex." Chassie grinned and pulled herself onto a barstool. "I can't sleep so I've turned into Betty Crocker. It's sort of embarrassing. I started baking. Bread, rolls, cookies, muffins, you name it. Trev and Ed can only eat so much, so poor Colt is stuck with the remnants."

"As a bachelor, I imagine he hates getting fresh baked goodies." India smiled. "Is the baby keeping you from sleeping?"

Chassie's hand caressed her rounded abdomen. "The fear of childbirth is keeping me awake most of the time. I hate doctors and hospitals." She shuddered. "And I can't convince my boneheaded men that I'd rather have a midwife deliver the baby at home, in our bed, where he was conceived, instead of in an impersonal hospital."

India admired Chassie for bucking conventions and living with and loving two men, despite the many tongues wagging in the community about the arrangement. "Sky was terrified of giving birth. But when the time came...she was fine. Afterward, she said the unknown was the worst part for her. It couldn't have been too bad because she went through it again fifteen months later with twins."

"I was really surprised Sky and Kade jumped on the McKay family 'let's have a kid every other year' bandwagon that our other McKay cousins are on." Chassie cocked her head. "Was that beep a signal the coffee is done?"

"Oh sure. Sorry, I'm not much of a hostess." She smiled sheepishly. "Then again, this isn't my house."

"Then again, isn't most of the décor in this place your doing?" Chassie asked.

"Yes. I didn't want such a beautiful house to be a typical bachelor pad. Luckily, Colt has great taste." India grabbed two mugs and moved on the other side of the counter. As she poured, she said, "Anyway, I think Sky and Kade decided if they were going to have more kids, they should do it sooner rather than later. They just didn't bank on twins."

"And twin girls to boot. If I decide to go through this again, I hope we have a girl." Chassie sighed. "We still have three months before we have to decide on a name, which is a good thing."

India spun her cup on the counter, biting her tongue because the question she wanted to ask was wildly inappropriate.

"I know tattooing me and Trev and Ed doesn't mean we know each other very well, even if Colt talks about you all the damn time—"

"Really? He talks about me?"

"Constantly, but just ask me whatever's on your mind, India."

"Are you talking about what first name you're gonna give the baby, or the last name?"

"First name. The baby's last name will be Glanzer, like ours."

"Ours?" India frowned. "But don't you guys have two names?"

"Not any more. Earlier this year, when Trev, Edgard and I celebrated our first...anniversary together, Ed legally changed his last name to Glanzer."

"Why?"

"Mancuso was his stepfather's last name. Since he's broken all ties with his family in Brazil, and he has no living relatives here in the US...it just seemed right he have our name since he's a part of us."

"That makes sense."

"Plus, as a bonus, Trevor knew it'd piss his dad off." She winked. "So enough about me, tell me about you and Colt. When did you and my cousin start..."

"Start dating? Two weeks ago."

Silence.

Chassie sighed. "I just bared my soul and that's all I get?"

"Yes, 'cause Indy ain't the kiss-and-tell type like some people I know." Colt set his hands on India's shoulders and leaned in, mock whispering, "Although, there is plenty to tell after last night, huh?" He kissed down the side of her neck. "Mmm. Mornin', sugar."

Goose bumps broke out in the wake of his warm kisses and sweet words. She closed her eyes and sank into him. "Morning."

"Thanks for makin' coffee."

"Like I had a choice."

She felt him grin against her cheek. "Is that a complaint?"

"No. Hell no."

His smile widened, if anything. "Good to know."

"But I am going to insist on no more betting today."

"You're the one who always starts it."

Chassie snorted. "You two are so whipped. It's as sweet as it is nauseating."

Crap. India had forgotten about their guest. She opened her eyes. "Chassie brought caramel rolls."

"Lucky us." Colt gestured to Chassie's coffee cup. "You ain't supposed to be drinkin' coffee, Chass."

"So don't tell." At Colt's continued hard stare, she said, "But I know you will. Fine. Dump it out, meanie. I probably better get home anyway."

"What are Trevor and Edgard doin' today?"

"Probably screwing around." Chassie slid off the barstool. "Nice seein' you, India. Nice boxers, Colt. Next time, I'll knock." She shuffled out.

"I like her," India said.

"She's ornery and sweet with a big heart. Kinda like you." He grinned. "Which is probably why she and I have gotten on so well over the years."

"Is that part of the reason you built out here?"

"Maybe. By the time I got my life back in order, Chassie had married Trevor, Edgard had moved in, and havin' family close, but bein' in my own place, appealed to me. I get along great with all of them, sometimes better than with my brothers. Heck, the four of us have even partnered up breedin' stock."

"But you still work at the McKay Ranch?"

"Yep."

"I don't understand how that works."

"The ranch is run like a corporation. We're all shareholders. We take care of the ranch as a whole, but we've divided it into four sections. Each one of my uncles and my dad is an original owner. But when the main owners started havin' sons, they divided their individual sections up again. So, we've all added separate parcels. Like Cord and my dad bought the Foster place a few years back. Colby and my dad bought an acreage north of Colby's place up in the mountains. That's where Kade was during Skylar's pregnancy."

"I'd wondered about that."

"It was easier for Kade to take off since there's only Kade and Buck on my Uncle Cal's portion and they haven't expanded."

India frowned. If Cord and Carson bought land, and Colby and Carson bought land, wouldn't it make sense...Carson and Colt would've bought land? "Did you and your dad buy other acreages together?"

"Nope. I bought land on my own that I kept separate from the McKay Ranch, which pissed them off. Because financially it ended up bein' a good investment, one that was solely mine."

One thing India and Colt never talked about was finances. "Like this place?"

"Technically, we all own the land my house is on. My other McKay cousins take care of their two sections, and they've added significantly to their holdings in the last ten years. We help each other out, but mostly we're responsible for what goes on in our area. So Colby, Cord, Dad and I run ours. My cousins Kade and Buck theirs. Quinn and Bennett theirs while Chase is off rodeoin'. My other cousins, Dalton, Luke, Brandt and Tell...I ain't gonna get into the clusterfuck that is right now."

India stared at him, too embarrassed to admit she didn't understand a word he'd just said.

"Am I borin' ya?"

"No, it's just a hard concept to grasp."

"Tell me about it. I'm glad it ain't my job to figure out who's owed what when it comes time to get paid."

For some reason, bringing up ranch business always made Colt tense. His hands were wrapped around his coffee cup so tightly she feared he'd break the ceramic.

"You hungry? The caramel rolls look delicious."

"Nah. I ate earlier." Colt smirked at her over his cup.

Cocky man. She smirked back when she remembered what he'd had for breakfast.

It was time to return the favor. She set down her mug. "I hope you don't mind if I indulge. I love caramel. So thick, and sweet and sticky." She peeled back the foil and dipped her finger in the center of the gooey mass. She sucked her finger provocatively. "Wanna taste? Mmm-mmm."

"Indy—"

"Colt." India leaned forward and let her sticky lips track the line of his jaw. "Take your boxers off." She breathed heavily in his ear. "Don't ask why, just do it."

His mug hit the counter and a second later his boxers hit the floor.

"Good boy. Grip the counter and spread your legs. Now watch me."

Colt managed to choke out, "Watch you do what?"

"Show you my favorite way to eat caramel." India recoated her fingers with the sugary goodness, scooping a dollop into her palm. Keeping her eyes on his, her hand circled his cock. "Might get a little messy."

"I live to get messy."

With the hand that wasn't stroking his brown-sugar coated shaft, she scraped the gooey topping off three caramel rolls and smeared it on Colt's chest. She took special care to paint both his nipples. Thoroughly.

Then she bent her head and tasted. Mmm. Sweet sugar and salty Colt. The perfect combination. She enclosed her mouth around his left nipple and sucked. And sucked. Worrying the pebbled tip with her teeth. Stopping to rub her cheek across his pecs. Each brush of her mouth and lips made those tight muscles dance.

Colt didn't utter a sound until she bestowed the same

treatment to the other side.

India followed the sweet trail down the center of his spectacular body. She drew small circles around his belly button, dipping her tongue into his navel. Several times. She enjoyed the way his six-pack rippled with each wet swipe. Then she dropped to her knees.

He growled. "Sweet Mother of God."

As she received her first up-close-and-personal look at his cock, she couldn't believe how...big it was. Yeah, she'd felt it inside her, but Colt had pretty much kept her hands off his junk. Mr. Chivalrous hadn't allowed her to put a condom on him at all last night. Or in the shower this morning. He'd slipped one on and hoisted her against the tiled wall as she'd been trying to gather her wits after her second water-pik-induced orgasm.

India looked up at him. "Packin' some serious heat there, cowboy."

He blushed. Colt McKay actually blushed. "I-I—"

"I'm not complaining." Keeping her eyes on his, she licked all the caramel from the head. "I'm not complaining at all."

"Goddamn that feels good."

"Why don't we quit talking so I can get to the really good part. The licking—" she flattened her tongue and licked from the root to the crown, "—more licking—" she lapped at the purple head, flicking her tongue over the pre-come seeping out the tip, "—and my favorite, sucking." India bent her head and swallowed as much of his cock as she could.

A strangled groan emerged and he swayed.

She sucked off the brown sugar sweetness until all she could taste was the muskiness of Colt. "You didn't tease me the first time you used your mouth on me, so I'm returning the favor."

"Christ," he muttered, "I'm so lasting about four more seconds."

Her fingers loosely wrapped around the base of his shaft and she stroked her hand up to meet her mouth going down all that delicious hard male heat. India curled her left hand around his right hip, stroking her thumb on the delicate skin by his hipbone as her head bobbed.

All at once, his balls tightened and she knew he was close. Especially when Colt started bumping his hips into her face.

She jacked his cock faster and focused her attention on the sweet spot beneath the cockhead.

"Yes." His cock twitched against the roof of her mouth. "That's it. Ah hell, Indy."

India sucked him as deep as she could, suctioning as hot bursts of semen hit the back of her tongue. She swallowed the bitter/sweet taste, losing herself in the satisfaction of pleasing her lover.

After she let him slip from her mouth, she kissed the tops of his shaking thighs and rubbed her face against his semi-soft cock, nestled in the dark hair covering his groin. Marking him with her scent as clearly as he'd marked her with his.

She rolled to her feet. Before India even met his gaze, Colt picked her up and set her on the kitchen table. "What are you doing?"

"I'm wantin' a little caramelly goodness of my own." He pushed her flat, keeping his hand in the center of her chest. "Don't move." Then his other hand was smearing caramel between her thighs.

"Colt—"

He lapped at the caramel as delicately as a cat. The pointed tip of his tongue traced the outline of her weeping sex, from the piercing above her clit, down through her cleft to the slit of her pussy, to the rosette of her ass. He swirled and licked and probed with that nimble tongue until her whole body vibrated. Colt drove her to the brink of orgasm, dangled her at the edge and then yanked her back at the last second.

"Are you going to let me—"

"Not yet."

He took great pains to erase all remnants of the caramel with his Hoover-like mouth. He inserted one finger in her pussy as he lightly tongued her clit. Then he inserted a second finger as he slurped at the sweet stickiness from the folds.

"How long—"

"Until I say." He began to fuck her with his clever fingers while his tongue flicked. "I like sweet caramel." He blew a cool stream of breath over her hot tissues. "But I prefer your sweet juices." Colt latched onto her clit and sucked without pause. His fingers curled inside her, gently rubbing at a spot beneath her pubic bone. The tension coiled tighter and when she exploded with a gasp resembling a scream, he chuckled against her wet flesh.

Every throb, every pulse, every muscle twitch synchronized into a whole body orgasm. Just as India caught her balance, Colt knocked her off balance again. She was flipped over face-first on the table.

Colt yanked her hips back until the lower half of her body hung off the table. Then his hot breath teased the skin behind her ear. "You have no fuckin' idea how many times I've whacked off to this fantasy."

"Your dick is hard again?"

"Yes. Fuck, woman, you'd tempt a eunuch." He positioned his cock and plunged in.

"Oh God you're good at that, McKay."

"Glad to know you think I'm good at something." Again, he stretched his torso across her upper back so he could whisper in her ear. "One of these times I take you from behind? I'm gonna be fuckin' your ass, not your pussy. You'd like that, wouldn't you? Maybe if I put a vibrator up this pretty snatch? So I'm fuckin' you in both places?"

She didn't respond.

"Answer me."

"Yes! Damn you, yes!"

"No shame in likin' it raunchy, sugar, now hold on."

He drove into her again and again. Slam. Retreat. Slam. Retreat. Slam. Retreat.

The shirt stuck to her back. She wished it was just Colt's bare skin sticking against hers.

"Only been an hour but I forgot how good this feels."

Something niggled in the back of her head. Something else they'd forgotten.

"Close. Here it comes."

It hit her. A condom.

"Colt, stop, we forgot a condom—"

"I can't stop." He pulled out. A groan escaped and she felt the heat of his ejaculate spraying her butt cheeks.

India looked over her shoulder at him. His hand still pumped his cock, but his gaze was focused entirely on her ass.

"I love these tattoos. But I gotta admit, I love seein' my come splattered all over them." He hugged her from behind. "Jesus that was hot."

"Mmm-hmm. And sticky."

"Shower. Now."

"And then?"

"You have an idea of what you wanna do today?"

"It has to do with having something hot, and hard and fast between my legs."

Colt nipped her earlobe and soothed the sting with a swipe of his tongue. "I'm likin' this idea so far."

"Cool. I brought extra protection."

"For?"

"I'm taking you for a ride, cowboy. On my motorcycle."

Later that afternoon, India lifted her head from Colt's chest. They were naked in his bed, after spending most of the day there.

She'd convinced Colt to take a ride on her bike. When they'd returned to his house, he'd ridden her. She was still a bit sweaty and a lot tired.

Colt's fingertips idly traced her spine. "You have this cute little wrinkle by your nose that tips me off the wheels are spinning in your head."

"Ah. I just wondered...what now? Are we still dating?"

"I believe we've moved beyond the dating stage to the 'seeing' each other stage." Colt tucked a strand of hair behind her ear. "Do we really need to label this?"

"Yes."

"Why?"

Because it scares me. "Because I don't know what we're supposed to do. Do we call each other and make plans? Is it a given we'll see each other every day? Do we take turns spending the night at each other's houses? Are we still going out and doing couple things? Or are we staying in and having sex nonstop?"

"I like that last option."

"Be serious. I've had friendships. I've had sexual relationships. But I've never had one that's been both."

"Me neither."

"Which leads me straight back to the original question:

what now?"

Colt absentmindedly stroked her cheek. "It took us time to become friends, Indy. It took us a lot longer to start dating. I imagine it'll take adjustments to bein' lovers. If I had my way, we'd speed up that adjustment period together every minute we weren't workin', but that ain't realistic. Let's just take it week by week."

"If we were together like that all the time, we might as well move in together or get married."

They both froze.

India backtracked. "You know I didn't mean it like that."

"More's the pity."

Her head screamed, *retreat!* "Um. Wow. Look at the time. I have to go."

Colt sat up and reached for the box of condoms on the nightstand. "Then let me have you once more, because I can't get enough of you."

She allowed him to kiss her but then she snatched the condom out of his fingers. "I am so all over bouncing on your cowboy pole...just as soon as we have a plan of attack for the next stage of our relationship."

"You're serious."

"Deadly."

"Fine. Monday night, we'll go to a movie." He grabbed the condom back and ripped the package open. "Tuesday night, we have a meeting, but afterward, let's go to your place. You can show me your sex toy collection and I'll prove why it's so much better to have a man fucking you than plastic." Colt rolled the condom on. "Wednesday night, ladies' choice. On Thursday nights, I work out with Cam, so it'll be an off night for us. Friday night, we can hit the meeting and then come out here, where I will fuck you nine ways 'til Sunday, which I'm hopin' will spur you into staying with me until Sunday night." He stretched his legs out and brought her across his lap. "Is that a good enough plan of attack for you?"

India wreathed her arms around his neck. "You didn't just come up with that on the fly, did you?"

"Nope."

"But...how did you know?"

"Because you're not as much of a free spirit as you pretend

to be. You have an orderly, logical streak, planning ahead is important to you."

"Thank you."

"Now that the plan of attack is planned, can I get to the attacking you part?"

"Absolutely."

Chapter Fifteen

Lovers Week One

"I never thought that meeting would get over," Colt said Tuesday night.

"It might've gone faster if you would've tried the trust game," India pointed out.

"That game don't prove nothin' about trust." Colt nuzzled the back of her head. "Jesus, I want you so fuckin' bad, Indy."

"Can you at least wait until we get into my apartment?" The instant the lock clicked, he shoved them both through the door and slammed it shut.

Colt tried to cushion the blow when India's back hit the wall. Luckily she didn't smack her head. Unluckily, their teeth clacked together, piercing her bottom lip.

"Ouch."

"Sorry." He gently sucked at the raised bump while strumming the pads of his thumbs down the side of her neck. Seductively. Delicately. "Better?"

"Mmm."

"Bed. Now."

India took his hand and led him into her bedroom, clicking on the lamp in the corner.

When they stopped by the side of the bed, Colt pinned her wrists behind her back. His mouth brushed her ear. "Tonight you're mine. You'll do as I say. Understand?"

"Yes." Good God it turned her on when his dominant side came out to play.

"Get your favorite vibrator and half a dozen of those silk scarves you love so much. Then strip and get in the middle of the bed."

"What are you going to be doing?"

"You'll see."

India rummaged in her drawer. How ironic that the vibrator was beneath the scarves. She draped the silken strips across the end of the bed, set the vibrator, a new tube of K-Y and a few condoms next to them and removed her clothes.

When she glanced at Colt as she spread out on the sheets, he was completely, gloriously nude.

Oh yeah.

Then he reached for a scarf and leveled her with the molten look that spelled pure trouble. "Hands above your head." He tied her left wrist to the metal headboard and repeated the process on the right. "Can I trust you to keep your legs in place?"

"No. You'd better tie them."

Colt growled.

He chose the narrowest scarf and carefully threaded it though the nipple rings. He tugged lightly and the sensation zinged from her nipples straight to her core. "Oh. Wow. Do it again."

He pulled a little harder. "Interesting that Miz India likes a bite of pain with her pleasure."

"Colt, I don't know about this."

"I won't hurt you. But I am gonna drive you more than a little crazy." He hung above her body, his knees bracketing her hips, his hands by her head.

"Why didn't you blindfold me?"

"Because I want you watchin' everything I'm doin' to you." Colt kissed her. Hot. Wet. Slow. He sat back on his haunches between her straddled thighs.

India stared at his erection and the slick spot the tip left above his navel. "Is that bad boy for me?"

He ripped open a condom and rolled it on. "How about if we get your first one outta the way?" he said, reaching for the vibrator.

A loud *bzzzz* reverberated as he cranked the vibrator on high. He placed the tip over the top of the piercing and left it there, keeping constant sensation on her clit.

"Oh God, I might set the new speed record."

"I could almost come from just lookin' at you all tied up and listening to you make those sexy-ass noises. Let go, there's plenty more."

Sure enough, the continuous contact sent her into a fast orgasm. A quick throbbing that both eased her and left her hanging on the edge, wanting more.

She'd barely caught her breath when Colt placed his mouth on the curve of her throat and sucked. He pulled the scarf back and forth between the rings so the silk constantly slid across her hardened nipples.

Between his marauding mouth and the sensual slide of the material, chills broke out from her neck to her knees.

Colt kept up the suckling kisses and erotic silken glide of the scarf, changing the pace at odd intervals by tugging gently on the silk, sending a spark of pain that immediately morphed into pleasure.

She gasped.

He chuckled and kept doing it. Again and again.

When India couldn't take any more, and felt the sticky warmth pooling between her thighs, she whispered, "Please."

"Please what?"

"Please make me come again."

His cheek rubbed against hers; his breath tickled her ear. "You'll come my way. It won't be on my cock. Not yet."

"I don't care. I just need—"

Colt took her mouth in a tongue-tangling kiss before that clever mouth moved down the center of her body. He scooted back on his belly until his face was on level with her mound.

She looked at his dark hair as he flicked his tongue across the piercing. Her arms jerked in her bonds and her legs twitched with every fleeting lick. She noticed he'd twisted the ends of the scarf around the palm of his left hand. Her heart thumped when he turned the vibrator on.

"Colt—"

"Loosen up, sugar." He swirled the end of the vibrator around her opening in the same manner as his tongue circled her clit. Three things happened simultaneously: he slid the vibrator into her pussy, he sucked on her clit and he tugged on the scarf.

India screamed.

Never had all her erogenous zones been targeted simultaneously. Her body was electrified, merely a conduit for sexual pleasure.

And Colt overwhelmed her with it. He fucked her with the vibrator, pressing the phallus against her pubic bone inside as he suckled her clit, then he'd slowly drag it out again.

The intense stimulation had her grinding her sex into Colt's face. He emitted a growling noise and continued driving her to the brink with his lips and tongue. She thrashed as much as the bonds would allow, the fabric burned her wrists and ankles, the sheets abraded her spine, but she didn't care.

Especially not when her orgasm broke free, reverberating in one long wave, as if every neuron in her brain sent a message to her body to tingle, explode and throb in unison.

She was so bowled over she couldn't scream. She couldn't breathe. Her eyes rolled back in her head. She finally knew what the French meant when they called an orgasm a little death—she'd briefly experienced heaven.

When the rhythmic pulses in her clit slowed, the vibrator disappeared.

"Look at me."

India opened her eyes to see Colt's cheeks were flushed, his lips glistened with her juices and his eyes were heavy-lidded with desire.

He ripped the scarves from her ankles, hiked her hips up, pressing the backs of her thighs to his chest. Aligning his cock to her pussy, he plunged in, his fingers tightened on her ass as he fucked her with abandon. "Jesus, you're wet."

"You have that effect on me."

"Yeah? Your effect on me is I'm ready to blow."

And he did, almost immediately. He was mesmerizing lost in his climax. She watched him, humbled by all this man freely gave to her—in bed and out.

He untied her arms and legs and carefully unthreaded the scarf from the nipple rings. Rather than bringing her into his arms, Colt laid his head on her chest.

India ran her fingers through his damp hair. "You okay?"

"Never been better."

She smiled. "Will you stay over?"

"I'd like to, but I can't because I have to be up early."

No bullshit excuses, just the truth.

"Too bad. I was gonna bake caramel rolls for breakfast."

He snorted. "You don't cook."

"Does that bother you?"

"Why should it?"

"I don't know. I'm not good at the sorts of things women around here are good at."

"Such as?"

"Ranch stuff." *Wife stuff.*

Stop that, India.

"Don't matter. You're good at all sorts of other things."

"But I wanna learn..."

"What?"

"The normal stuff," she blurted. "Will you teach me?"

"Be my pleasure." Colt kissed the tip of her breast and then her mouth and hopped up.

India watched him get dressed.

He sat on the edge of the bed beside her. "I'll see you tomorrow. Ladies' choice, remember?"

"I've already decided what we're gonna do."

"Yeah? What's that?"

"Two-step."

"I'm hopin' that's a sex position we haven't tried."

"No. This is the normal stuff I'm talking about. I want you to teach me how to cowboy dance. In private, where no one can see my two left feet and my inability to keep time."

Colt's eyes searched hers. "Why do you wanna learn to dance?"

"Don't you love to dance?"

"Well, yeah, but that don't mean I expect you to take it up just to please me."

"And if I want to please you, Colt? What then?"

"Indy—"

"Forget it. Stupid idea." She peered at her fingers gripping the edge of the sheet, feeling the sting of embarrassment. She never should have suggested—

He tipped her chin up. "If you really wanna learn, I'd be honored to teach you." His thumb swept over her bottom lip. "You constantly surprise me, India Ellison. Goddamn. You have

no idea how much I—" He kissed her with such emotion she felt
a lump rising in her throat.

"Sleep," he said gruffly and left her staring after him.

Three days later, Colt laid on his back staring at the wispy
fabric draped above India's bed. While relaxed from a round of
fast and fun sex, and content to just be around India, naked or
not, he was tired of looking at the back of his eyelids. He
sighed.

"Stop sighing like a teenage girl."

"Are you done yet?"

"No."

"Can I move now?"

"No."

"I just wanna peek at what you're doin'."

"No."

"Please?"

"Dammit, Colt, sit still."

"I hope you're drawin' me with a really big dick."

India peeked over the edge of the sketchpad at him. "You
don't need me to embellish that appendage, McKay."

Colt grinned. "Now who's the sweet talker?"

"Besides, this isn't a nude. You just happen to be nude as
I'm sketching. Now, stop interrupting my artistic flow."

"Fine." About thirty seconds later, he said, "Who's gonna
see this picture anyway? Because I don't want it hanging in
your tattoo shop."

"Don't worry. I'll keep it away from the slavering masses of
women who trail after you like lovesick puppies."

"Only woman I want slavering and trailing after me, all
lovesick, is you, sugar."

No response. *Scritch scratch. Scritch scratch. Scritch scratch.*

"This secretiveness ain't givin' me warm fuzzies about what
you're drawin'."

"I'm not exactly the warm fuzzy type, Colt. Neither are you."

"I know, which is another reason you need to show me
because I wanna make sure you're not drawin' devil horns on
me. I don't know why you're doin' this."

She looked at him again, a bit curiously. "I'll tell you if you promise not to freak out."

"No dice. I will freak out if the reason is embarrassing or lame."

"Don't you trust me?"

He didn't answer.

India closed her eyes and sagged back into the pillows, clutching the sketchpad to her chest. A minute or so passed.

"Indy?"

"The real reason is...you're beautiful. Men aren't supposed to be, but you are." Her eyes opened and she stared at him with an intensity that fired his blood. "Your face, your body. God. Every single inch of you is...perfection. Sometimes the light hits you just so and it takes my breath away. I can't believe you're..."

"What?"

"Here. With me."

Talk about taking his breath away. Colt rolled to his knees. "There's no place I'd rather be."

"Do you ever wonder...if we've wasted time not being together like this, before this?"

"No. We can't go back. Any time I spent with you, as your friend wasn't wasted time. Our friendship is what got us to this point. And it's what'll get us to the next point."

"The next point? What's that?"

Marriage. Babies. Happily ever after. One week into dating and India wasn't ready to hear that yet, so he kept it light. "Where you show up naked at my house ready to do my bidding."

"Maybe you'll rethink that statement when you see what I've drawn." India watched him as he crawled toward her. With each inch he edged closer, she hugged the sketchbook tighter.

"Lemme look at the picture, Picasso."

"No way."

"I want to see how you see me."

"No."

"Please? With caramel on top?"

She shook her head. "Back off."

"Huh-uh. Don't make me tickle you to get what I want."

"You wouldn't dare!"

157

"Don't dare me. I rock at double-dog and triple-dog dares and don't get me started on truth or dare. Plus, I know all your ticklish spots. Hand it over."

"Come and get it, McKay." She attempted to roll off the bed.

His hand circled her ankle and he tugged her back on the mattress.

India shrieked and tried to wrench free, which only increased his determination.

Colt attacked her feet. She yelped and swatted at him with the sketchbook. He snatched it from her with one hand. "Hah!"

"Hey! Gimme that back, it's mine."

"In a sec. I just wanna look." He studied it before his eyes met hers. He flipped the page back to her, jabbing his finger at the twin images. "You really see me this way? With turquoise stars and orange and purple flames tattooed around my pierced nipples?"

She giggled. "Gotcha. You really thought I was drawing nudie pics of you, huh?"

"You little tease." He threw the notebook over the side of the bed and tickled her until she screamed.

The touches turned from playful to passionate. And then he was inside her, face-to-face, skin-to-skin, heart-to-heart. The more time he spent with her, the more amazed he was by her. By everything they were when they were together.

India curled her fingers around his neck. "I wasn't kidding, earlier. You are so beautiful, Colt McKay. Beautiful inside and out."

"Same goes, India. Same goes." He kissed her and the world fell away.

Chapter Sixteen

Lovers Week Two

Colt hated cleaning the garage. So, when a sultry, "Hey, cowboy," drifted through the open garage door, he thought he might've been hearing things.

"India?" Colt's gloved fingers tightened around the shovel handle.

"In the flesh, baby." Pause. "Literally."

"What're you doin' here? It's the middle of the day."

"The tattoo biz is dead and my sister is running the store. So I thought to myself, I wonder what my big, sexy cowboy is doing." Her footsteps echoed as loud as the sudden thumping of his heart. "Since I'm not busy, I thought I'd come out and see if I can help you. I even have my cowgirl boots on."

Colt turned around so fast he almost got whiplash.

Holy hell. Cowgirl boots were the *only* thing India had on.

The shovel in his hand clanked to the concrete floor.

"Sadly, I don't own any other western wear."

"I'm not complaining." Colt's gaze slowly tracked her sexy body, from the pointed tips of her red nipples to the pointed toes of her red boots. His cock hardened. His mouth watered. "But I'm hopin' you didn't ride your motorcycle out here in that get-up."

"And if I did?"

"Cam'll have to arrest me."

"Why?"

"For killin' every man who laid eyes on you undressed like that."

Satisfaction glinted in her eyes. "A little proprietary, aren't you?"

"If that means you're mine, only mine, then hell yes."

"I am yours, Colt."

His eyes ate her up with a hunger that bordered on obsessive. "Prove it."

"How?"

Without breaking eye contact, he grabbed a horse blanket from the pile on the workbench. He tossed it on the concrete in front of him. Then he began to unbuckle his belt. "You'd better be over here, on your knees, ready to suck my cock by the time this zipper is down."

She hit the ground like she was sliding bases.

"That's good." Colt peeled his jeans down his thighs and his blood-engorged cock slapped his belly. "Like what you see?"

"Mmm-hmm." India licked her lips.

He circled the tip of his cock around her mouth. "Open. Take it all."

Her lips parted and she swallowed in a drawn out tease.

"The rest of this ain't gonna be your pace, it's gonna be mine. Fast and hard, Indy. That's how I'm gonna fuck your sweet, perfect mouth."

Her moan vibrated up his shaft.

Colt threaded his fingers through her hair for a decent grip. He pulled out and eased back in. Three, four, five slow thrusts. Once his shaft was coated with her saliva, he increased the pace.

She'd closed her eyes and kept her neck arched at an angle where she could take him deep.

It was a fucking turn on to watch her. How sexy it was as his cock disappeared between her red lips. How her fingertips dug into his thighs with enough force to leave half-moon shaped marks. How the wetness from her mouth freely ran down her chin and neck. He loved the raw power she had over him in her submission. The occasional scrape of her teeth. The teasing flicker of her tongue.

It was too much. Too good. Despite the cool temperature of the day and the garage, sweat beaded on his forehead and his whole body burned hot.

When his balls contracted, he shortened his strokes and increased the grasp on her head.

"I'm there. Right...now. Oh hell, suck. Suck hard. Suck it all. Ah. Jesus. Your mouth is so wet and tight...fuck!"

India held him upright as he came. And came. And when his cock was empty, she licked his softening shaft and nuzzled his balls, bringing him down from the sex high with tenderness.

He looked down at her and touched her cheek. "That was awesome. And I love your obedience. Love it so much, in fact, that I'm gonna return the favor."

She lifted both pierced brows. "Meaning I get to demand your obedience?"

"No. Meanin' I'm gonna grab some ropes and see how long you can keep it up."

Thursday night, the loud click of India's bedroom door opening echoed in her room. The mattress dipped. "India? You awake?"

"I am now."

"You probably weren't even sleepin', Little Miz Troublemaker," Colt drawled. "I can't believe you left a message on my cell phone callin' me a dickhead."

She smiled in the darkness. "I knew that'd get you over here in a hurry after your workout with Cam."

"You pissed off about something?"

"Just that I didn't see you today."

"That's it?"

"And I was lonely."

He laughed softly. "So you insulted me to get me to come over?"

"Yeah. Might be masochistic, but I do love fighting with you. I love the making up part."

"Me too." Colt whipped the covers back. "Especially when you're already nekkid."

"All for you."

"It's not supposed to be for me tonight, remember?"

"But I missed you. Are you mad?"

"I'm still debating." His teeth latched onto her right nipple, his left hand circled her wrists and pressed them above her head.

161

She arched, anxious to lose herself in the passion that always flared between them. His avid mouth was on her breast, sucking at the hoop piercing her nipple.

But he stopped.

"What?"

"Have you been touchin' yourself while you've been waitin' for me to get here?"

Crap. How had he known?

"Will I find your sweet cream if I slide my hand between your thighs?"

Distract him. She moaned and arched harder.

"Answer me."

"Yes."

"Part your legs."

His rough palm was cold as it slid down her belly, over her mound. He slipped one long finger inside her pussy.

Eyes closed, she murmured, "That feels good."

"How good?" Colt added another finger, pumping both deep, adding that delicious twist at the end she loved. "As good as when you got yourself off?"

"Better. It's always better with you."

"Then you should've waited." He removed his hand.

India froze.

"You're a bad girl, Indy. Makin' me worry for nothin'. And while I was worryin' you were gonna rip me a new one for some reason like you're prone to do, you were here, diddling yourself, bold as you please." His breath was hot in her ear. "Bad girls get punished. Roll over and take your licks."

"But—"

"Don't make me tell you twice." Colt released her wrists.

While she rolled onto her stomach, she heard him taking off his clothes. Heard him open a nightstand drawer. Heard the crackle of plastic as he ripped open a condom. Blood whooshed in her ears as her excitement rose.

"Get on all fours." The bed dipped.

"What are you gonna do?"

His hard, hot upper body covered her back and his chin came over her shoulder. "Bad girls don't get to ask questions. Do I need to gag you?"

"No."

"Then be still." Colt trailed love bites from shoulder to shoulder. Then his tongue slowly followed the line of her spine from her nape to her tailbone. And back up. And back down.

Goose bumps spread across her skin. She moaned at the eroticism in his teasing touch, the wetness of his tongue, the coolness of his breath, the rasp of his beard, the silky swish of his hair, the tiny bite of anger guiding his movements.

And his scent drove her crazy. India knew he hadn't showered after leaving the gym. The dark, male musk of his sweat coated his skin and she breathed it in, hoping that scent would linger on her and the sheets after he left.

Colt lightly sank his teeth into the tattoo on her right butt cheek. He flicked his tongue around the design. Then he let his tongue lead the way to the left butt cheek, and he briefly lapped at the crack of her ass. Another bite. More licking.

Her whole body shook. "Oh God, Colt. I'm—"

His lips were on her ear. "You took your licks like a good girl."

"I thought by 'licks' you were going to spank me."

"Would you like that?"

Yes. But India bit her lip instead of confessing.

A beat passed, then *whack whack* on each of her butt cheeks. "Answer me."

"Yes, okay? I've always wondered what it'd be like, not that I've ever let a man spank me because of some of that crap from my past, but I trust you not to take it too far."

"Good answer, sugar. Another time we'll explore that secret kink. With a paddle. Maybe a ridin' crop. Definitely my hand."

India shuddered.

"It is punishment not to lick you where you most want my tongue, bad girl." He nuzzled the back of her head. "I should fuck you and not let you come, since you already got off tonight without me, but makin' you come gets me off. Lower your chest to the mattress and leave your ass in the air."

She set the side of her face on the bed and stretched her arms above her head.

"Brace yourself." Colt kneed her stance wider, tilted her hips and plunged in. His withdrawal was fast. His returning stroke was fast. As fast and hard as he liked.

His selfishness shouldn't be a turn-on, but it was. Normally he was an incredibly generous lover. India closed her eyes and let his need wash over her.

Slam. Slam. Slam. Slam. Slam. The slap of his skin against hers as she listened to his choppy breathing had her clenching around his cock. That familiar pulsing sensation rippled through her deepest tissues, sending her straight over the edge into a short orgasm.

Colt's hips pistoned faster. His fingers squeezed her ass and he began to come. "Fuck. Fuck."

India craved that burst of male heat inside her, not trapped in a condom. She wanted to stand up and see his seed trickling out of her sated and swollen sex.

"God, woman, the things you do to me."

After he pulled out, India collapsed on the bed. Vaguely she heard the toilet flush. The rustle of his clothes. Then his yummy scent surrounded her.

"Mmm. Can you stay and punish me some more since I tricked you?"

"No." He kissed the tattoo between her shoulder blades and tucked the covers under her chin.

"Next time, if you're missin' me just ask me to come over, okay? Because if it happens again, I *will* spank your ass good and red for pickin' a fight. Sweet dreams."

Chapter Seventeen

Lovers Week Three

"Oh yeah, baby, right there."

"Colt, will you shut up?" India hissed.

"Can't. It feels too goddamn good."

"People are staring at us."

"Let 'em. Harder." He arched his neck. "Like that. Goddamn you've got magic fingers, Indy."

"That's it. I'm done."

"No! Please. Don't stop."

India wrapped her hands around the shopping cart handle and pushed to the frozen food section.

Within thirty seconds Colt came up behind her, curling his hands and his body over hers. "What's wrong?"

"Don't ever ask me to rub your neck in the grocery store again."

"Why? It wasn't like you had your hand on my dick."

"I might as well have with the 'oh baby' porn noises you were grunting."

He nipped her earlobe and licked the sting, brushing his lips to the center of her ear. "And to think I didn't utter a sound last night when you gave me a handjob at the movies."

"Colt—"

"It was hot as hell, havin' your buttery fingers strokin' my cock. I had to clench my ass cheeks together when your thumb rubbed the sweet spot below the head. I was so fuckin' hard, India. You did that to me. You *do* that to me."

And she thought he'd lost his sweet-talkin' ability. The man could make her wet and weak-kneed with just words.

He blew in her ear. "I think I behaved admirably by not shoutin' out your name when I came all over your hand. I think I oughta be rewarded."

"You were rewarded."

"Hmm. Maybe I oughta reward you."

"I'm listening."

"You fulfilled one of my fantasies, so turnabout is fair play. Tell me, sugar, what's one of your unfulfilled fantasies?"

"The first one that pops to mind?"

"Uh-huh."

"I'm with a man, who has a really big—"

"Indy," he warned.

"Kitchen. A man who knows the difference between simmer and burn, a man who can whip and stir, steam and cream. A man who keeps his promises of heating things up."

"I get it. I'll teach you to cook. But you so aren't getting any cock...tail shrimp tonight, if you waste all that dirty talk in the grocery store."

"Oh, don't you worry. There's plenty more where that came from."

"That's what I'm countin' on."

Three days later, India was cleaning up the kitchen at Colt's house, when he shouted from the living room, "Indy, you okay?"

"Almost done. You need anything?"

"I'd take a soda if you're offerin'."

India wrapped tinfoil around the leftover pieces of her first chicken dinner and shoved the plate on the shelf in the refrigerator. As she reached for a Diet Pepsi, she accidentally knocked over the can of whipped cream from the back.

Heh heh.

The laugh track from the TV echoed. She vigorously shook the can and kept it behind her back, hiding it behind his recliner after she entered the living room.

Colt glanced up and bestowed the wicked grin that was hers alone. Cheeky man.

India leaned over and set the soda on the end table. As she

straightened up, he snagged the ends of the dishtowel draped around her neck and hauled her on his lap.

He swallowed her tiny shriek with a kiss heavy on seduction. She found herself plastered to him as he lowered the recliner completely horizontal.

"Mmm," he murmured against her throat, "much better."

"What are you doing?"

"Don't you want to mess around?" He brushed warm kisses across her lips. "Because I could kiss you for hours. Here," he briefly let their lips connect, then nibbled a path to her ear, "and other places."

"What other places?"

"Lemme think. Right here." He opened his mouth where her neck curved into her shoulder and sucked until she whimpered. "And here." That agile tongue circled the hollow of her throat and rained wet kisses down to the top button of her shirt.

"Anywhere else?"

"Oh yeah." His deft fingers began to unbutton her blouse. He didn't say a word until the material flapped open to reveal she wasn't wearing a bra. He groaned and filled his hands with her breasts. Squeezing, rasping his thumbs over the nipples until they contracted into tight, aching points beneath the hoops.

Colt watched her face as he touched her. Gauging her reaction to better torture her next time. She let him think he was in charge, but she couldn't stop a smirk from forming.

"Why the devious smile, India Blue?"

"No reason. I thought you were gonna show me all the places you'd like to kiss me and your mouth is nowhere near where I want it to be."

"You're so impatient."

She slid his palms down her ribcage to her hips and shimmied closer, letting her bare breasts sway in front of his lips. She eased back when his tongue flicked out to swipe at a hardened nipple. "Or maybe you need an incentive."

Without waiting for his response, India leaned over and grabbed the can. She sat up and squirted a dollop of whipped cream on her left nipple.

Colt's eyes nearly popped out of his head.

"Put your mouth on me, Colt. Lick me, suck me. Show me

how you wanted to kiss me."

"Jesus Christ."

The mechanism in the recliner went *sproing* as it snapped back into a chair.

Then he was upright with his lips pursed around her nipple, sucking off the sweet white stuff like a vacuum. Opening his mouth wider and wider until he seemed to suck her whole breast inside.

The cold spot from the whipped cream evaporated in his heated, hungry mouth. She arched into him, grinding into his cock, her blood pumping in cadence with him drawing her nipple in and out.

He snatched the can, tipped it upside down and sprayed a thick mound on her right nipple. This time he licked a tiny swath until just the pink tip poked out.

Slowly. Round and round. A measured lick here and there. His tongue started at the bottom swell of her breast, flattened around the sides, tapered to a fine point over her breastbone. As the circle grew smaller and smaller, he went slower and slower. He zeroed in on the rigid aching nipple, letting his tongue toy with the hoop, while his right thumb lightly feathered the skin above the waistband of her jeans, causing her belly to tremble.

When he'd lapped up every drop, he sank his teeth into her sticky flesh, toeing that fine line between pleasure and pain, knowing just how much pressure she could stand.

White-hot desire lanced through her.

She'd been rocking the seam of her jeans, which was directly in line with her clit, against the hardest part of him. The instant his teeth and tongue and hands and mouth came together, the throbbing between her legs synchronized and ignited an orgasm that left her gasping.

Once the ringing in her ears stopped, India realized the growling noise vibrating against her throat sounded suspiciously like a satisfied male chuckle.

Hey. How'd she get off...track? She'd meant to tease him. Make *him* lose control. So why did she have whipped cream smeared all over her chest and her sex was spasming?

Just lucky.

Time to spread the luck around.

Colt scattered sticky kisses back to her lips and devoured her mouth. He tasted sweet and spicy and darkly male.

She used her teeth on his jawbone. Kissed his dimples. Blew in his ear until he shivered. "Take off your sweats."

He went utterly still. "What?"

Her tongue darted out and flicked his earlobe and he moaned. "I'm going to squirt whipped cream all over your cock, Colt. I'm going to lick and suck it off. Then I'm going to suck you off. You're going to come in my mouth and I'm going to swallow every creamy spurt."

"Jesus."

"Any more questions?"

"Hell no."

India grabbed the can, climbed off the chair and shut off the TV.

In record time, Colt's sweats and boxers sailed to the floor.

The little vixen trailed the fringed end of the dishtowel over his thighs and stomach. His flesh rolled beneath her touch and he recognized the power she had on him, body and soul.

It was surprisingly sexy to give up control.

"Last thing. Keep your hands on the armrest until I say otherwise. If I feel those mitts in my hair or on my face, I'll stop and tie them together with this towel. Understand?" She snapped it once by his head for good measure.

Colt nodded. Damn. Was this domination stuff as much of a turn-on for her when he did it?

"Good." India dropped to her knees and scooted between his legs. She rubbed those soft breasts and pebbled nipples over the coarse hair on the inside of his thighs. "That feels good. Do you like that?"

"Hell yes."

He went rigid as she studied him, as if deciding where to start. The tip of his cock jerked. The thick vein running up the center pulsed; pearly liquid seeped out the purple head.

With an evil grin she put the nozzle at the base of his shaft and squirted a wide line straight up.

"Holy shit! That's cold!"

"Not for long." She bent her head and zigzagged her tongue up the length of his erection.

It took every ounce of control not to grab her head and force her mouth where he wanted it. Not to touch her while she was tormenting him.

She swirled more sweet stuff around the head of his cock. Then she sat back and admired her handiwork. "Mmm. Looks like a big mushroom, don't you think? And isn't it lucky I love mushrooms?" She daintily closed her lips over the rim where the cap met the shaft and sucked.

Colt's hips shot up, a reflex for her to take him all the way in her mouth.

"Huh-uh. Not yet. I've still got half a can of creamy goodness to mess with. You were the one who wanted to mess around, weren't you, Colt?"

He groaned.

She tortured him. Fleeting licks from his balls to the twitching tip. Then she'd suck him hard until the head hit the back of her throat. Bringing him to the edge again and again. Leaving him hanging there by a thread and then starting over. Hot mouth. Cool spray of whipped cream. The wet lap of her tongue.

His thighs clenched. His knuckles were white on the black armrest. He gritted his teeth. Sweat dripped from his temple. He didn't touch her. But he knew his eyes were absolutely wild and probably begging. Finally, he panted, "Enough."

India smiled. "You've been a very good boy. You can touch me now." She curled her hand around the root and began to pump as her wet mouth moved up and down. Clasping her lips tightly as she released him from her mouth, opening her throat as his cock slid back in into that warm cavern. Creating a rhythm that made him pant and squirm.

Colt's hands cupped her face; his thumbs traced the center of her hollowed cheeks. Then his hips thrust higher.

"Faster. Like that. Oh God, India. Don't stop. Oh Jesus. Oh fuck." He gripped her head as he erupted against the roof of her mouth. She sucked and he felt her jaw working as she swallowed and swallowed until he was fully spent.

After his cock quit throbbing and he could think again, he sank back into the recliner.

She stood.

Colt pulled her onto his lap. He aligned her back against the front of his body, hugging her tightly. "Would it be lame if I said thank you?"

"No."

"Thank you. That was..." He sighed. "Words fail me. I didn't invite you over, expecting that, India."

"I know. That's why I had such a fantastic time blowing your expectations all to hell."

"Blowing me to heaven and back is more like it."

She released the catch on the recliner. When they were horizontal, she snuggled into him and whispered, "Aren't these cooking lessons going great? I think I'm a natural."

Chapter Eighteen

Lovers Week Four

It was another crappy, boring day.

Damn rain meant India couldn't ride her bike. No tattoo customers had braved the lousy weather. No Sky Blue customers either. She'd been stuck inside for four lousy days. She was sick of her own company.

You're sick of staying away from Colt.

True.

India kicked the door shut and bobbled the box of lavender soap when she saw him leaning against the doorjamb, looking pretty as you please. Dark hair tousled and damp from the wind and the rain. Stubble coating his jaw. Trouble in his eye.

Crap. She could never resist him when he looked all gorgeous and scowly.

Go on the offensive.

"Colt? What are you doing here?"

He patiently returned her cool stare. "I'm here to ask why I haven't seen you."

She dropped the soap on the counter and pointed to the boxes scattered around the showroom. "I've been busy."

Colt gave her that you're-full-of-shit eyebrow lift.

"And you were out of town."

"I was in Guernsey for two lousy days, India, two days in which I didn't hear from you once."

"Hey, bucko, the phone lines run both ways."

"Is that so?" Colt began to stalk her. "I thought we were beyond this fightin' just so we can make up stuff."

"But it's so fun."

He growled.

"Besides, didn't we talk about not spending every waking minute together?"

"You talked. I listened. And I disagreed."

India's pulse doubled. He'd used that matter-of-fact tone before he'd stripped her, boosted her against the tile in his shower and screwed her until the water ran cold and her vocal cords shorted out from shouting his name in rapture.

Thinking about showering with him and experiencing his hot, naked male stamina is not helping you retain the upper hand, India.

Right. And she *so* had the upper hand when the man had her in full retreat until her spine hit the wall.

"Got nothin' to say?"

"Fine. What do you want?"

"You," he said tersely, slapping his hands on either side of her head. His mouth swooped down on hers in a kiss that wasn't gentle, wasn't meant to soothe, but to chastise. His mouth punished, forgave, and seduced—all at the same time.

It was a kiss that smacked of ownership.

It was a kiss that knocked her for a loop.

It was a kiss that was four long days overdue.

After he'd thoroughly scrambled her brain cells, Colt whispered, "Sweet Jesus, you piss me off sometimes, but I missed you, Indy. Come home with me tonight so I can show you how much."

She ducked under his arm. "I can't."

"Why not?"

Tell him the truth? Or lie?

He didn't give her time to decide. "What? Are you sick of me?"

"No!"

"Then what?" His gaze roamed over her. "Are you sick?"

"Sort of."

"Explain."

She huffed out a nervous stream of air. "Dammit, I got my period after that last time in the shower."

"That's why you've been scarce?"

"Yes."

He looked utterly confused. "Why didn't you just tell me?"

"Because it's not usually a topic for discussion between men and women when they're first dating. Plus, I feel gross and I'm not good company. I thought I'd spare you."

Colt kissed her hard and quick. "I don't care. I want to be with you no matter what your mood or what your hormones do."

"Really?"

"Really. We're way beyond the first dating stage, Indy, and don't pretend what's going on between us is only about sex."

"Oh yeah, Mr. 'I Disagreed'?"

"Don't get me wrong. I love getting nekkid with you." He kissed her. "All." He kissed her again. "The." Another kiss. "Damn." And another. "Time." He grinned. "But I'd be just as happy hangin' with you as bangin' you."

"How poetic, McKay."

"I am tryin' like the devil to get the shine back on my silver tongue." He fingered the gold hoop in her eyebrow. "Come over anyway. You can sit on the couch with a heating pad and a bag of Hershey's Kisses. I'll even watch chick flicks with you."

"How'd you know—"

"That you crave Hershey's Kisses that time of the month? We've been friends for almost three years. I've noticed all your little quirks and your hormonal breakdowns."

"Why didn't you say something?"

"Because I was too much of a gentleman to mention it. Now that I know you prefer my ungentlemanly ways..." He brushed his mouth across the crown of her head. "Sometimes I think I know you better than you know yourself."

He was so damn sweet that she teared up. "Colt—"

"Hey now, none of that. I'd rather you were throwing wrenches at me instead of crying."

She kissed his chin. "I'll be over at seven. But I'm warning you; in my hormonal state, I expect a lot of kisses. And chocolate for dessert."

"Sugar, I'll give you as many kisses as you can handle."

$$*$$

After an amazing week with India, didn't it figure his weekend started out crappy?

Colt's morning had gone to shit after the engine on his four-wheeler blew up. If that wasn't bad enough, he'd gone to check cattle and found two dead cows and one dead calf that'd been gnawed on by coyotes. Then he'd sliced open his forearm on a piece of metal sheeting in the barn when his mother called demanding he show up for Sunday night supper. He spilled gas all over the floor in the garage and the fumes gave him an instant headache.

It was enough to drive a man to drink.

By the time he finished his daily chores and returned to the house well after dark, he needed a beer. Or a shot. Anything grain alcohol based.

Days like this, it flat-out amazed him he'd passed the three-year mark without ingesting a single drop of booze.

India had left a message on his machine and on his cell phone and he ignored both. Pissy, testy, fighting the temptation of addiction; he wasn't fit for company.

He needed a distraction. Driving into town and running on a treadmill at the gym didn't appeal to him. He was too wired to sit on his ass and watch TV or climb into bed and sleep it off. He wanted to hit something—just not hit the bottle.

In the spare room he slipped on a pair of boxing shorts, his sparring gloves and circled the punching bag. Starting slow, he wanted to stretch out this beating and not tire himself out too quickly.

Right jab. Right jab. Left jab. Reverse the sequence.

He hit the bag over and over. Then he moved to the speed bag and pummeled it until he could scarcely hold his arms up. Only then did he take a breather. The workout mats were slick with sweat. Colt's entire body was soaked, even his hair dripped. His eyes stung. The self-inflicted physical punishment usually helped him focus on one thing: not chugging beer until he passed out.

But tonight it didn't work.

So, Colt began his workout again. By the time he'd suffered through the third round, he'd almost reached that level of an exercise high. He wanted to wallow in that feeling of invincibility. Of strength. He spun around to rest his forearms on the weight bench bar and saw India leaning in the doorway, gawking at him.

No hello. No pleasantries. He tried to level his breathing

and demanded, "How long have you been standin' there?"

"Long enough."

Goddamn, she looked good. She wore leggings the color of rich coffee and a floaty sheer pink tunic that hit her mid-thigh. No shoes. No makeup. No extra jewelry. No bra.

"Tell me, do you always beat on that thing so hard?"

"Only when I've had a lousy fuckin' day."

"Been a bad one?"

"You have no idea how bad."

India crossed her arms over her chest. "Try me."

"Look, Indy, I'm in a piss-poor mood, I'm shitty company, and I don't feel like makin' small talk."

"Did I suggest we sit around and shoot the breeze?"

"No. But you oughta know I'm feelin' a little mean, more than a little raw around the edges and I can't promise I wouldn't take it out on you, so it'd be best if you went on home." Colt faced the heavy bag again. "I'll call you tomorrow."

"Oh, I see how this works. You can demand *I* buck up and spend time with you when I'm a physical and emotional train wreck, but when *you're* having the same issues, I'm just supposed to accept a pat on the head and go on my merry way like an obedient girlfriend? That sucks, Colt, and it's not fair."

He ground his teeth together. "I didn't ask you to come over."

"I didn't think I needed a written invitation."

"Jesus, India. Will you just drop it?"

"Fuck that." She stomped behind him. "You demanded complete honesty in this relationship and that includes both of us. Which means you don't get to hide this side of yourself from me."

"I'm hidin' it from you for your own damn good."

"What? Do you turn into a werewolf or something?"

"You're fuckin' hilarious."

"I'll keep cracking jokes until the crack of dawn because I'm not going anywhere, McKay, so you might as well talk to me."

"I already told you; I don't wanna talk."

"So let's fuck."

Colt wheeled around. "You don't want to fuck me either, because I ain't a nice guy right about now."

"I don't care."

"Yeah? Even when I warn you haven't begun to see my aggressive side?"

"So show me. I'm a big girl. Maybe I like it rough."

"You don't know what you're askin'."

"Maybe you don't know what you're denying me. Or yourself."

He snarled. "Don't push me."

India raised her chin. "Even if I do, I know you won't hurt me."

"I'll use you. Hard."

"It's not using me if I'm a willing participant."

"A willing participant? In rough sex? You're sure?" Colt stalked her. "I'll have you any way I want, as many times as I want, until I've had my fill of your hot little body. You understand, once I start, I won't stop. Not even if you beg me."

"But I am begging you to let me be what you need. I don't know what that is unless you show me."

Just like that...Colt lost it. He didn't kiss her; he inhaled her. The second he touched her, his cock inflated. His heart rate kicked up. He slid his hands over the curves of her hips, then hooked his thumbs in the waistband of her leggings and pulled them to her feet. His finger traced the crack of her ass, past that tight pucker to the sticky slit of her pussy.

He ripped his mouth free. "Christ. You're already wet."

"That's what seeing you half-naked, sweaty, beating the shit out of a punching bag does to me."

His answer was a low growl as he yanked her shirt off. Colt dropped his boxing shorts and brought them both to the mat with India on the bottom and his hands beside her head.

Colt surged inside her. Pounding into that hot, pliant flesh. Over and over. Harder and harder. Not kissing her. Not looking at her. Not touching her. Just fucking her.

India's legs circled his lower back as her hands spread across his upper back. Bringing him closer.

Thrust, thrust, then a grinding withdrawal.

So perfect. Her pussy was so smooth and wet and hot.

The mat was slippery with sweat. He was slippery with sweat. Sandwiched between Colt and the mat, India became slippery with sweat and they scooted sideways.

Colt hardly noticed, he was so focused on getting to that

point of no return, each stroke all the way in, then all the way back out.

Thrust, thrust, grind. Thrust, thrust, grind.

She didn't say a word, just raked her nails down his back and arched her hips hard. Colt knew her reactions well enough by now that he instinctively increased the side-to-side movement on every upstroke and downstroke.

That simple change set India off. She gasped, her cunt squeezed his cock like a vise and her nails gouged his ass with enough pressure she probably left bloody half-moon shapes on his skin.

He didn't care. He felt powerful. His balls lifted. He threw back his head, waiting for that pulsing rush to start so he could finish.

"Colt. Wait. No condom."

He finally looked at her. "I know. Because I wanted to do this." He pulled out, sat back on his knees and beat off. The roughness of the glove abrading his cock took him to that point between pleasure and pain. The muscles in his belly, his groin, his anus tightened. He shouted as spurts of his hot seed shot out, dotting her torso, marking her as his.

Spent, he sagged back to catch his breath. But only for a minute.

When he opened his eyes, India was still all stretched out before him. Waiting.

Colt ripped off the gloves with his teeth, scooted her down, tucking his knees in her armpits. He traced the outline of her full, beautiful lips with his thumb. "Now you're gonna lick me clean. Open wide." He leaned forward on his hands and fed his semi-hard cock into her mouth.

India moaned around the root of his shaft.

"See how good you taste on me?" He pumped in and out of that wetness and suctioning heat until he was almost completely hard again. Then he pulled out. "Now suck my balls. Get them wet."

Her eyes were closed as she licked each one separately and blew across the dampness. Then she sucked both into her mouth and gently rolled them over her tongue.

Colt almost came when she released his nuts and her tongue ventured back to tickle the strip of skin in front of his anus.

"Enough." He sat up and kissed her thoroughly before dragging her to her feet. "Bedroom. And there won't be any talkin' unless I say so, got it?"

She nodded.

In his room, Colt stripped back the covers. "Get in the middle of the bed on your hands and knees." He lit a candle on the dresser and grabbed the lube.

He moved into the space between her calves and ran his hands up the outside of her legs to her hips. He bent his head and tongued the tattoo on her right butt cheek.

India sucked in a quick breath.

Then he turned his head and tongued the tattoo on her left butt cheek.

Another hissing intake of air.

Colt flattened his tongue and dragged it up and down her spine, over the infinity symbol—two long, twisted black lines—a tattoo that started above her butt and ended at the gigantic butterfly spread between her shoulder blades. No traditional tramp stamp for his India. Her skin was a canvas; every marking on her was a work of art.

"You're so beautiful. So sexy. I could lap you up." Colt scooted beneath her. He curled his hands around her ass and pulled her pussy to his mouth, so she was sitting on his face. He licked her folds and suckled her pussy lips and fucked her entrance with his tongue. When she was whimpering and grinding her hips, he latched onto her clit and sucked until she screamed. And while India was still coming down from her orgasm, Colt slid out and licked her again. From her piercing to the pucker of her ass.

He painted that sweet rosette with his saliva. When she mewled cries and thrust her hips back, he spread her ass cheeks with his hands and thrust his tongue into that tight hole. Over and over. Licking. Sucking. Making her loose and ready.

She softly whispered, "Oh God."

Colt kissed his way up the crack of her ass and her arched spine. His body covered hers and he pressed his forehead to her nape. "Your ass is mine. No condom. I want you to feel every inch of me sliding into you. I want you to feel me coming inside you."

India made that mewling sound again.

He lubed up his fingers and scattered kisses across her shoulders as he prepared her. One finger. Then two scissoring inside her until she relaxed. Colt rolled her over on her back.

Her dark gaze stayed on his hand sliding up and down his hard cock as he applied lubrication.

"I'll go slow. At first. But we'll see how long it lasts once I'm buried balls deep in your tight ass. Let me see that pretty pink pucker."

India brought her knees by her shoulders and closed her eyes.

"Huh-uh. I want you to watch me take you."

She lifted her head the same time Colt put his hands under her ass and lifted her across his thighs.

Colt rubbed the wet head of his cock over that slippery rosette. "Don't clench." He pushed until the tip popped in through the ring of muscle.

Her breath hitched.

"Let me in. Like that. Look at us, Indy. See how hot it is as I'm pushin' inside you?" Colt watched as his cock slid into her ass completely.

India clenched around him.

When he looked at her, she wore a smirk. Very carefully, he lowered his body over hers, not moving his cock, until they were nose to nose. Colt angled his head and kissed her. Sweetly, at first, then with heat. He began to thrust. "Every part of you belongs to me now."

She arched and canted her hips, pushing his shaft deeper as her pelvis sought contact with his.

Colt knew he wasn't going to last. Indy's ass would be sore no matter how hard or easy he fucked her, so his greedy male nature urged him to fuck her hard.

So he did.

She loved it.

He pounded into her relentlessly, losing his mind when the friction of their groins sent her into a screaming orgasm. Her cunt and anal muscles contracted around his cock. Four deep, hard pumps and her body sucked his orgasm right out of him, as he shot inside that tight gripping channel.

Colt collapsed on her, kissing her neck, her mouth. Letting his cock soften before he withdrew. "You okay?"

"Uh-huh." She twined her fingers in his hair. "Colt? I like that you showed me your rough side."

"Good. Because it's early and that was just round one."

Chapter Nineteen

Colt had been summoned to a Sunday night McKay family dinner and he'd insisted on bringing India along. Which was why India's stomach was tied in knots as they pulled up to Carson and Carolyn's house.

The queasiness pissed her off. Why did she feel like a kid from the wrong side of the tracks being invited to the popular kid's birthday party?

She already knew Colt's family. Correction, she was friendly with the women who'd married into the McKay family—AJ and Macie. She'd met Channing once or twice. Carolyn was a loyal Sky Blue customer. She'd done tattoo work on Keely. But as far as really knowing them? Hell no.

Colt squeezed her hand. "You okay?"

I'd be fucking peachy keen if I was sucking down a fuzzy navel right about now. "Yeah. Why?"

"I dunno you seem...tense. Unlike yourself." His gaze moved from the high neckline of her long-sleeved blouse to the hem of her ankle-length suede skirt and red cowgirl boots.

"I'm fine. Just a little tired. You kept me up way too late last night."

"Was that an objection?"

She flashed back to how thoroughly he'd claimed her, tamed her, proven to her his mastery over her body, proven he trusted her by showing her his dark, commanding, rough side without apology. He'd fucked her, one way or another, eight times last night. Her belly churned for an entirely different reason than nerves, but from pure lust. "God, no. Not at all. Were you worried I didn't enjoy it?"

"Maybe." The ragged edge of his thumb rubbed across her

knuckles. "I was rough. More than a little, and a lot out of control."

"Are you ashamed?"

He shook his head. "I loved every second that you trusted me enough to let me lose control with you."

"I do trust you, Colt. Besides, if I hadn't liked it, I would've told you. I'm not exactly a shrinking violet."

"And thank God for that." He appeared to struggle with his next thoughts, so she jumped in and changed the subject.

"Dare I ask how many McKays are going to be in attendance?"

"Everyone in my immediate family. Ma decided to keep it simple." He scowled. "I'm sure Skylar told you how hard it is keepin' everyone straight with our extended family. And that ain't counting the West side."

India allowed a smirk. "Does that mean Blake isn't going to be here?"

"Nope."

"Pity. I like him."

At Colt's half-snarl, India kissed the back of his hand. "You're so easy."

"Only when it comes to you, sugar. Lemme come around and help you out."

After he'd opened the door, she said, "I'm capable of bailing out of this monster rig on my own."

"I know. Maybe I wanna steal a kiss before we head into the lion's den."

"Oh. Good plan."

He tugged her close enough she felt his heartbeat against her chest. His kiss was surprisingly tender and soothing; she hadn't realized she'd needed pacifying.

The sound of footsteps on gravel, then a loud, "Eww, gross."

"Yeah, gross."

Colt eased back from the kiss. Once India's boots hit the ground, they faced the intruders.

Three boys. India recognized Kyler McKay and Thane McKay but not the last one with the same dark hair and blue eyes that ran in the McKay family.

"Uncle Colt, you were kissin' India?" Kyler said in

astonishment.

"Yep."

"Hi Kyler, hi Thane," India said. "Who's this?"

"This is my nephew, Gib McKay, Colby and Channing's oldest boy. Gib, this is India."

"Hi Gib."

"India is your Aunt Skylar's sister."

"India also draws tattoos. Really cool ones. She has needles and ink and everything." Kyler frowned and touched her arm. "Hey, how come you covered up your tattoos? That snake is so awesome."

India resisted jerking her arm back.

"Good question," Colt said.

She really resisted sticking her tongue out at him.

Kyler blurted, "Are you gonna get married? Like Uncle Kade and Aunt Skylar done?"

"Why? You thinkin' of proposing to my girl if I don't get on the ball?" Colt teased.

"No way! Girls are gross."

"I'm sure your mothers wouldn't appreciate that opinion. Or your Aunt Keely," Colt said dryly.

Kyler shot a nervous look over his shoulder. "She'd kick our butts."

Colt rubbed his palm up her arm when she shivered. "Let's all go inside. It's getting chilly out here."

"We can't go back in yet."

"Why not?"

Kyler sighed. "Grammy said we were bein' too wild and riling up the babies, so she sent us outside to run off some energy." He scrutinized Colt from his boots to his ballcap. "You wanna race to the end of the driveway?"

"Please?" Gib said.

"Please?" Thane added.

The knot in India's stomach tightened. *Please don't make me walk in there by myself, Colt, please.*

"Maybe in a bit."

"That's what all grownups say," Kyler grumbled.

"Hey, *I* never say no to you guys."

"But you promised you'd give us a chance to beat you." Kyler's chest puffed up. "I'm faster than I was last time."

Colt turned to her and winked. "Wait here. I'll be right back." He faced his nephews. "Be prepared to get your butts whupped. On your mark. Get set—"

Gib jumped the gun.

Thane followed.

Kyler took the lead, whooping and hollering, with Colt running in fourth place behind the boys, taunting them.

India tried to imagine Colt at that age. Surrounded by brothers and cousins. All boyish charm and athletic grace. Did he have an uncle who'd drop everything to race him?

Four shadows tore up the driveway. Colt lagged behind until the very end when he put on a last second burst of speed and beat them all.

His competitive streak evidently didn't allow his nephews to win. But they didn't mind. They were planning rematches, making big promises of defeat, and right then, India knew it wasn't about competition but about anticipation. For the boys and their uncle.

"Don't wander off, guys. Stay right in front of the house, you hear?"

Affirmative grunts.

Colt wasn't even breathing hard when he grabbed her hand and led her up the porch steps. "You're awful quiet."

"I don't talk all the time."

He snorted.

A blast of sound and heat hit her when the front door opened.

She froze.

"Come on, it ain't that bad." He kissed the skin below her ear. "Okay, that was a total lie. But I promise not to desert you."

The huge kitchen was filled with people. Big people, little people. Women. Men.

India half-expected everyone to turn and stare when she walked in, but no one noticed.

Finally Carolyn McKay looked up from an enormous steel pan on the cook stove. "Colton! Do you think you can steer your brothers and your father out of here so we can get supper done?"

"Sure, Ma. Where do you want them?"

"Dining room. The table needs all the leaves."

Colt squeezed India's hand and approached the group in the corner.

Macie descended on her. "India Ellison, you little devil. So, you and Colt are a couple, huh?"

"I, for one, am not surprised," AJ said.

"That'd make one of us," India said under her breath.

"Oh pooh, you guys spend all your time together and have forever. It was only a matter of time before you realized..." AJ waggled her eyebrows. "The friends to lovers angle is *so* romantic."

India's face heated. Colt's mother was right over by the sink. "How can you be so sure we're...?"

AJ laughed. Macie laughed. Channing laughed. Hell, even Carolyn had a grin on her face.

"What?"

Keely came from behind her and wrapped an arm around her shoulder. "We're sure, because Colt is a McKay."

"All McKay men are...territorial," AJ said.

"You mean virile," Macie corrected.

"Very virile," Carolyn agreed.

"Eww. Mom! TMI!" Keely said.

Carolyn flapped a towel at her. "Oh, your poor virgin ears, Miz McKay."

"Virgin?" AJ sputtered.

"And don't forget fertile," Macie said, rubbing her belly.

Channing added, "Yes, very fertile."

All eyes zoomed to AJ. "What?"

"Care to add anything to the 'fertile' pile?" Macie said sweetly.

AJ's mouth dropped open. "He told his brothers? Already?"

"Cord told *everyone* already," Keely said wryly.

"But I'm like, barely two months along!"

A dark-haired blur rammed into Channing's legs. "Mama!"

Channing bent to grab him but Keely intercepted. "Huh-uh. This ain't your first rodeo, Chan. You know you're not supposed to pick up Braxton or Gib when you're pregnant."

"I feel fine."

"Mama!" The boy squirmed toward Channing.

Keely passed him over. "Braxton, you are off the list as my

favorite nephew. Where's Parker?"

"With Carter."

"And Kyler took Gib and Thane outside, thank goodness."

"Can you at least try and have a girl, AJ? Five nephews with two more on the way is a bit too much testosterone in this already testosterone-laden family." Keely shot India a sly look. "India has three darling little nieces to spoil and play dolls with."

"Eliza would much rather throw rocks than throw a tea party," India said.

"That, I have to see." When Keely sighed and ran a hand through her hair, India noticed Keely looked really tired. Distracted. Not her usual full of mischief self.

"I'm sure Kade and Sky would love it if you came over, Keely."

"Me too. Because of my travel schedule I haven't been home enough in the last year and it looks to be worse next year. I've only seen those sweet twins a couple times."

"They are sweet. And not sweet. Thank God Colt came over and helped me take care of them when Kade and Sky went out of town."

"He did?"

"Yeah, the girls adore him. He's so awesome with them even when I was pulling my hair out within six hours."

Everyone turned and stared at her.

"What?"

"Nothing," Channing said carefully. "It's just, well, we're surprised."

"About what? Colt is amazing with kids. All kids. He helped me out at the community center, and I know he's looking forward to being around Chassie's baby."

AJ, Channing and Macie glanced away. Carolyn gave her a curious look.

"Doesn't surprise me Colt is great with kids," Keely said cheerfully. "He spoiled me rotten when I was growing up. He's always been my favorite brother."

Pause.

Keely ducked as her sisters-in-law threw things at her. "I know when I'm not wanted." She snuck out the side door.

"She just wants to go drink beer with the boys," AJ said.

"Some things never change."

The women chatted amongst themselves. India listened, but didn't contribute much, either verbally or with dinner preparations. She felt like a fifth wheel.

India wanted a drink something fierce. Stressful times like this made the crutch of alcohol more appealing.

Just one wouldn't hurt you.

She peeked around the corner of the living room, looking for Colt. He held a sleeping toddler on his lap and was in deep conversation with Carter. Cord, Colby, Keely and Carson were congregated by the bay windows drinking beer.

A half-empty beer bottle sat on the sofa table.

A sense of urgency, a need to flee swamped her. She wouldn't be missed if she snuck outside for a breath of fresh air.

No one would miss that bottle. No one would know if you had a little nip of liquid courage. No one would blame you.

India told the voice to *shut up* and practically ran outside.

Kyler, Thane and Gib were racing in front of the porch, playing hide and seek between the pickups. The night air had become chilly and she shivered, wishing she'd worn a coat.

The McKay family dynamics weren't different from other families. Yet, she had a hard time figuring out where Colt fit in. With two older brothers and two younger brothers, he could almost be considered the middle child.

The invisible child. The pleaser. The intermediary.

But according to the way Colt described himself, he was the rebel, the bad seed, the black sheep, even before he'd become an alcoholic.

India didn't see him that way. And after spending just a short amount of time with his family, she wondered if any one of them saw Colt at all. The real Colt. The man she saw. Or did they still see him as Colt, the drunk? Colt, the charming womanizer? Colt, the screw up?

Didn't they see the man with the big heart? The quiet, contemplative man who'd learned from his mistakes? The sweet man? The helpful man? The man who dropped everything to run a race with his nephews? A man who helped out at the community center with kids he didn't know, as eagerly as he'd volunteered to help out with his own family's kids whenever he was asked?

Colt would be a wonderful father. Involved. Caring. Loving. And not for the first time did she think he'd make an even better husband.

"Whatcha thinking about so hard?"

She jumped at the sound of Cam's soft drawl drifting to her from the right side of the porch. "Cam. I didn't know you were out here."

"Yeah. I know you didn't."

"You enjoy sneaking up on people."

"Habit. Although, I'll point out I didn't sneak. I was already here when *you* snuck out."

"And when did you slink away, deputy?"

"As soon as humanly possible."

"Why?" It was weird having a conversation with someone she couldn't see. Almost like he was a ghost. Or she was in a confessional.

"My older brothers are pissed off at me for some things I said. Dad ain't bein' real friendly either. I ain't about to apologize. If pesky Keely wouldn't have forced me to come by showing up on my doorstep, I wouldn't even be here tonight."

"You guys are still fighting? That happened a couple weeks ago."

"How'd you know about it?"

"That was the same night I called Colt to help me with Sky and Kade's girls. I knew he was upset but he didn't get into specifics."

"Just as well."

Kyler, Thane and Gib ran inside.

The sound of sloshing liquid drifted to her. India recognized the sound of a half-empty bottle of booze and her mouth watered.

"So you never answered my question, India. What're you thinking about?"

"I'm contemplating my place in the universe. Or my navel. Take your pick. They seem to be one in the same these days."

"Smartass."

"Sorry. I needed a second to clear my head because it is overwhelming. What are you out here thinking about?"

"I'm a trained soldier. It isn't my job to think. It's my job to do what I'm told."

"Is that why you went into law enforcement? Just another set of orders to follow?"

"Maybe. You have to admit...the uniforms are sexy as shit."

India laughed. "And every woman loves a man in uniform."

"Loves. Right."

Rather than quiz him on why he was so determined to keep Domini at arms length, she asked, "Do you miss being a soldier?"

"Yes." More sloshing liquid. "And no."

"Well, that cleared things up a whole bunch for me, thanks."

Cam's chuckle wasn't particularly pleasant. "Welcome to my world."

She shivered as much from his tone as the temperature.

"You want my coat?"

I want a drink of whatever you're having.

"No. Thanks, though. I should head back inside. Probably time to eat."

"They'll come looking for us. Or maybe I oughta say Colt will come looking for you."

"You don't sound too happy about that prospect." India faced him, or where she thought he might be lurking. "In fact, several times, like at the basketball game, you've questioned whether I should be with Colt because he ends up injured around me."

"Sorry for snapping, I was on edge about Domini's situation that night." Pause. "Besides, why would you give a shit what I say or what I think?"

"I don't. But if you think Colt doesn't listen to you or care about what you say or what you think, you're an idiot, Deputy McKay."

She could tell that statement caught him off guard. "I wouldn't torpedo the first decent relationship Colt's ever had, India. Far from it."

"That's good to know."

"Although, you drive that motorcycle too damn fast."

India flashed him a cheeky smile. "You'll have to catch me first to prove that, copper."

Cam laughed.

"So you're keeping your torpedo launcher away from me...because you think I'm gonna keep Colt on the straight and narrow?"

"No. It's Colt's responsibility to stay on the straight and narrow, not yours. Despite the fact you two wage war over the dumbest shit, and fight just so you can make up, you're good for him. You're a good person, Indy. A lot of the people in his past haven't been, including some people in his family. He deserves a woman who understands him. Who sees his past and doesn't judge him for it. Who sees him as the man he is now, not who he used to be."

"Amen. Maybe you oughta share that insight with your family."

"Believe me, I've tried."

The porch door banged and Colt stepped out. "Hey. What're you doin' out here without a coat on?"

"Just thinking." She wouldn't out Cam. If he wanted to pipe up, that was his business. "It got a little stuffy in there."

"I understand that. You okay?"

No. I could use a big, stiff drink. "Of course."

"Good. Come on, supper's ready."

Of course.

She'd never admit a fallacy. Instead, she'd just slap on a happy face even if she was bleeding on the inside.

India was like that in A.A. too. Willing to deal with other people's issues, while skirting her own. Did she ever feel...overwhelmed? Did she ever have that urge to drink until she passed out?

Probably not. Of all the people Colt knew, India seemed to have the addiction thing whipped. She had total control of her demons and some days he wished he was as confident in his sobriety as she was.

No one noticed India's quiet demeanor at the supper table. She smiled. Laughed in all the right places but that restrained laughter never reached her eyes.

The only time a portion of the mask slipped was when she watched his nephews. A wistful look would soften her features. The same look she got watching her nieces. But if Colt let on he'd noticed? He knew her back would snap straight. Directly followed by a determined lifting of that elfin chin.

It drove him insane she had to act so freakin' tough all the time when he knew she wasn't.

When the kids began to get restless and whiny, Colt took it as a sign for them to leave.

After five minutes of silence cruising down the gravel road, he said, "Sorry you had a sucky time."

"I didn't have a sucky time. Why'd you think that?"

"Because you were awful quiet."

"It's sort of hard to get a word in edgewise with your family, so you can hardly blame me."

"Blame you? For what?" Colt slammed on the brakes and threw it into park in the middle of the gravel road. "For Christsake, India, will you at least be honest with me?"

"Hey! Do you mind giving warning next time so I can brace myself for whiplash?"

"Funny, I was just thinkin' the neckline on that shirt makes it look like you're already wearing a neck brace."

"Since when do you critique my clothing?"

"Since when did you start dressing like my mother?"

Her mouth dropped open. "Omigod. You are such an ass."

"Why does that make me an ass?"

"Because it's none of your goddamn business what I wear."

"Yeah? So tell me. Why did you wear a long-sleeved shirt?"

She gave him a stony stare. "Because it's October, Einstein."

"Fine." He let his gaze focus on her nose, then her eyebrow, her ears and finally her breasts. "But where are your hoops? And studs? Why'd you take all of your piercings out?"

"I don't wear them all the time."

"Yes, you do. That's what I'm talkin' about. Were you tryin' to look more acceptable to my family?"

India's defiant posture said it all.

"Why do you give a damn what my family thinks about your tattoos, piercings and funky clothes, India? I don't. I didn't take you there so you could change who you are to please them."

"Why did you take me there?"

Because you're mine. Because I wanted everyone to see that I'm worthy of love from an amazing woman like you. "To please myself."

"To please yourself? Jesus. You are such an asshat, jerkwad...fuckface!" India jumped out of the cab and slammed the door with enough force the whole truck vibrated.

She'd gone beyond calling him a dickhead in a helluva hurry.

And now she was hurrying away from him.

"Goddammit, India! Get back in here."

He didn't hear her response but he did see her flip him off in the glow of the headlights as she walked down the middle of the road.

Colt climbed out and chased after her. "Hey, I'm not done talkin' to you."

"Tough shit, I am done talking to you."

She kept walking.

He kept fuming. "Just get back in the truck, India, this is ridiculous."

India whirled around. "You know what's ridiculous? That I actually tried. I put forth an effort to be—how'd you put it?—more acceptable to your family. And to what end? It isn't me that they aren't seeing clearly, Colt, it's you."

"What the hell are you talkin' about?"

"I could've shown up, painted fucking purple, with yellow feathers in my hair, wearing a slave choker and chain and it wouldn't have made a difference. I'm not the one who needs to make the effort because *I* know who you are. They don't. It pisses me off." She flounced off again.

She was upset. For him? Because his family didn't understand him like she did?

"Indy, wait—"

"No. I'm too mad to deal with you right now."

"You can't walk home."

"Watch me."

Each twitch of her sexy little ass was like fuel on the fire. He wanted her. Now.

So Colt started after her. He caught her in about fifteen steps and picked her up, throwing her over his shoulder.

She kicked and screeched but he held onto the back of her legs as he spun around and headed back to the pickup.

"Let me down!"

"Nope."

"If you don't, I-I'll bite you in the ass, McKay, I'm not kidding!"

"I'll bite you back. And you already know how much I like your ass."

She screamed with frustration, pummeling her fists into his butt.

By the time they'd reached the truck, she'd quit flailing. She had a tight grip on his belt loops. "Are you gonna run if I put you down?"

"No."

Colt slid his hands up to brace her back as he lowered her feet to the ground. "Sugar, look at me."

She was breathing raggedly, more out of anger than exertion. Her head fell back.

Their eyes met. And Colt was lost.

"Sweet Jesus, India, when you look at me like that..."

"Like what?"

Like you love me. Like I'm a man worthy of you.

But he suspected she didn't know everything he'd ever wanted was visible in her eyes. So he backtracked—chickened out really—and focused on the one thing she would admit to: overpowering lust.

"Like you want to fight me and then fuck me."

India didn't deny it.

"Are we done with the fightin' portion? Cause I'd sure like to fuck you. Right here, right now. Against the dirty truck as you're shootin' me dirty looks."

Her response? She launched herself at him. Her mouth slammed into his in a kiss so raw it felt as if she'd knocked the wind out of him.

Colt pushed her against the pickup. His hands raced everywhere as he tried to find a single section of her skin. Dammit, of all the times to be buttoned-up. He hooked his fingers at the hem of her shirt, between the lapels, and jerked until buttons flew and her warm flesh greeted his eager hands.

India didn't protest, in fact, ruining her shirt only made her kiss him harder. Her hands dove into his hair. Not for a leisurely, tender stroking, but she pulled his hair into tight fists as her lower body ground against his fly.

Goddamn he wanted to suck on her skin. Mark her. Bite her, but the ferocity of the kiss made it impossible for him to release her lips even momentarily. He growled in her mouth, bumping his cock into her belly. His hands scraped up her back, maneuvering around to cup her breasts. When his thumbs rasped over her nipples, he didn't feel the rings.

When he broke his mouth free and he ate a path down her throat, she arched, baring all to him. One tug and her bra cups opened. Rather than look, he let his mouth do the walking, straight to her left nipple.

Yes. A ring. A smaller one than what she'd been wearing, but she hadn't taken it out in a fit of propriety. He sucked and lapped and bit and worshiped that tiny bit of metal until she moaned. He suckled her breast deep enough the ring tickled the back of his tongue. Another moan escaped as he switched to the other side and did it again and again and again.

"Colt. I need..."

"What?"

"You. I need you."

"You've got me."

His cock, already straining behind his zipper, jerked when India's hands dropped to his waistband. She unhooked the belt buckle, popped the button and eased down the zipper. Her fingers snaked into his boxers and she circled her hand around him and squeezed.

Colt hissed at the intense pleasure. Feeling the velvety smoothness of her palm on his shaft. The tightness of her grip as she stroked from the base to the wet tip.

"Lift me against the door. You wanted to fuck me so bad, do it. Like you mean it."

With her hand commanding his cock he couldn't remember why this wasn't the best idea ever...wait. "Condom," he rasped. "We don't have a—"

"So fucking what? You didn't use a condom last night when you came on my belly. Or in my ass." India teased his ear with her hot breath. "I want to feel that heat in my cunt. I want to feel your cock sliding and pounding inside me without latex. Your wetness mixed with mine. Just hardness and heat. Just you, Colt."

Like he could deny her that.

Like you could deny yourself that.

He yanked his jeans below his knees. Then he boosted her up, fighting with the material of her skirt until it bunched at her waist. "Help me."

"I am." She wrapped her legs around his hips and pulled her thong to the side. "I'm ready. Please. Colt. Now."

Colt bent his knees and drove deep in a single thrust.

India dug her fingernails into his shoulders. "Again. Hard like that again."

His slow withdrawal only made the hard, fast plunge more rewarding. Again. And again. Over and over.

No kissing. He'd crack her teeth if he put his mouth on hers. He lived in the moment, the feel of her hot pussy tightening with every stroke. The sharp bite of her nails through his shirt. Her irregular breathing fanning his cheek. The earthy scent of his lover filling his lungs as he filled her body with his.

She drummed her heels into his butt. "Do that little grinding thing. Like that."

"Come on, India. Come on my cock. Lemme feel those sweet pussy muscles tightening around my dick as you're comin' hard." He grabbed a handful of hair and yanked, moving her head to where wanted so he could bury his lips in her neck. Nuzzled and licked the hot spot that'd send her into orbit.

"Oh! Yes." India gasped. Her pelvis canted closer as she arched her lower back and her knees squeezed his hips. "Don't stop. Oh God, Colt, please don't stop."

Colt didn't move his mouth. He kept his rhythm uniform, and clenched his ass cheeks as he fought off his own climax. The second her body relaxed, he hammered into her. Losing his mind in the slickness of her pussy, her whimpers burning his ear and how fucking fantastic, how perfect it felt to have his come filling her up. After the last pulse, he reconnected with her mouth and kissed her with the gentleness his body had lacked.

He kept kissing her. She kept letting him. He tried to convey that being with her was everything. *Everything.* He loved her with his heart, his soul, his mind, his body. And being half-naked, against his dirt-coated pickup, in the middle of nowhere Wyoming, after he'd fucked her mindless, was just icing on the cake.

India retreated to brush soft kisses over his cheeks, and his temple, his forehead, his eyebrows, his eyelids. All the while her hands stroked his shoulders and his chest and his neck. As if she was trying to convey the same thing to him.

The moment was perfect.

Chapter Twenty

Lulled by the sound of the wheels clacking on the pavement and Colt's presence beside her, India fell asleep.

The next thing she knew, Colt gently shook her awake. "Hey. Come on, sleepyhead."

She blinked and realized they weren't at Colt's place but hers. "I thought we were going to your house?"

"You're tired and yours was closer."

"Oh."

It didn't appear Colt was going to get out of the truck. Was he sick of her company and just dropping her off?

Or maybe he's waiting for an invitation.

India laid her head on his arm. "You coming in?"

"Do you want me to?"

"Yes. And I'd like you to spend the night."

"I'll have to get up early."

"I know. I don't care. I just want you with me."

He kissed the top of her head and parked.

They held hands as they climbed the stairs. Colt's quietness was unnerving. Not because he chatted nonstop, but something was wrong.

India led him into her bedroom. She stopped at the side of the bed and faced him. Sliding her arms round his waist, she rested her cheek against his chest.

He sighed and seemed to sag against her.

They embraced for long time.

"You tired?"

"A little. You?"

"Yeah. Maybe we should crawl in bed."

"Sounds good." He disentangled himself and stepped back.

"Sit. I'll help you get your boots off."

"I'm capable of—"

"I know you are."

"My feet probably smell."

"I don't care. Sit." She gave him a little push. She grabbed the heel end of his right boot and tugged. It slipped free so fast she lost her balance.

"Maybe you oughta let me do it."

She tossed the boot by the door. "I'm fine." Then she grabbed his left heel. The boot slid free easily. "Now that I've done the hard part, I'll let you get the rest."

Colt shucked his clothes while she did the same. She rolled down the covers and turned off the light. They crawled in their respective sides.

It was all very orderly.

India cuddled up against Colt's naked back. "You're warm. Mmm. It's like having my own electric blanket."

"Getting cold at night. Probably need that electric blanket soon."

Now they were talking about the weather in bed. She waited a minute, but he didn't draw her into his arms like he did whenever she slept in his bed. She scooted up and placed her chin on his shoulder. "Colt, what's the matter? And don't tell me nothing."

Silence.

"Did I embarrass you at your parents' house?"

"No. Why would you think that?"

"You aren't going to try and pretend you're acting normal right now?"

"And fuckin' you up against my truck in the middle of the goddamn road is normal?"

"Is that what this is about?"

"Yeah. Jesus, India, I ripped your damn shirt. I pulled your hair, for Christsake. How can you even want me next to you?"

"Knock it off, McKay. I could've said no at any point and you would've stopped. Don't you doubt for a second that I didn't enjoy every second." She put her mouth next to his ear. "And you told me you hated that shirt anyway, so no big loss."

He laughed softly.

She moved so she could roll him on his back. She brushed the hair from his forehead. "I wouldn't have asked you to stay if I didn't want you here next to me."

"Why?"

Because I love you. Now was not the time for that confession.

"I've been so rough with you. Last night. And now tonight." Colt angled his head and kissed the inside of her wrist. "You deserve…"

When he didn't finish, India said, "What?"

"Tenderness." He squeezed his eyes shut. "I can give you passion, but I've never given you…"

He had given her softness and gentleness; he just hadn't realized that's what it was. But here was the opportunity she'd wanted to show him her softer side. "Then let me give you tenderness, Colt."

His eyes flew open.

"Let me give you sweetness. Let me make love to you." *Let me show you how much I love you, Colt McKay.*

"Indy—"

"Please." She traced the outline of his jaw. "If you hate it, I promise I'll let you fuck me as hard and raw as you want."

He managed a smile.

India threw a leg over his hip and straddled his belly. She reached up and knocked the pillows to the floor. "There. Now I have room to work." She set her hands by his head on the mattress. "Close your eyes."

He did.

She pressed a soft kiss on his lips. And another. And another, until there was no break and they were kissing nonstop. Not frantically, unhurriedly. She eased back, latching onto his wrists and moved his arms up above his head so she could run her fingers across the muscles of his biceps, triceps, and forearms. Touching him, feeling his cock jerk against her butt made her all the more determined to go slow.

India slid her lips down, flicking her tongue over the sexy dimple in his chin, trailing openmouthed kisses over his neck, past the hollow of his throat, between his pecs. She let her mouth follow the curve until the pebbled nipple brushed her lips.

Colt hissed.

"Mmm," she said, lapping at the flat disk. She blew across the wetness and worried the pointed tip between her teeth. She switched back and forth between the two nipples until his upper body arched into her from the attention.

"I hope you're not spending so much time licking and kissing me there because you're secretly measuring me for a tattoo?"

Her chuckle against that sensitive flesh brought another groan from him.

"You have nice nipples."

"Yeah? What makes them nice?"

"Big. Round." India's tongue drew a full circle. "Not much hair. A pretty color. Brownish-red, but not too much red."

"I can't believe I'm askin' this, but nipple color matters?"

"Of course. Some guys' nipples are ugly. They're too small or centered weird on their chest. Or eww, they're buried beneath too much chest hair. Yours—" she watched his eyes as she tongued the tip, "—are perfect."

"Glad you think so."

"So sensitive too. I know you love it when I do this." India sucked the whole nipple into her mouth.

He groaned.

India kissed and nuzzled every inch of his chest. Enjoying the chance to take pleasure in his body, not just his cock. She gave him credit; he left his arms above his head and didn't attempt to seize control.

Good behavior should be rewarded.

She wrapped her fingers around his shaft and slid her hips down his belly until they were groin to groin. She pressed her lips to his as all that male hardness slipped inside her on a slow, sweet glide.

A sighing moan filled her mouth, but Colt didn't attempt to break the kiss. India followed the contours of his arms and clasped their hands together, stretching her upper body completely across his.

She rocked on him, only allowing his shaft to withdraw halfway on each downstroke. Once he was buried balls deep, she'd rub side to side, loving the combination of the rasp of his pubic hair over her clit and the piercing.

It was a level of sexual comfort and closeness she'd never experienced, the heat of Colt's body beneath hers, the fullness of his rigid sex filling her. The scents of sex and his cologne and her lotion mixed together. Hearing their stuttered breaths, at times in unison, at times staggered, and the whisper of rough skin on soft.

Colt finally broke his lips free. His neck arched and his fingers tightened around hers. "So close."

"I know. Let me take you there." She trailed kisses down the arc of his neck and sucked on the spot between his collarbone and throat that brought his swift intake of breath. His hips pumped in a steady rhythm. He whispered her name as his cock jerked inside her, bursts of heat bathed her vaginal walls.

Her inner muscles started to spasm in time to the pulse pounding in her clit and she clenched those muscles around his cock, trying to prolong their pleasure.

He muttered, urging her to tip her head up so he could fasten his mouth to hers. God, she loved kissing him. Absolutely freakin' loved the give and take of their kisses, sometimes passionate, sometimes flirty, sometimes sweet, but always with an edge of heat.

She released their joined hands and pushed up. "So? Did you hate that sweet, sweet lovin'?"

"You even have to ask?" His hands roamed up and down her back, from her shoulders to her ass. "You and me nekkid is always spectacular, but that felt like we were..."

"What?"

"Connected on a different level." He paused, in speech and movement. "Did you feel it?"

"Absolutely."

"Good." His hands landed on her hips and he rolled with her, laughing at her surprised squeak as she looked up at him. "Now that you've shown me sweet, sweet lovin', I might give the gentle approach a shot next time."

His tenderness would be her undoing.

Colt buried his lips in her neck, sending goose bumps dancing across her skin. "Indy. I..."

She couldn't handle a confession from him. "Snuggle me up, cowboy. I'm cold and tired and it's been a long day."

Colt was gone by the time India woke up the next morning. No note, no anything. He hadn't even made coffee. She started the coffeepot and detoured to the bathroom.

When India grabbed a towel to shower, she dislodged the "monthly" calendar she'd shoved between the stacks.

Since she'd sobered up and since her mother's death from ovarian cancer, and her sister's accidental pregnancy, she'd kept track of her period and other women's issues on a separate calendar in the bathroom.

Her gaze zeroed in on the big red X's. She counted forward.

Holy shit.

They'd had unprotected sex at her most fertile time.

Twice last night alone. Once the night before when he'd pulled out at the last minute.

Dammit. What if she'd gotten pregnant? She unclipped the pen attached to the top and used it to mark off days. They'd had sex a lot to make up for the five days she'd had her period.

India freaked out. She counted again. No mistake. She jumped up and ran into the living room so she had more room to pace and freak out.

This was not happening. Not happening.

God. What'd she been thinking? How could she've been so stupid? So irresponsible?

It takes two to tango.

Colt had brought up the condom issue right before he fucked her against the truck. She'd been so...intent on having him in his riled up state, all sexy and masculine and needy that she hadn't been thinking clearly. Just like he hadn't been thinking clearly the night before when he'd used the withdrawal method.

Still, they both knew better. Especially since her sister and his cousin had an unplanned pregnancy due to a moment of recklessness.

But hadn't Skylar and Kade turned that oops into a happily-ever-after?

Yes.

So had she subconsciously wanted to get pregnant?

No. She wouldn't do that to Colt. She loved him. She couldn't wait to tell him how much she loved him. But she didn't want to start the conversation with, "These last six weeks have been the best of my life and I love you like crazy...and speaking of crazy, guess what? I'm pregnant!"

The poor guy had no choice but to marry her. Seems that's how the Ellison women find husbands; they trap them by getting knocked up.

Colt had suffered through enough gossip.

India sat on the floor and tried to come up with a workable plan. She had two days left of her most fertile time. If she could avoid Colt, she could avoid sex.

Isn't that a bit like closing the barn door after the cows get out?

Yes, but it was the only option that made sense—even when it made no sense.

✳

Late the next morning, Colt was standing outside shooting the breeze with Trevor and Edgard after they'd sorted cattle for the upcoming sale.

"Chass said Carolyn called a McKay family supper last night?" Trevor asked.

"I think you mean a summons," Colt said dryly.

"How'd that go? You took India, right?"

"Yep. It went fine."

"Really?"

"Sure. It ain't like Indy's a stranger to anyone in the family." Although she had dressed and acted like one, Colt figured India wouldn't appreciate him sharing that tidbit.

Edgard and Trevor exchanged a look.

"What?"

"I guess Chass was worried how it played out, bein's half of ya'll ain't talkin' since Cam blew up at your brothers and Carson a few weeks back."

Colt sipped his coffee. "Seems Cam's been avoiding everyone in the family, 'cept for me. So yeah, conversation at the dinner table was subdued. But there was enough babies cryin' that we all pretended we didn't notice the strain."

Trevor said, "What the hell did Cam say that pissed everyone off anyway?"

"Chassie didn't tell you?"

"Chassie doesn't know," Edgard said. "It's driving her crazy, which means..."

"She sent you two to get the dirt."

Edgard grinned. "Yep."

"You guys are such suckers," Colt scoffed.

"Oh, she ain't gettin' the family dirt for free," Trevor added. "Me'n Ed have her repayment choices all planned out."

"I'll just bet you do." Colt never would've thought his sweet little cousin would be living openly with two men. At first, Colt had suspected Chassie's intimate relationship with Edgard came about only because of Trevor's need for a sexual relationship with his former rodeo partner. Colt'd worried Chassie would do anything to keep her husband happy, including welcoming an old lover into their lives and their bed. Not that Chassie discussed Trevor and Edgard's past, but it was obvious to him how the two men felt about each other. Yet, the more time Colt spent with the trio, the more he realized they were all truly happy together, and in his mind, that was what mattered.

"Spill the family beans, cuz," Trevor said.

So Colt did.

When he finished, Edgard whistled. "That's harsh, man. Does that mean things aren't back to normal between you guys?"

He shrugged. "Define normal. It's about the same as it was before. We're in the slow season so it ain't like I gotta see them everyday, which is probably a good thing."

"What's India's take on it?" Trevor asked. "Even though you just started datin', you two've been friends for years."

"India agrees with Cam. In fact, we had a huge fight about it last night after the family dinner." He told them an abbreviated version of what she'd said.

"You'd be wise to keep her. She's a smart one."

"No argument from me," Colt said. "I know Cam will come around and clear things up with Cord and Colby when he's ready. He's stubborn, but he ain't the type to hold a grudge."

"Are you?"

"Maybe. My resentment and Cord and Colby's distrust of me has been going on for years. Workin' my ass off like I used to before I hit the bottle regularly ain't changed their opinion of me. I'm at a loss on how to fix it."

"Ain't your responsibility to fix it. Sure, Colby and me go way back, but that don't mean I agree with everything he's ever done. He and Cord've been outta line toward you for a helluva long time, Colt, so in my opinion, they need to do a little groveling, not you," Trevor said.

Edgard put his hand on Trevor's shoulder and shoved him sideways. "Way to be compassionate, Trev."

"What?"

"Not all families love to be shitty to each other like ours did."

"So what do you suggest Colt does, *Dr. Phil?*"

Colt saw the playfulness and how Trevor didn't attempt to shake off Edgard's touch. It meant the world to him these two gruff, private men were comfortable enough with him not to hide their feelings.

Which led him right back to the issue at hand with his brothers. He sighed.

A big red diesel Chevy turned and barreled up the driveway. Cord's truck. And was that Colby in the passenger's seat?

What the hell?

"Speak of the devils," Edgard murmured. He ran his hand down Trevor's back before dropping it from view. "We'd better get goin'."

"Tell Chass thanks for the muffins."

Edgard and Trevor chatted with Cord and Colby for a few minutes before they disappeared up the driveway.

Colt stood his ground and waited, hating that he felt nervous.

Colby climbed out first. "Mornin' Colt."

"Mornin'. What brings you guys by?"

The truck door slammed in response.

"Didja need something?" Did I do something wrong again?

"No. Gotta say, it's sad the only time we show up at your place is when we need something."

"A damn shame," Cord added.

"You're both welcome here any time."

"Good to know."

Both men leaned against the truck. Colby still favored the leg he'd busted up rodeoing, and had taken up a cockeyed position. Cord crossed his arms and his legs, keeping his face shadowed beneath his hat brim.

"So why *are* you here?"

Colby tipped his head up and looked Colt square in the eye. "To apologize for bein' a prick to you."

Whoa. Not what Colt expected.

"I ain't gonna make excuses about what I said a few weeks back, 'cause it's over and done. We both know it was wrong. We all know this situation has been buildin' for a while. You've pissed me off so many times since I quit the circuit and started workin' on the ranch that I'm surprised we ain't come to blows before now."

"Hell, I've been pissing you off since I was born," Colt said.

Colby shot him a smile. "Ain't that the truth."

"And Colt, you and I did come to blows," Cord added.

Just another blackout drunk moment Colt didn't remember.

"So until Cam pointed it out a couple weeks back," Colby continued, "I hadn't considered I'd kept up that shitty attitude toward you even now that you're clean. Because I was used to actin' that way, I realized I didn't know how *not* to be mad at you, bro."

Silence.

"Then when you built this house, away from us, and up the road from Trev, who'd always been *my* best friend, I guess I was pissed *and* jealous. Makes me an immature fuck to spout off the shit I did to you. You didn't deserve none of it. Jesus. I don't know if I can ever apologize enough."

"You don't hafta—"

"Lemme say my piece. I'm sorry I—*we*—didn't kick your ass when we saw you losin' the battle with booze. You shoulda been able to turn to us, Colt, instead we turned you against us. I don't blame you for wantin' to distance yourself. No wonder you prefer Kade and Buck to us, at least they had your back when you needed it."

Colt glanced away.

"As long as we're spillin' our guts, I'm sorry I didn't try harder to include you in my life with Channing either. All Gib could talk about on the way home from dinner last night was you."

"He's a great kid."

"And I'm really fuckin' sorry you've borne the brunt of the work in your sobriety while I was workin' banker's hours because I've got a wife and kids to go home to.

"Bottom line is Cam was dead on and it pisses me off I was too stubborn to see it. I didn't believe you could change, even when the proof was right in my face for the last three years. And it sucks that if Cam didn't have the balls to speak the truth, we all probably would've gone on like this for years, huh?"

"Probably."

Another moment of silence.

Cord shifted his stance. "I ain't got much to add. Colby pretty much said it all. But I will say I'm just as much a sorry sonuvabitch. Maybe more. Christ, Colt, I'm so fuckin' sorry. It never shoulda gotten to this point. We all know the strained relationship Dad has with Uncle Casper. As the oldest kid I swore it'd never happen to any of us. I'll be damned if I didn't sit back and let it happen.

"When you sobered up I wasn't sure it'd stick. Hell, I watched you strugglin' that fall when you returned from treatment until you found an A.A. meeting. And what did I do the instant AJ and I got married? I quit hangin' out with you. I even went a step farther than Colby; I justified my actions by convincin' myself you were better off with A.A. support than with ours."

"Look, I ain't gonna lie. I needed A.A. I wouldn't have survived the first year if it hadn't been for A.A." If it hadn't been for India. "I dealt with a lot of shit I didn't want any of my family to know about. So blame on the 'backing away' response is equal."

"I'm supposed to tell you from Carter that although he ain't around as much as he'd like, he feels guilty," Colby said. "Especially since all of us banded together and knocked some sense into him when he needed it. Must've seemed like we couldn't be bothered to do that for you."

Colt looked back and forth between his brother's hangdog

faces. "Lemme ask you something. Did your wives put you up to this?"

"Nope. AJ's been worried," Cord said. "But she's been feelin' too crappy to do much but yell at me for knockin' her up."

"Same with Channing. Though, I gotta say, if either one of them were in top form, along with Macie, they woulda thrown their lot in with Keely and kicked all our asses. Keely knew what was up. Might've saved us all some grief if we woulda listened to her."

"What about Ma? Any of this her doing?"

Colby shook his head. "I'm pretty sure Ma's in worse denial than the rest of us. First thing she said after Cam blew up was she raised us to treat each other better."

"That's it?"

"Uh-huh. And Dad..."

"You don't gotta explain nothin' to me about Dad," Colt said.

Both Colby and Cord smiled.

This time the silence wasn't filled with tension.

Colt said, "I appreciate you guys comin' by and bein' up front with me. It'd been easier to ignore it."

"No lie there."

"So we okay?" Colt asked.

"I reckon. Except Colby and I would like you to help us draw up a more structured distribution of ranch duties."

"Jesus. Dad'll hate that."

"Tough shit. That ain't his decision," Cord said. "This ain't a monarchy."

Wow. Bucking Carson McKay's iron rule about "doin' what needs done" and receiving apologies from both his brothers? This was shaping up to be a damn fine day. The family changes would take some getting used to for all of them, still, Cord and Colby had taken the first step to making things better and Colt admired that. He could work with that.

But they could all use a little levity. "So, do we give each other a big group hug now, or what?"

Cord said, "I vote for the 'or what' option."

"Meaning?"

"Let's dick with Cam. I'm beginnin' to think our little brother feels left out of our family dramas."

Colby scratched his chin. "You know, we *have* been treatin' him with kid gloves since he settled back here. Maybe it's time we..."

"What?"

"Take the gloves off," Cord and Colby finished together.

Colt grinned. "I'm in."

$$*$$

Colt returned home hours later to find the light on his answering machine flashing. Probably a telemarketer. Most everyone he wanted to talk to called his cell. He hit play anyway. Two messages.

"Colt. It's India. Look, I'm going to be really busy the next couple of days. I hope you understand it'd be best if we just did our own thing until the weekend. I'll call you then."

Beep.

He hit pause on the machine and dialed India's cell. She picked up on the second ring. "Hello?"

"What the hell is this? You're too busy to see me all week?"

"I explained in the message."

"Like hell you did. What's really going on, India?"

Silence.

"I know you're there."

"I need a break."

"From me?"

"From you, from us, from this..."

"How long is this break gonna last? Or is it a permanent break?"

"No! God no. I swear to you, I just need some time alone to think." She paused. "Don't you ever need that?"

Yeah, he did. Didn't mean he liked it. "So do you have an end date in mind for this moratorium on seein' each other?"

"How about Thursday?"

He bit back a growl. "Fine."

"I won't be at the meeting tomorrow night either."

There went that plan. "Can I at least call you?"

"No. Thursday is not that far away, Colt, I think you'll survive not talking to me for two days." Softly, she said, "I'll miss you. Take care," and hung up.

"Goddammit." He hated this. Especially since he didn't know what'd sent her into full retreat.

His family? Maybe.

Or maybe...he'd spooked her by his intent to tell her he loved her last night, before she'd stopped him. Why would that scare her? She had to know how he felt.

Guess he'd have to wait until Thursday to find out.

The message light still blinked. He hit play. "Hi, Colt, it's Ginger Paulson. I don't know if you remember me, but we met a couple weeks back at the community center? My son Hayden was in a class and we talked when I picked him up? Anyway, if you could call me back, I'd appreciate it. There's something I'd like to discuss with you." She rattled off the number and he scrawled it on the scratch pad by the phone.

Yeah, he remembered her all right. The redhead. He dialed her number. "Ginger? It's Colt McKay. What can I do for you?" He waited while she explained. A big grin broke out when she finished. "Sure I can meet you. Tomorrow night? At Dewey's? It's a date."

Chapter Twenty-one

The bell on the front door clanked.

India threw her sketchbook on the counter and stretched. Talk about a slow day. She slapped on a smile and entered the main part of the store, which showcased the Sky Blue product line.

"Good morning. Something I can help you with?"

The woman turned around. Carolyn McKay.

India tried not to let her smile slip. She'd known Carolyn for a few years, in a professional capacity, as India the saleswoman who tempted Carolyn with new Sky Blue products. Was she supposed to act differently now that she was dating Colt?

"Hi Carolyn. How are you?"

"Fine. And you?"

I'm dragging ass because your son fucked me senseless and we didn't use protection, so I could very well be pregnant with your grandchild.

Not a good answer. TMI, as Keely would say. "I'm good. You looking for something in particular? I'm afraid the lavender and sage hand lotion is backordered until next month."

"Thanks for letting me know. But that's not why I'm here."

"Oh?" *Brilliant response, India, maybe you oughta be totally stupid and her if she's here for a tattoo.*

"Did you have a good time at our house Sunday night?"

"Yes. The food was wonderful. Colt has always told me what a great cook you are."

Carolyn beamed. "Really? Sometimes I wonder if any of my family pays attention to what they're eating. It's good to hear my efforts are appreciated." She paused. "Do you cook?"

"God no. Seems pointless for one. I tend to go for fast and easy." That hadn't come out right.

A knowing look entered Carolyn's eyes. "I see. My niece Chassie tells me Colt is a good cook, not that he's invited his father and me over for dinner."

Colt's choice of dinner guests was not India's issue. "He is a great cook."

"He's cooked for *you*?"

Crap. She'd fallen right into that one. "Yes. Since I can't crack an egg, I have to reciprocate in other creative ways." Ooh. And didn't that sound totally suggestive?

"I'm sure."

"That's not what I meant—"

"And it's not important. Anyway, I was surprised to hear you were dating my son. Aren't there...rules against that sort of thing?"

India frowned. "Rules?"

"A.A. rules. About a sponsor not becoming intimately involved with a sponsoree."

Carolyn was fishing. The relationship between the sponsor and sponsoree wasn't spelled out on purpose, according to the A.A. guidelines. If she'd done any sort of research—and India would bet money Carolyn McKay had read up on A.A—she'd know that.

What Carolyn wanted was confirmation India was now—or had been—Colt's sponsor. India wouldn't betray that confidence, especially since early on Colt demanded everything about his A.A. life be kept from his family, as was his right.

India said, "With all due respect, Carolyn, I'm sure you understand I'm not at liberty to discuss A.A. business with you."

"Oh sure. I just wondered. I worry."

"You worry about Colt? Or about me dating Colt?"

"Both, I guess."

At least she hadn't lied. "Why?"

"Can I be honest with you? You look like a straight shooter."

India took it to mean she looked low-class and acted crass. "By all means."

"My worry is that Colt has come to rely on you too much."

"Too much?"

"At first it was understandable, he needed the support of others who'd been through the same types of...things. But it's been a couple of years. Isn't time he weans himself from A.A.?"

Weans himself? Jesus. Was this woman for real? Did she understand anything about what an addict goes through every damn day? "Recovery is a lifelong process. It doesn't have a shelf life. Or a convenient timeframe. And the level of involvement in the A.A. program is just as individual as the journey it took to get there. We don't demand or command members. Participation is strictly voluntary."

"I realize that. I'm not talking only about A.A. I'm talking about you."

"What about me?"

"Do you realize Colt's pulled away from his family almost completely in the time he's been with you?"

"I hate to argue with you on the family issue, but that's not true. Colt spends lots of time with Cam. And with Kade, Skylar and the girls. He helps Buck out. I know for a fact he, Chassie, Trevor and Edgard have breakfast together most Sunday mornings."

That didn't placate Carolyn. In fact, it seemed to distress her even more. "Which is all good and well, but Colt doesn't come over to our house for Sunday brunch or supper. He doesn't have much to do with Cord or Colby or their families unless I organize it. He and Carter used to be close, but not now. Can you explain that away as easily?"

"Carter lives in Canyon River. Maybe because Colt works with his brothers almost every day, he needs a break in his off ranch hours?"

Carolyn's owl-eyed expression said India was clueless. "A break? There are no 'breaks' in ranching. For any of us. Especially in such a large-scale operation as the McKay Ranch. Especially in a family business. And him needing a break from his family is just plain ridiculous."

"Maybe it'd be healthier if you did take an occasional break from one another. God knows Skylar and I get along better when she's not in my face all the time."

"You might be that way, India, but Colt isn't. He never has been until he met you. I know my son."

"No, Carolyn, that's the crux of your problem. I don't think you know Colt at all," she said softly.

"And you do? Since you've come into his life he's built a house in the boondocks. He doesn't go to dances or to church. He never goes anyplace where he might meet a decent woman to settle down with now that he's cleaned up his act."

Decent woman. Evidently a woman who loved her son body and soul, who accepted him as he was, who believed Colt McKay was the most loving, most sincere, most thoughtful, most wonderful man she'd ever known...didn't qualify as a decent woman.

Oh. That stung. Big time.

Don't cry. Don't you give this woman a reason to offer you false comfort.

Yet, even as she was bleeding inside, India knew Carolyn wasn't being malicious. Only acting on a mother's concern, as misguided, misinformed as that concern might be.

"Look, India. That might've come off sounding a little harsh. I like you. I always have. I just want you to understand not to take it personally when Colt—"

"What? Moves on? Decides he'd prefer a sturdy, native Wyoming ranch woman to a tattooed, pierced freakshow like me?" India leaned across the counter. "That way of thinking is *exactly* why he's distanced himself from your family. None of you know him anymore, nor have you taken the time to get to know him. And that is just plain sad."

"How are we supposed to get to know him if he's with you all the time?"

"Who Colt chooses to spend his time with is his business. Is that what this is about? He's choosing me over you?"

A startled look darted across Carolyn's face. Her eyes teared up.

"But the thing is, he's *not* always choosing me. He has a life you don't even know about. A life that has nothing to do with the ranch."

Carolyn's mouth opened to protest. India stopped it with a wave of her hand.

"Did you know Colt plays in a charity basketball tournament a couple times a year? Did any of you bother going to cheer him on? No. Did you know he takes boys in the Little Buddies program horseback riding on his land? So he can talk to them one on one about staying away from drugs and alcohol? No. And he did go to a dance, a community dance. For charity. Were any of the McKays, besides Colt and Buck—"

"Are you talking about the dance Colt brought a date to? A nice girl who he embarrassed when he was found in a janitor's closet with...you? Trust me, we heard all about that one. Just like we've heard about all the rest of his sexual escapades for the last twenty years."

India felt all the blood drain from her face.

Carolyn's eyes went wide as if she were surprised she'd spoken out loud. "I'm sorry, that didn't come out right. I'm just frustrated. None of my boys are talking to each other or to me. And I thought..."

"If you warned me to stay away from Colt it might fix your family problems?"

"Heavens no. I'm warning you to expect that type of response and attitude from people around here, who always expect the worst from the wild McKays. I'm afraid there's more than a little trouble that'll come your way if you are involved with my son."

"I welcome it." She pushed back from the counter. "If you'll excuse me, Mrs. McKay, I have a tattoo customer scheduled that I need to get ready for."

India spun on her heel and managed to walk to the backroom with dignity she didn't feel.

$*$

A whispered voice pierced the silence and darkness.

"You ready?"

"Ready for what? What's happening?"

"You know."

"No, I don't. What's going on? Where am I? Indy? Is this some kind of sex game, sugar? Because I can't see it to enjoy it."

A slice of awareness glimmered on the edges of his subconscious.

Colt couldn't move. It felt like a thick rope was wound around his body from his shoulders to his knees.

Where was he? At the ranch? He heard laughter. Smelled

dust and coffee. He stomped his feet. It wasn't dirt beneath his boots but concrete.

Strong hands grabbed him by the arms and dragged him. His heart nearly beat out of his chest. "Okay, enough of the rough stuff. Or are you givin' me back some of what I gave to you? I said I was sorry."

The blindfold was ripped from his eyes. He blinked until Bert's face came into view.

"Bert? What are you doing here? Where's India?"

"The time has come for you to face your fears."

"But I have faced them. I haven't had a drink in years!"

Colt looked around. He was in the middle of a circle. The circle of trust, just like the A.A. meetings. Except this circle was composed of his family, Cord, Colby, Carter, Keely, his mother, his father, his uncle Harland, his cousins Dag West, Quinn and Bennett McKay, not his fellow A.A. members.

He looked at Dag. Then Uncle Harland. "But you're both dead."

They just stared at him with vacant eyes.

"You ready, Colton West McKay?"

"Ready for what?"

"To let go."

His gaze zoomed around the circle. Where was Kade? Cam? Chassie? Trevor? Edgard? Buck? The people he counted on?

Where the hell was India? The one person he trusted most in the whole world?

She's not here when you need her. She's just like the rest of them. She will let you down.

"He's not ready yet."

Colt's head whipped around because every other part of his body was immobilized.

Blake West grinned at him. "But I'll give you a little push in the right direction, cuz, to get you started."

"No."

"Trust me."

"I don't trust any of you!"

Blake shoved him hard.

Without the use of his arms or legs, Colt braced for impact, knowing not one person in the circle would jump to catch him. They'd just let him fall. Like they always had.

He jackknifed up, throwing his hands in front of his face to protect himself and connected with nothing but air.

His eyes opened. He was in his bedroom. The alarm clock read four a.m.

It took a second for him to get his heart rate back to normal and realize it'd just been a dream. A weird fucking dream, but a dream nevertheless.

Rather than dwell on all the hidden meanings any counselor would have a field day with, Colt focused on one thing: India. She was missing from the dream, missing from his life and he missed her something fierce. He needed to talk to her as soon as possible.

Chapter Twenty-two

The next day, India's Ink had a customer. Not India's favorite person by any stretch, but she was so bored and lonely she welcomed the diversion.

"So where've you been, Cat? I haven't seen you around." India lined up the ink cups and wiped an alcohol pad across the faded pink rose tattoo on Cat's ankle.

"Oh, I had family stuff in Denver. Then I worked in Canyon River while Macie was flitting off to another one of Carter's art shows. I can't believe she's pregnant again. Three kids in five years is crazy."

India didn't point out her sister had three kids in three years and she didn't find it crazy in the least.

"Sometimes I wonder if Carter doesn't keep her pregnant because Macie will wake up and leave his poor artist's ass if she wasn't tied to him in some permanent way."

Not a flattering comment for Cat to voice about her friend and boss. "It's a good thing Domini fills in for you."

"A *good* thing? Right. I'm lucky she doesn't lock the damn door and hide in the storage room when I'm gone." She sighed dramatically. "Dommy is sweet and all, but she should not be allowed out of the kitchen. I can't believe Macie made me train her for front work. What a waste."

India figured Cat's pronunciation of "Dommy" as *dummy* wasn't accidental. "I still think it's lucky for you or else you couldn't flit off to Denver every month."

"My great aunt was in the hospital. That hardly counts as flitting off," Cat huffed.

Cat's weeklong trips to Denver had been going on for over a year. Who picked up the slack? Domini.

Domini complained to India, well, as much as Domini complained about anything, which was almost not. Since Domini grew up in a different culture, making waves as a lowly employee had been frowned on. So India's suggestion that Domini take her concerns to Velma and Macie was met with a horrified and vehement no.

"My aunt had knee replacement surgery. There were orthopedic patients up the wazoo. She said some were diabetics there for amputation. Yuck. Which makes me glad Cam McKay keeps his fake leg covered up, because I'd barf if I ever saw it. I mean, can you imagine? Eww."

"Cam McKay is a decorated war hero. Eww, doesn't exactly come to mind when I see him."

"He is a total hottie, too bad he's a cripple."

A cripple. India's tongue would be bloody by the time she finished this job. Why had she taken it?

Right. Rent was due. Again. And she was short of funds. Again.

"Anyway, I can't get past how icky it'd be to get naked with him and see that...stump. And he's missing part of his hand." She shivered. "It's uncomfortable since he has a thing for me because he's always in the diner."

Talk about cocky. Cam had a thing for Domini.

"I'm just re-inking this tat, right?"

"Yes. I debated on having you do it at all, since it is a Kat Von D design. The guy who originally did it worked with Kat before she became famous."

Please. If she had a buck for every time she'd heard that line in the last few years, she'd be flush with cash. After dipping the needle gun in black ink, she stepped on the pedal and her hand started to vibrate. She gently set the needle on Cat's skin.

India was grateful conversation stopped for a few minutes, even when she knew it wouldn't last.

It didn't. Cat chattered on about her life. What she did, who she did. All gossip, all mind-numbingly boring to India, but Cat didn't notice. She must've taken India's silence for rapt attention because she kept going.

She mostly tuned her out until she heard Cat say, "So rumor around town is you're dating Colt McKay."

India slid her hand a fraction of an inch to thicken the

outline. "Who'd you hear the rumor from?" She concentrated on keeping the line the same diameter and not letting the black bleed into the pink.

"Macie. Is it true?"

"That Colt and I are dating? Yes."

"Friends with bennies now, huh?"

India's grip tightened on the tattoo gun.

"Macie said you came to a McKay family dinner at the big house. I've gotta say, I'm impressed. Very few people get invited into the sacred McKay family realm if you're not married to one."

"I'll remind you my sister, Skylar, is married to a McKay."

Cat gave her a droll stare. "And I'll remind you about the number of McKay shindigs you've been invited to because of that association. Zero. Am I right?"

"Can you turn your leg a little?"

"It shocked me to hear you and Colt were together." Cat laughed. Not a nice laugh, a mean laugh. "A few of us around here wondered if you weren't gay."

"Me? Gay?"

"Come on. With the bull dyke swagger, the piercings and the excessive tats, not to mention the motorcycle, the addiction issues, the funky haircut and the tough girl attitude?" She slurped her Diet Coke. "Granted, single men are slim pickin's unless you're in the market for a dumb cowboy."

A loud click echoed in the room. India sat up and heard it again. She scrutinized her tattoo gun. Did it seem overly hot? She smacked it on her hand. It'd be just her luck if the damn thing died on her. She stepped on the foot pedal, let go, and waited for the noise to sound again. Nothing. Weird.

"Is everything all right?" Cat asked.

"Just fine. I'm switching ink colors."

"As long as you're not changing colors."

India wished she could change customers.

"When I heard you and Colt were 'dating'," Cat made quotes in the air, "I thought as your friend, I should warn you. Don't get suckered in by his charms, because that cowboy talks sweet. And before you know it, you'll be watching him doing the same sweet-talking routine on another woman as soon as he gets bored with you."

"You telling me you've dated Colt?"

Cat attempted an innocent look. "Would you be upset if I said yes?"

Yes. No. Lie. If you say no she'll get pissy and clam up. India settled for, "Maybe."

"I didn't 'date' him, but I did sleep with him a couple of times."

"When was this?"

"Right after I moved here...maybe three and a half years ago. We were dancing at the Golden Boot, one thing led to another...and we ended up back at his place." Cat paused. "Then a week or so later we were at a party and ended up in somebody's bedroom again. Anyway, he fucked me and never called me. What kind of man does that?

"My friend Mimi went to a party at the Boars Nest, his old house, like a month later, and Colt was fucking some stripper, right in front of everyone! And when he finished with her, he passed her off to another guy."

Yeah, and then Colt probably passed out. Those drinking escapades were a thing of the past, in Colt's past, and had no bearing on their future.

Still, India had to concentrate on keeping her hand from shaking. "Why are you telling me this about Colt if it happened years ago?"

"Because a leopard doesn't change his spots, India. Knowing the truth about him will save you a lot of heartache. You wouldn't be the first woman in this area to fall for his lies and lines and you won't be the last." Cat pushed onto her elbows and looked at India over her shoulder. "Besides, didn't Blake West ask you out?"

"Yeah he did."

"What happened?"

Colt happened. "We decided to stay friends."

"Was that before or after you and Colt hooked up?"

"Before."

"See! That's what I mean. You and Colt had been friends forever, and when his cousin starts paying attention to you, a cousin he's always had a rivalry with, then Colt becomes interested in you? Isn't that just a little...ironic?"

It wasn't as if India hadn't thought of that. And discounted it. She opened her mouth to protest, but Cat wasn't done.

"Almost as ironic as Carolyn McKay waltzing in here yesterday."

"She's a regular customer of Sky Blue."

"But I'm betting she didn't come in here to buy lotion. I'm betting she came in here to talk to you. Did she warn you off Colt?"

India looked up. "Why would she do that?"

"Because you're not the type of woman she wants her darling son dating, are you?"

"My, my Cat, what a tangled web you weave. I'm finding it impossible to follow a single thread."

Cat gave her a superior sniff. "What do you mean? It's obvious."

"Not to me. First you say Colt is going to dump me because he dumps every woman. Then you say his mother is worried we're going to have a permanent relationship, so she comes to warn me off?"

"Which brings me back to my original point. You being at the McKay family dinner. I think that tipped Mama McKay off Colt's fling with the local tattooist might go on a little longer and she had to do something to stop it."

Fling. As if.

"So what did she say to you?"

None of your goddamn business.

"Because you looked upset."

Maybe it's because I look like I could use a big bottle of scotch.

"Probably not as upset as you were knowing Colt came into the diner with another woman last night."

"Who?" Dammit. She shouldn't have asked. It'd be just like Cat not to tell her. And then for India to find out it'd been Colt's sister-in-law and to get pissed off for nothing.

"That gorgeous redheaded lawyer who moved to town earlier this year and took over her father's law office...Ginger Paulson?"

That'd explain Colt's evasiveness about the woman talking to him at the community center. "Maybe it was business."

"Oh honey, it sure didn't look like they were talking business." Cat gasped with mock distress. "Oh, India, I'm really sorry I opened my big mouth and told you when you didn't know."

No, you aren't sorry you miserable pot-stirring, gossiping, lazy-assed bitch.

Rather than allow catty Cat the satisfaction of seeing how badly she'd upset her, India shrugged. "I appreciate you telling me. Like you said. I'm just dating him. No big deal, nothing permanent, we're having some laughs. It's not like I'm picking out wedding dresses and invitations."

Suspicion darkened Cat's eyes. "Really? You're sure you're not upset?"

"Positive," she lied. "Besides, I am getting what I want from Colt McKay."

"What's that?" Cat asked.

India's lips twisted in a parody of a smile. "Now where would be the fun in telling you, when I want it to be such a big surprise for him?"

Colt was stuck in hell—the foyer at the back of the building between the tattoo studio and the stairs leading to India's apartment. He'd been there for the last twenty minutes.

He racked his brain trying to remember whether he'd slept with Cat, but it was pointless. There was a period of eighteen months that'd been a total blur. But he did know in the years he'd been sober, whenever she'd come on to him at Dewey's, he'd let her know he was not interested. In fact, he'd been downright rude to her on a couple of occasions.

So...his rudeness, not calling her after a two-night stand...he could see why she had it in for him.

What sickened him, as much as Cat's tactics to turn India's niggling doubts into full-blown doubts, was that India hadn't defended him. Not once. She'd demanded clarification on a couple of points. But never once had she said, *you're wrong. I know Colt. I know his heart. I know his soul. I know the man he is now, not the man he was.*

Not fucking once.

And what was up with her cryptic claim, *I am getting what I want from Colt McKay?*

A gut-level fear froze his breath in his lungs. Was India just another person who took what they wanted from him, expected his support, but when push came to shove, couldn't offer it in return? Support or trust?

A leopard doesn't change his spots.

Colt shifted the bouquet of flowers and lumbered up the steps, not bothering to tiptoe. They'd tiptoed around these issues plenty, it seemed, and the time had come to face them dead on.

India heard the stairs creak and knew Colt had come calling a day early. Her heart leapt for joy and she set the tattoo gun on the tray table. "Almost done, give me one sec." She hustled to the backroom.

The foyer was empty. Ever since she'd tossed the wrench at his head, Colt kept his distance when she was working. But really, had he been in such a damn hurry he'd left the back door open? Her hand curled around the doorknob and she pulled the door shut. A click echoed in the enclosed space.

A familiar click.

Heart pounding, India opened the door to determine her ears weren't playing tricks on her.

Click.

She hadn't heard him go upstairs until just now. Which meant...he'd heard every word.

You mean he knows you didn't defend him.

Colt didn't understand how a woman like Cat operated. The only way to keep their relationship private, and not fodder for Cat's gossip mill, was to ignore her.

But Cat taunted you and you fell for it.

Heartsick, India dragged her feet returning to her tattoo station. She picked up the tattoo gun and dipped the needle in the ink.

"You okay?"

No. "Yeah."

"Well, then, as I was saying—"

"You know what, Cat? The truth is, I have a vicious headache. Let me concentrate on this last petal and you'll be done."

Numb and weary, she shifted into autopilot as she finished adding in the last of the pink to the rose.

After she swabbed the area and Cat admired the tat refurb, India taped a bandage on it. "I'll ring you up out front."

Cat stopped. "Ring me up? What do you mean?"

"You didn't expect me to re-ink you for free, did you?"

The look on Cat's face said exactly that.

"That'll be a hundred bucks."

"For a re-ink? A new tattoo doesn't cost that much."

"Ah, but those aren't special Kat Von D tats, are they? I had to take extra care not to wreck her design, and that's much harder than starting from scratch."

"Seems a little pricey."

India just hoped it hadn't cost her everything.

Chapter Twenty-three

Rather than pace until India came upstairs, Colt found a vase and put the flowers in water. Then he paced.

Did he admit he'd overheard the conversation? Did he play dumb and see if she brought it up first?

Yeah, he'd go with that option.

He wandered to her bedroom. The bed was unmade. The sheets were twisted into a knot. Pillows were strewn across the floor, as if she'd thrown them. That made him smile. She was a restless sleeper.

The scents of cinnamon and lemon lingered in the air. His gaze landed on the silk scarves piled on the dresser. Between her scent and the memory of what he'd done to her with the scarves, his cock started to stir. Not good to greet her with a hard-on. He backtracked to the bathroom.

Makeup, washcloths, empty coffee cups littered the bathroom counter. He washed his hands and was looking for a hand towel when he saw the calendar.

Whoa. Why did India need a calendar in the bathroom? Curious, Colt picked it up. Several days were X'd out. Some in blue. Some in red. He flipped the page. Days were marked for the following month. Not hard to figure out what the red days meant.

A weird feeling arose as he looked at the dates. A *yes* was scrawled on the blue X'd square three days ago. The night they'd had sex against the pickup. A *yes* was jotted in the blue X'd box for four days ago. The night she'd spent at his place and he'd fucked her nine ways 'til Sunday. A *no* was written in the blue X'd box for the last two days in which he hadn't seen India at all. A blue X marked today and tomorrow. Then nothing until four weeks from the first blue X. Exactly four weeks.

Son of a bitch. Colt knew enough about biology to understand why India was marking the days. This was a fertility chart and blue indicated her most fertile time.

I am getting what I want from Colt McKay.

He didn't have to tax his brain to figure out what India wanted from him: a baby. She wanted a baby so bad she'd...steal it? She didn't care if it wasn't what he wanted?

Jesus. He wanted kids some day. He wanted kids with India, but he wanted a say in when and if that happened. Not for her to take away his choice by staging a "do me right here, right now" stunt that ensured he couldn't say no.

You could've said no. By saying yes you reverted back to the behavior you used to be known by. So are you really mad at India? Or yourself?

Colt couldn't breathe. He couldn't think. Had he put his trust in the wrong person? He stumbled out of the bathroom. When he reached the living room, India opened the apartment door.

Her gaze zoomed to the flowers on the table and then back to him. "What are those for?"

"They're not given out of guilt, if that's what you're thinkin'."

She frowned. "Why would I think that?"

Was India really going to play dumb? "I heard you and Cat talkin'. Brought to mind Ma tellin' me when I was a kid that eavesdroppers never hear anything good about themselves. Guess she was right. But then again, I didn't exactly hear you leaping to my defense, Indy, when Cat started in on my character—both past and present." He looked at her with a mix of misery and anger. "I expected more from the woman I'm dating."

"How was I supposed to respond? Anything I said would've been the wrong thing."

"Some of the things she said were an outright lie. Any positive response about me or our relationship would've been better than the flip crack that we're just havin' fun and you weren't pickin' out wedding announcements."

"Aren't we just having fun? Dating for kicks? Nothing serious, right? Especially since you were out with another woman last night?"

"Just like that, you believe what Cat told you?" He threw up his hands in total exasperation. "You believe what Cat thinks she saw? Without askin' me? Without trusting me?"

"You're a fine one to talk about trust, McKay."

"Don't you go there. This ain't got nothin' to do with me not playin' some stupid trust game in A.A. meetings."

"Fine. It's not a game. But it is about trust. So I'm asking you now, Colt. Who was she?"

"No, you're not asking me, you're *accusing* me. Expecting me to defend myself when I've done nothin' wrong. When the reason I haven't explained anything to you is because I haven't talked to you in the last two goddamn days. *You* said you needed space, remember?"

She moved to the wall separating the living and dining rooms, folding her arms across her chest. "That is not the issue."

"You're damn right that's not the issue. You immediately jumped to the conclusion I was seein' another woman behind your back." He resisted the urge to shake her. "Do you honestly think if I was sneaking around that I'd do it in the restaurant next to your business? In the same building as your apartment?"

India bit her lip and looked at her feet.

Colt expelled a bark of laughter. "Don't you go all wet-eyed and coy on me. You'd be better off pickin' a fight because you know it's impossible for me to resist the hellcat in you. Then you'd get what you want from me, just like you told Cat you would."

Two red spots appeared on her cheeks.

"I wondered what that comment meant. I'd foolishly hoped you were bein' cryptic with her because she's a mean, gossipy hag and it'd drive her crazy." He paused. "Then I found the calendar in the bathroom. I know exactly what you want from me."

"What? You had no right—"

"And neither did you. No right at all, to be another person in my life who takes away another one of my choices. To take something from me I would've freely given to you, if you just would've asked."

Tears shimmered in her eyes. "I'm not the only one who jumps to conclusions, Colt."

He said, "Tell me I'm wrong."

She countered with, "No, you tell me *I'm* wrong."

A standstill.

Jesus. He had to get out of here. Now. He shuffled to the door, everything inside him heavy as lead. Like dead weight, which fit since he felt dead inside.

"That's it? You're just leaving?"

For now. "Yep."

"Great. So what happens now?"

"I don't know. I need time to think."

"But—"

"I gave you time to get your head on straight, more than once in this relationship, I expect the same courtesy from you."

"Fine." She pushed off from the wall. "But I sure hope you don't plan on finding a bottle to help you pass the time while you're off *thinking.*"

And he thought he'd felt sick before. "Spoken like a true A.A. sponsor. Thank you for the support."

"Shit. Colt, I'm sorry. I didn't mean it the way it came out, I just can't think... Fuck. I can't believe this is happening and I know I'm doing this all wrong."

Yes, you are.

"I'm just frustrated and you know how I get and say such stupid impulsive things—"

"No, I don't know. Because I thought I knew you, India. And I thought you were one of the few who knew me. But I guess I was wrong about that too."

Colt didn't look back as he left.

Go after him. You need him. You love him. Weren't you mustering up the guts to tell him how you felt? How can you let him walk away?

Let him go. You don't need him, especially after his hypocritical behavior. He jumped to his own set of conclusions without letting you explain.

India sank to the floor and wept, knowing it was pointless, knowing it'd make her feel worse. She was so numb in body and mind and spirit, she couldn't even move. She couldn't even crawl to her bed. She just laid on the floor, curled in a ball, and cried. And cried. Big sobs. Hiccupping sobs. Silence as tears streamed down her face.

What had she done?

What had he done?

She'd never wanted a drink so badly in her life. Or to smoke a big, fat joint. Or to down a bottle of sleeping pills so she could sleep the day away.

Her mind flitted between all the choices, in greedy glee, the old voices and vices taunting her. *You've been good for so long, don't you deserve to cut loose? Just once? No one will ever know. Surely one wouldn't hurt you.*

One what?

One of anything. Pick. There are so many choices.

But what if I get caught?

By who? Could your life honestly get any worse?

No.

YES. Another voice piped in. *Don't let eight years of sobriety go down the drain because of an eight-minute fight. Do something besides sit around and give your demons control. Take a walk. Talk to someone.*

The only person India wanted to talk to was Colt.

Screw him. It's his fault you're in this state anyway. Get in your car and drive to the package store. No one will know. Don't you miss it? Don't you remember? The tart taste of white wine on your lips? The bubbly feeling of beer on your tongue? The fiery burn of tequila sliding down your throat?

India's mouth watered.

A mental snort sounded as voice number two reappeared. *You might as well throw yourself down the stairs. Drinking again is suicide. You know that. Colt is not to blame. And if you use him as an excuse for a relapse, you'll never have the chance to repair this misstep in your relationship, because part of you will always fault him, even when it's not true nor his fault. You're stronger than this.*

Goddammit, she *was* stronger than this. But she didn't have the strength to ride out the voices alone. She needed help.

Wasn't that what she always reminded fledgling A.A. members? No one is ever cured of alcoholism. Some days are easy; some days are hard. No matter if you've been sober a week or two decades, there's no shame in asking for help when you need it.

There wasn't. But there'd be a whole lot of shame if she gave in to temptation.

India rolled to her back and stared at the ceiling. Squinted at it mostly, because her eyes were so swollen and bleary from crying. She suffered from the mother of all headaches. Her mouth was as dry as the Wyoming prairie. She was exhausted. Heartsick. Her body hurt. Her mind was scrambled. But she knew if she laid there wallowing in self-pity another second she'd never get up. Or she'd give in.

One step at a time.

She slowly pushed to her feet. Shuffled into the kitchen. Poured herself a glass of water. Once she'd accomplished those simple tasks, she was ready for the hard one. She scrolled through the contact list on her cell phone. When his number flashed, she selected it and hit dial. He answered on the fourth ring.

"Hey Bert. It's India. No, I'm not doing so good. Yeah, I realized I'm not invincible. Do you have time to talk to me? Face-to-face?" The tears came again. "Thank you. Come on up, the door is unlocked. I'll put on the coffee."

Chapter Twenty-four

Colt's head spun every which way. When he parked in front of his empty house, he realized it was the last place he wanted to be. Running wouldn't fix anything, but time away might give him a different perspective.

He called Cam and left a message. "I'm droppin' off the grid for a couple days, bro. Don't round up a search party for me, I'll be fine. And if anyone in our family asks, let 'em know I ain't on a three-day bender. Later."

Next he called Chassie's. "Hey Trev. How's Chass? Yeah, well you knew she was ornery when you married her. It's funny that it takes both you guys to handle her. Look, I'm leavin' for a couple days and I wondered if you and Ed would keep an eye on my place? Nothin's wrong." Colt sighed. "That ain't entirely true. Just some shit I need to sort out on my own. I appreciate the offer. You guys are great. Thanks."

Food packed, gear packed. Two rods, one tackle box, zero cell phone.

When things got tough...the tough went fishin'.

Two days later...

India burst into Dewey's when she noticed the sheriff's department cruiser parked in front. She stalked over to Cam, who was sitting at his usual space in the back booth. "Tell me where he is."

"Who? Colt? I haven't the foggiest idea."

"Bullshit."

"I'm serious, India. He left me a message saying he was leaving for a few days, and not to worry because he wasn't on a bender."

India winced.

"You wanna tell me what's going on?"

"Domini didn't tell you?" After India talked to Bert, she'd called Domini. Usually India relied on Skylar for personal problems, but she was dealing with two sick babies and an equipment breakdown at the factory. The last thing Skylar needed was more stress.

So India had sobbed on Domini's shoulder for half the damn night. In addition to being a great listener, Domini gave practical advice. Which was why India had allowed a cooling off period before she set about making things right...only to realize Colt had all but disappeared.

"No, I haven't talked to Domini, besides when she swings by to refill my coffee. She's been a little busy around here."

"Why? Did Cat take off again?"

"Huh-uh. Cat got fired."

"What! When?"

Cam beckoned her closer. "You didn't hear this from me. But after Domini's, ah, talk with you the other night, she was furious. She got Macie and Velma on a conference call and gave them what-for. Said she was sick of covering for Cat's incompetence and sick of not being able to keep employees because no one wanted to work for, or with, Cat."

"Holy crap. What'd Macie say? She and Cat are old friends, aren't they?"

"*Were* friends. Evidently Cat said some crappy things when she was in Canyon River and Macie was already upset. Coupled with the fact sweet Domini tossed out the ultimatum of keeping Cat and losing her, they fired Cat. Domini is the new manager." Cam grinned. "I'm so damn proud of her. I knew there was fire beneath that ice."

"I'll congratulate her later." Her eyes searched Cam's face for clues. "So you really don't know where Colt went?"

"Nope."

"I'm worried about him. Really worried." She held up a hand. "Not that he's crawled inside a bottle, but I hate thinking he's hurting alone."

"Me too." Cam considered her over his coffee cup. "Did you cause that hurt?"

India looked him straight in the eye. "Yep. I'm not proud of it. But since I caused the hurt, I intend to heal it."

"I think you already have."

That was a weird statement. "So what's your advice?"

"Talk to my mother. She may have an idea of where he's gone off to. But don't call her," he warned. "Face to face is always best with her."

"Thank you."

Right. Talk to Carolyn McKay. Their last conversation had gone so well. But this wasn't about Carolyn. This was about Colt. He was all that mattered.

She closed the shop and drove out to the McKay homestead.

Her bravado faded a bit when Carson McKay greeted her on the front steps. "Mornin', India. Something I can do for you?"

How had she not noticed Colt was the spitting image of his father? In another thirty odd years, Colt would look exactly like this man. Handsome. Regal. She couldn't wait to watch the transformation take place as she and Colt grew old together.

The truth of that statement pumped up her courage to meet that suspicious blue gaze—so much like Colt's—dead on.

"Yes, Carson, there is something you can do for me. I need to talk to your wife."

Chapter Twenty-five

"I'm thinkin' about getting a dog."

His horse, Laramie, snorted.

"I'm serious. Maybe a blue heeler. He'd keep you in line."

Laramie snorted again.

Colt laughed. "Then again, I probably wouldn't have any better luck keepin' a dog in line, than I do keepin' anything else in my life in line. 'Cept maybe for this fishin' line." He chuckled again. "A great joke lost on a horse."

If he didn't know better, Colt would swear Laramie rolled his eyes.

He shifted on the log. Time to move. His ass was sore. He tugged on the fishing line. Nothing. He walked over to where he'd ground-tied Laramie. "You ready to hit the trail?"

After hiding out at his favorite fishing hole for three days, Colt was ready to head home. The pine-covered hills on either side of the small pond, and the rock cliff on the backside, made this site inaccessible, except on foot or horseback.

Few people were aware of this slice of paradise. The terrain was too dangerous for livestock, which also meant nothing worth selling would grow on it. Wasn't like the sage, rocks, cactus, and scrub pines were unique. Yet, for some reason, those elements served to hide this area well.

He and Dag had discovered this place one year when they'd drifted off West land. They'd likened themselves to Lewis and Clark—explorers, discoverers, adventurers. Every year after that, they'd load up the horses, basic supplies and spend a couple days roughing it. Fishing. Bullshitting. Planning. Later in their teen years, they drank like fish as they fished, bullshitted, and bragged about their future plans.

Dag had dreams of becoming a rodeo star. Living in California. Colt was one of the few who hadn't laughed at Dag or his dreams because Dag might actually get to live his fantasy. Whereas Colt knew he'd never have that choice. He'd live on the McKay Ranch for the rest of his life.

Thinking back on those times, Colt realized he'd been happy in that knowledge. That surety. He didn't have to choose a career; his heritage had chosen it for him.

So when had that security become a bad thing? When had he started resenting all he had? All he was? He wished he could pinpoint the exact moment. Attribute his sour attitude to an event, or a slight, or an epiphany. But he couldn't. He'd just woken up one day, and his first thought wasn't, *I'd better get cracking, I have a lot to do*, it was, *Fuck this. When the hell did I sign on for manual labor, every goddamn day for the rest of my life? When did I decide I didn't want to travel and see the world, but I want to view it only from Sundance, Wyoming?*

He hadn't. And it'd been the first time Colt felt he hadn't been given a choice. So he'd acted out. Not as a ten-year-old boy, but as a twenty-something man. Drinking, fighting. Resentful of his heritage. Resentful of his family. Feeling...inferior. To Cord, who'd had a kid. To Colby, who'd had a rodeo career. To Cam, who'd been a soldier and a hero. To Carter, who'd gone to college. To his sister, Keely, the precious, precocious, beloved baby girl. To his father, who'd seemed to prefer all his brothers to him.

No one can make you feel inferior without your permission.

Easy to hear; hard to believe. All that counseling in rehab made a big deal about turning points. Colt experienced more than a few in his life. Some good, some bad, and he'd reached another one last night. A major one.

As he'd laid on his bedroll looking at the gorgeous display of stars, listening to the coyotes' mournful howl, the small animals rustling the underbrush, watching the antelope cautiously approaching the water's edge, he had that moment of clarity: he was exactly where he wanted to be. He always had been. He was living the life he'd forgotten he'd wanted. Now he needed India in that life on a permanent basis.

India. Man he loved that woman. Loved her like he never thought he'd love another person. They were great together. Good for each other. They were more than friends, even more than lovers. They were soul mates.

So first order of business after he got home and rid himself of the stench of fish and the great outdoors was to sit down with India for a rational discussion about their future. Pregnant or not, he wanted his ring on her finger and her in his house and bed forever. It was that simple.

Something startled Laramie and Colt reached for the lead rope. "Easy." He ran his hand down Laramie's neck.

Sure enough. The distinctive sound of hoof beats echoed in the canyon walls. Before he could yell out, Laramie shivered. He turned his head and flared his nostrils.

Only one horse caused that reaction in Laramie: Sheridan, Carson McKay's mare. The equine pair had successfully bred several times, until Carson took Sheridan out of the breeding program. A fact Laramie hadn't forgiven Carson, as he tried to bite him or kick him at every opportunity.

"Is that horse of yours gonna charge me, son? Or is he tied?"

"I'll tie him." Colt tied Laramie to a good-sized pine and ignored the stallion's angry snorts. "I'm hopin' you didn't come lookin' for me because there's some kind of emergency at home?"

"Nah. Everything is fine."

"How did you find me? I didn't tell anyone where I was goin'. Didn't think anyone knew about this place."

"You've always come here when you need some thinkin' time." His dad didn't look at him as he tied Sheridan to a tree, away from Laramie. "I'm probably the only one who knows this is where you spent that week after Dag died."

Guilty. He'd never told anyone where he'd gone. It surprised him his dad had known.

"So am I in trouble?" Jesus. Sounded stupid to say. He was a grown man, not a disobedient boy.

"Guess that depends on your idea of trouble." His dad squinted at him. "Your India came to the house today."

"Yeah? What for?"

"She was lookin' for you, but I suspect she came to give your ma what-for." Carson gestured to the log and they both sat facing the water. "Did you know your mother stopped in and had a chat with India at her tattoo shop this week?"

Colt managed a terse, "No," through clenched teeth.

"I didn't either. I doubt I coulda stopped her if I woulda known. That woman gets her mind set on something..." He huffed. "Evidently they had harsh words. India said she didn't need our approval to date you. She didn't see where Caro got off tryin' to tell her what kind of man you are, when she doesn't really know you."

"Indy said that? To Ma?"

"Yep. Caro was a little stunned. She was even more stunned when India said she agreed with Cam, that we're all a bunch of idiots and hypocrites. Demanding you change and when you do, not believing that you have." His dad picked up a rock and threw it in the pond. "I'll admit that accusation threw me for a loop."

"Why?"

"'Cause it's true. 'Cause we've all been pretty selfish for years. And yeah, I'm includin' myself in that group. It pisses me off I was so busy judgin' you, that I didn't see what was happenin' right in my own damn family. Saw your brothers had followed my lead and were wrongly judgin' you too. It took Cam to bring it to a head." He scowled. "Although, now that I think back, Keely mentioned something along those same lines, what's the point in changin' if no one believes you can." He shot Colt a sidelong glance. "I'll admit she was right. *To you.* Be no livin' with that girl if I admit it to her."

Colt smiled.

"Son, I'm just gonna say this flat out. You know I ain't a spillin' my guts kinda man. I'm better at showin' my feelings than my dad was, but I ain't nearly the father I oughta be. I know that, especially when I see how good Cord and Colby and Carter are with their boys. I'm damn proud of them. They're good fathers and good men. I struggle with wantin' to be more like that even now that you kids are all grown."

Would his father gloss over and say something nice about him...just to have something positive to say?

"Yet, of all my boys, I feel I failed you the most."

Thud. The other boot officially dropped.

"Not because you hit bottom. Not because of the alcohol."

"Then why?" Colt demanded.

"Because you're too goddamn much like me for your own goddamn good. You have been since the day you slid outta your mama, all wide-eyed, cooin' charm and smilin'." He paused. "Know the first thing Caro said to me after she gave birth to Cam? You must've been about two and a half."

"What?"

"Don't let me love Colt more than the other boys. I thought it was some weird hormonal pregnancy talk, so I kinda patted her on the hand and told her it'd be all right. But she was insistent I understand. Musta been mother's intuition because she knew from the get-go."

"Knew what?"

"Knew that you're a carbon copy of me. People say that of Cord, but it ain't true. You look like me, you act like me, hell, you probably even think like me. Caro knew every time she looked at you...she'd see me. See my strengths and faults and want to fix the bad ones and bolster the good ones. Caro knew she'd play favorites. She knew she'd let you get away with anything, so she left it up to me to even things up."

Colt was absolutely tongue-tied.

"Now that I think about it, it chaps my ass, her passin' the buck to me. I ended up bein' harder on you than I shoulda been. Harder on you than I was on your brothers, that's for damn sure. Expected more outta you too. And if you did something wrong, goddamn if I didn't feel like *I'd* done something wrong. And when you did something right?" His laugh was bitter. "Well, I didn't heap praise on you, now did I?"

"No. Dad—"

"Lemme finish. As things changed, we expanded the ranch, you showed us all up by buyin' land we all scoffed at and forged your own way. Then your brothers came home, and I shoulda taken you aside. Made sure you knew how important you were—are—to the ranch and to me. But I shoulda warned you too. I knew you were drinkin' too much. I knew you were whorin' around. Thing was, I didn't know them things because I'd been listenin' to gossip. I knew them things because I'd lived them."

Not another *back in my day* lecture, Colt thought.

"Your uncles and I were the original McKay hellraisers. I was the worst of the lot. I drank too much, smoked pot, drove my truck like a fuckin' idiot, charmed my way into the pants of every woman that'd have me—married, single, old, young, if they had a pussy they were fair game."

Colt reached behind the log and handed his dad a bottle of water. The man's mouth had to be parched with the way he was babbling on. It was as scary as it was fascinating.

"Thanks." Carson took a long pull off the bottle. "Oh, and you'll get a kick outta this. I told my old man to fuck off. Repeatedly. Told him I didn't give a shit about his stupid piece of Wyoming dirt. I just wanted to get the hell away from him because he was a mean, old bastard."

"Jesus. What did Grandpop say?"

"Told me to get my ass back on the tractor and finish mowin' the south hay field because I had no choice. The McKay Ranch was my only choice. I imagine you must've felt that way a time or two yourself."

"You might say that."

"Anyway, about that time, I met your mother. I ain't gonna get graphic and gooey, but sweet baby Jesus, did I want that woman in the worst way. She was an innocent eighteen-year-old beauty. I was a hard-edged, twenty-four-year-old cowboy who got by on charm and looks and lived to raise hell. I convinced her to marry me, over her family's objections, over my family's objections, hell, over everyone's objections.

"Sad to say, I didn't change once we said them vows. I still drank. I still went to the bars and fought anyone who looked at me cross-eyed. And if they looked at your mother? I tried to kill them. I still did whatever the hell I wanted, whenever I wanted. Within three years we had one baby and one on the way, we were livin' in a trailer, hand to mouth. She shoulda left me. Many times. I thank the heavens she didn't because she's the only one who could ever get through to me when I hit rock bottom."

The idea of his staid, gruff, in control father, hitting rock bottom, startled Colt into blurting out, "No shit?"

"No shit. I've been there, son. More than once, sad to say. Didn't know that about your old dad, didja?"

"No."

"That's because Caro's pulled me up by the bootstraps every time I fell and covered my ass. 'Bout the time you rolled around, I'd gotten my ducks in a row, became the responsible man I needed to be. And ain't it ironic that you were around that same age when you saw the writin' on the wall?"

He took another drink.

"What I'm sayin' is I'm proud of you, Colton. You're a stronger man than I ever was. What you done, you done on your own. As much as I admire that, I wish it hadn't played out that way. I'm sorry. I wish I coulda been a bigger man and a better father and not let you deal with so much shit on your own."

Don't cry. Don't you dare cry. Be a man.

Fuck all if he wouldn't shed a tear when he'd just gotten everything he'd ever wanted from the man he admired most in the world.

A gentle breeze wafted by, filled with the scents of sage and dirt, of horseflesh and water. Smells he'd always associate with home.

Colt didn't look at his dad because he suspected the man wasn't completely dry-eyed. He allowed a couple minutes to compose themselves before he cleared his throat. "Thanks, Dad. I needed to hear it as much as you needed to say it. We're both livin' proof that people can change. And it can stick."

He kicked a clod of dirt. "Will you give us all another chance? I figure, maybe it's time we worked to earn your trust instead of the other way around."

Colt didn't mention his brothers had already come to that determination. "It'd be good for all of us to start fresh. It's been a long time comin'."

"Good. And if you wanna take a month off and go to Hawaii, then so be it. You've earned it." His dad turned and smiled. "'Course, part of me is hopin' you'll be there on your honeymoon with India. I like that little gal. She's a spitfire. Gotta say, it takes real guts to confront mama bear Carolyn McKay about one of her cubs."

"Or a deathwish," Colt muttered. "What happened?"

"India said her piece. Caro said hers, something about India surpassing her expectations and being exactly the type of woman you needed. They both started cryin' and carryin' on and were best pals by the time I hightailed it outta there." Carson stood and scratched his head. "Now I'm afraid I'm gonna come in from checkin' cattle someday and hear my wife's gone to town and gotten herself a tattoo."

"Tattoos aren't bad, but look out for the piercings."

"Son, there's just some stuff I don't wanna know."

Chapter Twenty-six

Colt unsaddled Laramie and brushed him down. He was dragging the packs to the back door when he saw her motorcycle parked in the driveway. He dropped everything and tore around the side of the house.

India sat on the steps, head in her hands, looking lost.

But she was here.

"Indy?"

Her head snapped up. "Colt!" She dropped the bundle in her hand, leapt to her feet and ran. Launched herself straight into his arms and peppered his face with kisses. "I missed you, you dickhead. I missed you so goddamn much. Don't you ever ever *ever* take off and leave me like that again, do you hear me?"

He laughed. He laughed and swung her around until she started laughing too.

"Oh God, stop. I'm dizzy."

"It's okay. I gotcha." He sat on the steps with India straddled on his lap. He picked up the bundle and it jingled. "What's this?"

"A present. I realized I never did any romantic dating type crap for you. I didn't bake you cookies, or surprise you with a picnic—"

"But the caramel incident counts as romantic. So does the whipped cream. And you showin' up buck-assed nekkid except for a pair of boots counts as the height of romantic behavior."

"Yeah? Anyway, I wanted to give you something tangible, so I brought you a bag of tokens from the pizza place in Moorcroft where we had our first date."

"As a token of your affection?"

"Pretty pun-tastic, huh?" She gave him a small head butt. "See? I knew you'd get it. You know me so well, Colt. Better than anyone ever has."

"Same goes. So you have to know my meeting with Ginger Paulson—"

India put her fingers over his lips. "You don't have to explain. I was a jerk. I trust you. Period."

He nipped her fingertips. "I'm gonna tell you anyway. Her son Hayden is Buck's little buddy. Hayden wanted to do something special for Buck, and Ginger thought I could give them some ideas."

"That's all?"

"Yep. So now—"

"Now you need to listen," India blurted. "First, I'm sorry. For not defending you, for acting like a lump of shit when Cat spewed all those horrible things about you. I lashed out at you when I should've lashed out at her. It'll never happen again and I'll beat the living shit out of anyone who casts doubts on your character."

"Including my mother?"

India snorted. "She's not afraid to come out swinging, that's for damn sure. But then again, neither am I. It surprised her that I'd fight for you."

"That's a little extreme, but apology accepted."

"Second, it was a cheap shot, questioning your commitment to sobriety after our fight. I should be your safe harbor, not the crashing waves dragging you down." India fiddled with the button on his shirt. "I'm the one who had doubts about whether I could hold it together after you left. I, ah, had to call Bert."

"Ah Indy." He rested his forehead to hers. "You okay?"

"Now? Yeah. Then? No. I was a mess. I needed help. I wasn't too proud to ask for it. That...feeling had been building for a while and I ignored it. So the near relapse reminded me I'd gotten cocky. I thought I had addiction whupped, but I don't. I never will."

Colt knew no matter what his dad thought about Colt being strong enough to fight his addictions on his own, he never would've made it this far if it hadn't been for India. And he was good with that.

"Lastly, the reason I asked for space was because it freaked me out when I realized we had unprotected sex more than once at my most fertile time. Making that chart gave me a plan of attack so I was fully prepared for if we dodged the baby bullet."

"What about the marks for the following month?"

"The Xs for the next month were so I'd know when I went on the pill, which days we'd have to use condoms until the pill was at full effect."

Now that Colt thought about it...the charts shouldn't have surprised him. That was exactly what India always did, planned for every contingency. "You want to go on the pill? Why?"

"I like sex without a condom. Which is the whole big 'oops' issue we have to deal with now, because we didn't use a condom, like three times, so I might already be pregnant." She searched his eyes. "You know I didn't do it on purpose, right? I'd never take that choice away from you."

"I know. And it wasn't just you, Indy, it was both of us throwing caution into the wind. If you're pregnant, you're pregnant. It wouldn't be a big oops in my mind anyway."

"What?"

"Your sister has little kids; my brothers have little kids. It'd be a great opportunity for them to grow up around family."

"That's your reasoning? We should have a baby so our kid will have cousins?"

"No. That ain't the reason." Colt cupped her face in his hands. "The reason is...I love you, India. I've loved you almost from the first moment I met you."

"You have?"

"Yes. I didn't fall for you because you were my sponsor and my lifeline to sobriety. I fell for you because you're *you*. You're everything to me. You have been for years."

"Omigod. Colt. Why didn't you tell me? We wasted so much time—"

"No. The last thing our time together was, was wasted. Don't you think there was a reason we didn't date other people after we met? Because we were already a couple. Platonic? Yes. But that don't make the years we spent together any less real or any less meaningful. In fact, I think it makes them *more* real because we know each other. Straight down to the bone."

She didn't attempt to hide her tears.

"Indy, you're my best friend. I love you. I'm *in* love with you. I want to spend the rest of my life with you. This is the real deal, sugar. I'm asking you to be my wife."

"Yes. God yes. A million times yes. Colton West McKay, I love you so much." India kissed him. So sweetly. So perfectly. With so much love and unbridled emotion he felt tears springing to his eyes for the second time in a day.

"Let's go inside." He set her on her feet and stood. Inside the house he spun her around.

She placed her hand on his chest. "What's wrong? You're so serious."

"You've shown you trust me in everything you do, and everything you are to me. It's time for me to do the same."

"You're scaring me a little." India reached up and cupped his face in her hands. "Talk to me. What's going on in that head of yours?"

Breathe. You can do this.

"Know that trust exercise you've been after me to do?"

"Yes."

"I'm ready."

She never looked away from him. "You're sure?"

"Positive."

Without another word, India led him into an open area in the living room and she stood behind him.

"Now what?"

"Cross your arms over your chest. Close your eyes. When you're ready, fall back. Straight back."

"That's it?"

"No, you have to trust me. I'll catch you. I promise. Even if you fall, I'll pick you up."

For the first time in his life, Colt didn't have a moment's hesitation about who to trust.

He closed his eyes and let go.

About the Author

To learn more about Lorelei James, please visit www.loreleijames.com. Send an email to lorelei@loreleijames.com or join her Yahoo! group to join in the crazy fun with other readers as well as Lorelei - http://groups.yahoo.com/group/Loreleijamesgang

Marking one's territory was never so naughty...

Take Me Again
© *2009 Mackenzie McKade*
Wild Oats, Book 2

Dolan Crane would love to hate the beautiful new veterinarian who's horning in on his territory. It's tough when the flame-haired fantasy come true makes his body burn with just a smile. The smart thing to do is forget about her, so perhaps a threesome arranged by his old college buddy is just what he needs to get her out of his head.

Divorcee Tracy Marx has followed her restless feet to Santa Ysabel to start a new practice—and maybe find someone to take her outside the boundaries of vanilla sex. Instead she finds trouble in the form of a cowboy whose dark, sexy gaze lights her up—and could also destroy any chance of success. The best thing to do is stay far, far away from him.

When Dolan shows up for the promised night of fantasy, he's shocked to find Tracy has traded her medical bag for a leather bustier and bondage gear. Tracy would like nothing better than to slap that smirk right off Dolan's face, but the prospect of being sandwiched between two men is impossible to resist—even if one of them is her adversary.

Besides...no one calls her chicken.

Warning, this title contains the following: Ride-me-cowboy sex, hot, explicit ménage scenes, light bondage, graphic language, and a heated romp in the hay.

Available now in ebook and print from Samhain Publishing.

Enjoy the following excerpt from Take Me Again...

As the music ended, Tracy Marx stepped out of the cowboy's arms. Damn. What was his name? Was it John? Paul? George? Ringo? A silent chuckle tickled her throat.

With a sultry expression, he smiled down at her, sliding his palms up her bare arms. "How about another dance?"

"Dance?" She glanced at him not really seeing him. Shamefully, her mind wandered to another—one who'd left her wanting with a single look. The flame had sparked again when their eyes had met once more.

The whole time they'd sashayed across the floor all she could think of was the dark-haired cowboy who appeared out of nowhere. Even when Tom—*yes, Tom was his name*—had suggested they find a quieter place to talk all she could think of was blue-black hair and eyes dark as the night.

She scanned the room in search of her mystery man. Disappointment hit her hard when the spot where he had last stood was vacant. Reluctantly, she drew her attention back to Tom and his question. "Can't. Promised the next dance to—"

Crap. Forgot that guy's name too. She never had problems with her memory. Guess she had too much on her mind tonight.

The stout cowboy she had met earlier sidled up to her. "Charles," he said slipping an arm around her waist to pull her back firmly against his body. "My turn."

Tom stiffened. His brows tugged down into a scowl. For a moment, she thought he might raise a ruckus.

Men were gutsier then she remembered. They could be so primitive. Give them a drink or two and they became throwbacks from the Stone Age, fighting to resolve all their disagreements.

Tracy released a pent-up breath when Tom finally tipped his hat. "Later, sweetheart."

"Not if I have anything to say about it," Charles whispered in her ear.

Her equilibrium was shot to hell when he twirled her around and into his embrace. His feet immediately started to move to the quick beat of the music. Lightheaded, she missed the first step, but caught the next one to glide across the floor. He held her confidently, guiding her into each move easily.

"So, little lady, where you from?"

Little? She was five-eight, one or two inches shorter than him. Judging by his solid build the man was a bull-rider. Of course, she'd been wrong before. "Nebraska," she answered.

Tracy wasn't prepared when Charles abruptly spun her twice, drawing her firmly against him on the final spin. But it was the knee wedged between her legs that made her attention perk up. He rubbed his thigh up hers. The large bulge in his jeans pressed against her abdomen was difficult to miss. The man was aroused. He ground his hips to hers emphasizing the point before giving her a devilish grin.

Good ol' Charlie expected a reaction, but she wasn't biting. *Not my type.* Besides she was just here to burn off some energy. Tomorrow was a big day for her.

Yeah. He might give her a good ride, but she was looking for something more, someone who could ignite a fire inside her with just a look. Someone like the cowboy she'd exchanged glances with before hitting the dance floor. Her thoughts wandered back to a pair of dark eyes. The bad boy persona the dark-haired cowboy wore screamed excitement and adventure. That's what she wanted—hungered for.

A light kiss pressed to her neck brought her back to the man that held her. "I've never seen you here before. Visiting?" His voice deepened as he rubbed his cheek against hers. The scent of sandalwood was strong. She preferred the light spicy scent of the dark-haired cowboy. It left her speechless and horny.

What was she saying? She didn't even know the guy.

"Yes. No." Truthfully, she wasn't sure. Her uncle had promised to help her establish a business in Santa Ysabel. Back in Omaha her mother had agreed to watch Sheldon until she found a home and babysitter. Again her chest squeezed.

It had been nine months since her sister's unexpected

death. Shelly had been thrown from a horse. Her head had struck the only rock in the field. Tracy's ex hadn't appreciated becoming a parent so soon, but she had no alternative. Her mother had enough health problems of her own. Lois Marx had a bad heart. Besides Tracy was Sheldon's godmother and she loved the three-year-old as if he were her own. Leaving Nebraska was a new start for both of them.

Charles chuckled. "Which is it?"

"What?" Blinking hard, she tried to recall what he asked. She had shit for a memory tonight. What she needed to do was pull herself together, but it was difficult when she had so much on her mind. Other than college, she'd never been this far away from home, never been alone. Even married she had lived only a mile away from home.

He eased his hold putting enough distance between them so he stared into her eyes. "Are you visiting or staying?"

Multiple choices—this should be easy. Yet she remained silent pondering his question.

Just pick one, a voice in her head chastised.

"Staying," she heard herself say.

There, that wasn't so hard.

Yet saying it aloud authenticated her decision and she wasn't sure it was the right one. What if she couldn't find enough work? What if the people in California didn't like her? She was a country-girl born and raised. What did she know about dealing with people of influence? What she did know were animals, especially horses.

An ear-to-ear grin tugged at Charles's mouth. His hand fell to rest on her ass. "Need a place to stay?"

His innuendo didn't escape her. She cocked a brow, grasping his hand to guide it back to her waist. "Got it covered, but thanks for the invitation."

His palm worked its way back down to ride the top of her ass. "Does that mean tonight is out?"

Men! She shook her head in disbelief.

Relief surfaced when the song came to an end. Hastily, she

stepped out of his embrace. "Thanks, but I have plans tonight. Now if you'll excuse me." Cutting through the crowd, she avoided Tom when he nodded at her, choosing instead to head for the line growing outside the bathroom door. It was as good as any place for her to catch her bearings.

Tracy probably shouldn't have ventured outside her uncle's estate tonight. But her fifteen-year-old cousin had recommended she check out Jester's party. She didn't want to speculate how Laurie knew about this place. From everything Tracy'd seen so far it was a meat market and the perfect place to pick up a one-night stand, which was exactly what she was in the mood for, but it would have to wait.

There would be questions if she didn't come home tonight. An inquisition was something she didn't need to deal with. But she might have stood a cross-examination for the tall, dark cowboy. She took one more look around the room and wondered if her mystery man had gone down the flight of stairs to the basement.

"Looking for someone, sugar?" The whiskey-smooth male's voice sounded familiar.

She turned and a smile fell across her face. "Rowdy."

He wrapped his arms around her waist and raised her off her feet to twirl her around, nearly knocking over two other women in line. They cast a disgruntled look, but remained quiet as she slithered down his firm body, raising her skirt to where it barely covered her butt. She gave the hem a tug as he settled her on her feet.

He held her at arm's length. "I couldn't believe it was you waltzing around the dance floor. What the hell brings you to this neck of the woods?"

"I could say the same to you." She took in his athletic build, knowing exactly what hid beneath his cotton shirt; lean strong muscles. Long powerful legs were encased in snug denim that rode low on his lean hips. Yep. She remembered the bulge between his thighs too. Hastily she jerked her gaze back to his face.

A wicked grin fell across his face. He pulled her back into his arms, giving her a squeeze. "Here with someone?" he murmured against her ear.

"No."

"That makes two of us." He nibbled on her earlobe. "How about I take you home, tie you up and have my way with you?"

Chills raced across her skin as his hair tickled her neck. The man was gorgeous. Peeking from beneath his Stetson, sandy blond hair framed his tanned face.

"Yes" was on the tip of her tongue. His sexy invitation almost made her forget she needed to call it a night soon. "Sounds delicious, but I'll have to pass. I work tomorrow."

His lips were soft trailing along her jaw line and cheeks, until his mouth whispered across hers. "Are you sure?" He caressed his tongue along the crease of her lips. "If I recall, we made some sweet music together."

Sweet music? That was an understatement.

Rowdy had been her first lover after the divorce. She had been scared and uncertain. He had been patient and understanding and joked around to make her feel comfortable. They had talked, but more importantly he had listened, asking questions and appearing genuinely interested in her plans for the future.

Little touches here—kisses there—and before the night ended she found herself locked in his arms, revealing some of her deepest desires. At the moment there hadn't seemed to be any danger in her frankness about her sexual desires. He was a stranger passing through town. Hell. After a couple of drinks and another tumble between the sheets, she had even told him about her darkest fantasy—a ménage a trois.

To her surprise he hadn't been judgmental. He didn't make her feel as if her wayward thoughts were disturbing or wrong. In fact, he appeared to be aroused by her confession, taking her in his arms and making passionate love to her once more.

Embarrassment heated her face. *I can't believe I revealed that fantasy.*

He smoothed a hand gently over her cheek as if he could sense her sudden discomfort. "It's me, baby." He looked at her with warm brown eyes. "I can make your fantasies come true."

He pressed his mouth to her ear. "All of them," he whispered.

Oh God. He remembered.

A spark sputtered low in her belly. The burn matched the heat flaring across her cheeks. Surely he was just teasing her. Even still, the thought of two men worshipping her body all night long was beyond exciting. It was downright sinful.

"Can't." She swallowed hard. "Not tonight."

Damn. Damn. Damn. It was already getting late and she didn't want to disturb her uncle's household. She didn't miss the disappointment on his face as he released her.

"When?"

"Maybe Monday. My weekend is booked solid."

"Monday it is. Give me your number." He pulled his cell phone out of his pocket and punched in her number as she rattled it off. "I'll call you with the directions to my house." He caressed her cheek. "Are you up for anything?" There was a spark of devilment in his eyes.

Anything?

"Yes," slipped from her mouth before she could think twice.

"I promise it will be a night dedicated solely to your pleasure." He kissed her softly. "Until Monday."

Eyes closed, lips still puckered, she murmured, "Uh-huh." He tapped her on the nose. Her eyelids rose.

He winked. "Later, baby."

She sighed low and long as she watched him walk away. Later couldn't come anytime too soon.